Murder on Cape Cod

A Cozy Capers Book Group Mystery

MADDIE DAY

KENSINGTON BOOKS
www.kensingtonbooks.com

KENSINGTON BOOKS are published by

Kensington Publishing Corp.
119 West 40th Street
New York, NY 10018

All Kensington titles, imprints, and distributed lines are available at special quantity discounts for bulk purchases for sales promotion, premiums, fund-raising, educational, or institutional use.

Special book excerpts or customized printings can also be created to fit specific needs. For details, write or phone the office of the Kensington Sales Manager: Attn.: Sales Department. Kensington Publishing Corp., 119 West 40th Street, New York, NY 10018. Phone: 1-800-221-2647.

Kensington and the K logo Reg. U.S. Pat. & TM Off.

First Printing: January 2019

ISBN-13: 978-1-4967-2288-1
ISBN-10: 1-4967-2288-4

ISBN-13: 978-1-4967-1507-4 (ebook)
ISBN-10: 1-4967-1507-1 (ebook)

10 9 8 7 6 5 4

Printed in the United States of America

For the multitudes of readers devoted to the cozy mystery. You know who you are.

Acknowledgments

I'm delighted to be starting a new series with a meta-premise: a cozy mystery series about a book group that only reads cozy mysteries. The concept and setting were a collaborative effort among my fabulous agent, John Talbot, my equally fabulous Kensington editor, John Scognamiglio, and me. Note: the town of Westham is fictional, but you might deduce from the name the general area of Cape Cod I imagined when I created it.

Thanks again to Sherry Harris, independent editor extraordinaire, for setting me straight on myriad details of my manuscript before I turned it in. Gratitude, too, to author Leslie Budewitz, who inadvertently reminded me with her own writing that Mac should love her job more than I had originally written.

While writing this book, I spent time at two beach retreat houses to turn out some word count and get in the Cape Cod mood. My dear friend Deb Hamilton loaned me her Plum Island beach house—decorated entirely with a lighthouse theme—twice during the winter of 2016-17, and even rescued me when I got iced-in after a storm. Love you, Deb. Thanks, too, to the West Falmouth Quaker House, where I've worked on several books. The cottage, where I polished this one and honed a few Cape Cod details shortly before the book was due, is a perfect retreat space: an affordable quiet house to myself with no Wi-Fi.

In preparation to write my fictional half-Wampanoag

detective, Lincoln Haskins, I toured the Mashpee Wampanoag Indian Museum on Cape Cod and read Paula Peters's book *The Mashpee Nine*. I hope to honor that part of Cape Cod heritage with my portrayal of Detective Haskins.

My protagonist Mackenzie Almeida's mother is an astrologer. I've learned a lot over the years about the practice from my college roommate Nani Vohryzek and my dear partner Hugh Lockhart, but any errors in attributing traits to the stars are clearly mine.

Amesbury police Detective Kevin Donovan again helped with a few bits of police procedure, and the state police on Cape Cod also supplied me with important local information. Thanks to author Annette Riggle Dashofy for a few critical assists with the scenes including EMTs.

Gratitude to my wonderful adult sons, Allan and JD Hutchison-Maxwell for helping with bicycle details (between them they know a lot), and to Allan for his astute comments on a near-final draft. I rented a tourist bike from Corner Cycle, Falmouth, and pumped several employees there for facts and practices. Thanks to the store, and to Tim and mechanic Rex, for real-life shop and rental color, policies (one that I lifted verbatim), humor, and murderous suggestions.

In the book, Mac buys the book *My Daddy* for her niece. This lovely work of art and storytelling is by my friend Susan Paradis. You should find one for the small person in your life.

Always, thanks to my backup crew, the Wicked Cozy Authors, for support, friendship, and both personal and professional inspiration. I love these women: Jessie Crockett/Jessica Estevao/Jessica Ellicott, Sherry Harris, JA Hennrikus/Julianne Holmes/Julia Henry, Liz Mugavero/Cate Conte, and Barbara Ross. Read their books.

My gratitude to Sisters in Crime, my Quaker congregation, Jennifer Yanco, and my sisters, sons, and main man, Hugh. I couldn't do it without you all. And to readers everywhere, I hope you like this new world and family of characters I've invented.

Chapter One

It's the little signs that end up meaning something. The fog. One man's odd restlessness. Another person's new confidence. The signs we ignore at our peril.

The weekly meeting of the Cozy Capers book group was winding down in my brother's lighthouse perched on a promontory in Cape Cod's hamlet of Westham. Gin Malloy, owner of Salty Taffy's candy store, lifted her wine glass. "Here's to a super-charged summer season."

"I'll drink to that." I, Mackenzie Almeida, matched my friend's gesture. I hoped the summer wouldn't be too rainy. I was lucky enough to own Mac's Bikes, a bike rental and repair shop, and we did a booming tourist business as long as the weather stayed fair. We shopkeepers depended on the three-month surge of vacationers for a large chunk of our income.

Tonight, at a little after eight, the lighthouse's arched windows stood open to the sea air, which blew in the damp scents of early June. The round rooms looked out onto the Atlantic Ocean, or would have if it weren't too foggy to see the water. Derrick Searle, my half-brother, hadn't contributed much to the cozy mystery discussion, instead drumming his fingers with a quick nervous movement, gazing out the window into the pea soup. Earlier he'd left the door to the lighthouse unlocked and had tacked up a note telling us to come in and start without him. He'd arrived out of breath after everyone else and without explanation, which was unfortunately typical of him.

Now he puttered around, picking up wine glasses and plates holding remnants of this week's treat. The members of the group took turns making a dish mentioned in the book under discussion. This week the town clerk had made a couple of killer pizzas for us to share, since Sherry Harris's *I Know What You Bid Last Summer* featured an Italian restaurant where Sarah Winston, the garage-sale-maven protagonist, often ate.

I stood to help Derrick but he waved me away.

"I'll do it, sis," he said in a gruff tone. He was the private lighthouse's caretaker and I knew he liked to keep the place tidy, a trait we shared.

The group, ten strong tonight, exchanged farewells and filed down the circular staircase.

"What are we reading for next week?" I asked.

"*Cracked to Death*, remember?" Gin replied.

"That's right." It was the third book in Cheryl Hollon's Webb's Glass Shop Mysteries. The group had decided to begin this season with a book set in June—thus starting with last week's *I know What You Bid Last Summer*—and then move ahead a month every week, so we'd go through an entire year by the end of August. *Cracked* was described as taking place during the dog days of summer. Our group, which read exclusively cozy mysteries, had contacted the author to make sure that meant July. She'd assured us it did.

"See you in the morning, Gin," I called, and waved to the rest, who headed for their cars. Me, I began my short walk home along the biking-walking trail that paralleled the coast. My shop was successful in part because of these paved trails that ran up and down the Cape from Provincetown to Woods Hole. I tried to hurry, smiling to myself because my boyfriend was meeting me at home. Tonight, though, the trail between the lighthouse and my tiny house behind the bike shop was almost unnavigable. It wasn't long past sunset but the fog was a wall of mist around me. I could barely see where I was going, and I felt my already curly hair gain a new layer of frizz.

I hoped all this damp didn't seep through my roof. I'd called out Jake Lacey, a down-on-his-luck handyman, about his shoddy repair job earlier. I volunteered serving dinner on Tuesdays in the late afternoon at Our Neighbor's Table, a food pantry and soup kitchen where Jake was a regular customer.

"Got my check?" he'd asked today as he handed me his plate.

"I'm sorry, Jake, but you did a terrible job on my roof." It was true. I'd hired him to replace some of the shingles on my micro-house after they'd blown off in a storm. He'd left gaps, some of the replacement shingles were poorly nailed on, and he hadn't even cleaned up the scraps and debris when he left. I gave him my sternest look. "I'll pay you after you've fixed the shingles and not before."

The woman behind him in line had raised her eyebrows at my criticism but didn't say anything. Norland Gifford, the volunteer on my right, who was our newly retired Westham police chief, cleared his throat. I guess I should have saved my comment for a more private setting.

Except Jake hadn't gotten his back up like he had in the past when anyone criticized him. Instead he'd lifted his pointed chin and waggled his head, wearing a smug expression on his worn face.

"I ain't gonna even need your money soon, Mac. You wait and see."

I'd peered at him for a second, having no idea what he meant. "Did you get full-time work?" He was known around town for not being able to hold down a job, which was the reason he was here getting free food, of course.

"Nah. This is better than no stinking job. It's good, wicked good." He'd grabbed the plate of pasta and sauce I'd dished up and moved down to the salad section.

"That's great," I'd called after him. There went my chance at a decent repair job from Jake. I guess I'd have to find somebody else since I wasn't going to do it myself. I could tune up a bicycle like nobody's business, but when it came to hammers and nails, I was all thumbs–and usually both of them got a good self-delivered whack within minutes of attempting anything in the field of carpentry.

Now I found the turn from the bike trail to the pathway that cut up to Main Street. Near the end of the path a hedge of scrubby coastal *Rosa Rugosa* separated the walkway from my postage stamp of a yard. The fragrant scent from the just-blooming native shrub mixed with the salt air and reminded me of my childhood here on the Cape. I slowed as I rounded a bend. I was scanning through the mist for the opening that would let me through the wall of roses when I tripped.

The obstacle in my path, oddly both soft and solid, was a sizable one. I yelled, arms windmilling like in a vintage cartoon. The air gave me nothing to grab hold of and I landed on my hands and elbows. I glanced down and back to see my knees resting on . . . Jake.

"Gah!" I shrieked and scrambled forward off of him. I crouched in place, my heart beating like the timpani in the Cape Symphony. Jake lay on his front with his head half-turned toward me, lips pulled back in a grimace, eyes unblinking.

"Jake!" I called. "Jake, are you all right?"

He didn't respond. I inched closer and couldn't detect any signs of breathing. I touched his temple but I didn't feel a pulse under his too-cool skin. His skinny legs were splayed at an odd angle, and his back was still, too still. No breaths moved it up and down. He was never going to enjoy another free spaghetti dinner—or anything else. Jake Lacey was dead.

Chapter Two

I pushed up to standing and pulled my phone out of the small bag I always wore when I went outside. My skin turned numb as I jabbed at 911, my shaking finger slipping a couple of times until the call connected.

Jake's straggly light-brown hair lay in skinny strands wet from the fog. The color of his beat-up old work coat almost matched his hair. I couldn't see any wounds. No blood stained his coat or marred his skin. I'd never seen a body before, not even an animal except roadkill, and then it was from the window of a car. My mother's parents had passed away before I was born, my other grandfather had died when I was traveling abroad, and we'd never had pets at home because of my allergies. What happened to Jake? Did he have a heart attack? A drug overdose? Did he even do drugs?

When the dispatcher asked what my emergency was, I said, "There's a dead person. It's Jake Lacey." I managed to keep myself from shrieking again. I was desperate to get home—my house was only a few yards away. I wanted to lock the door and pretend this never happened. But I couldn't. I was a responsible adult, and a body on the path was out of order. I didn't like disorderly things.

"What is your location, ma'am?" she asked.

"I'm on the path behind the bike shop."

"What town, ma'am, and what's the name of the shop?" The dispatcher's voice was infinitely patient.

Oh, yeah. The local police used a regional dispatch center. "Sorry. Westham. Mac's Bikes." I gave her the address.

"And how do you know this person is dead?"

One of those awful catastrophe giggles threatened to burble up. I swallowed it down. "He's not breathing and his skin is cold. It hardly even feels like skin." I turned away from the sight of his body. I had to.

"Do you feel safe?" she asked.

"Yes." After a beat it occurred to me to add, "Why shouldn't I?" I gave a quick glance around the fog-shrouded path that looked like a scene in a mystery filmed on the Scottish moors. Shouldn't I feel safe? Did she mean someone had killed Jake? That was awful. Murder, here?

I'd never felt myself in danger in Westham, not when I was little, not since I'd been back. I knew some of the bigger towns on the Cape were plagued with higher crime rates than we had. Just because the long curving peninsula was a scenic tourist destination didn't make Cape Cod immune from robbery, addiction, domestic abuse, and other bad things. On the contrary. But they mostly didn't happen in my town—as far as I knew, anyway. Jake had probably felt safe, too. The thought stabbed me with sadness for him. I shivered, from the shock as well as the cool damp of the night. It had still been warm and sunny when I'd left for the Cozy Capers meeting and I wore only jeans and a Falmouth Road Race t-shirt with my sandals.

"Is anyone with you?" the dispatcher asked, startling me.

I'd forgotten she was on the line. "No." Nobody living, that is.

"Officers are on their way. Do you feel comfortable staying where you are?"

"I guess." I'd feel a lot more comfortable once Jake was someone else's responsibility.

"Please keep this call open until the officers arrive," she instructed.

"Okay." I didn't dare stash the phone for fear I'd press the wrong button, so I stood holding it, like an unfortunate statue. The fog damped all sounds, but a dog barked faintly in the distance, and a big truck downshifted out on the highway a few miles away.

It seemed selfish to feel sorry for myself, but I wished I'd never found Jake. Since I had, I rued not leaving my back porch light on. If someone had killed Jake, they might still be around. My breath grew shallow. I glanced quickly behind me on the trail, but of course I wasn't able to see a thing through the pea soup. I couldn't wait for this nightmare to be—

"Mac?" a deep voice called. My boyfriend appeared in the gap in the hedge. "Who are you talking . . . ?" Tim Brunelle's voice trailed off as he spied Jake. "Is that Jake Lacey? He doesn't look good." Tim hurried through the opening in the bushes, made one giant step over Jake's body, and took my face in both hands. "Are you all right?"

I gazed six inches up into his tanned concerned face.

"I'm all right, kind of. But," I gestured at the ground without really looking, "Jake isn't." I could finally hear a siren growing closer. It was about time.

A couple of minutes later the path was transformed. A cruiser had rolled down the trail, barely fitting onto the narrow path, just. The police car now trained spotlights on Jake's body. Two bag-carting EMTs rushed in from the street—and then stopped rushing. Ambulance lights strobed over the tops of the buildings from the direction of the town's main drag. A bicycle patrol officer in a uniform polo shirt and black shorts leaned his bike against the hedge, pulled purple gloves out of a back pocket, and squatted next to Jake. Another officer was already stringing yellow plastic POLICE LINE DO NOT CROSS tape over the path behind me.

Tim held my cold hand in his big warm one. He was a tall man with luscious lips, dark blond hair to his shoulders, and well-toned abs, but right now what mattered was the comfort of him standing beside me. Victoria Laitinen, the recently promoted Westham Chief of Police, stood facing Tim and me. Victoria had pulled her white-blond hair back into a neat bun, the way she always wore it, and her petite figure was trim in the navy uniform of the town's police force.

"You simply happened across Mr. Lacey here," she said, blinking and setting her lips.

She and I had been high school classmates but not friends, and I remembered that look from twenty years ago. I let out a breath. "Yes. I was walking home from the lighthouse," I pointed behind me, "and I tripped over Jake. I wasn't looking down, and the fog was so thick I didn't see him."

"You didn't see anyone else in the vicinity?" Victoria asked. "Hear any noises?"

"Nope. Nobody and nothing."

"You, Mr. Brunelle?" Victoria turned her all-business gaze on him. "Did you also trip over the body?"

"No, ma'am." Tim was unfailingly polite and unshakable. "I was supposed to meet Mac at her house. When I got there," he pointed toward my backyard, "I heard her talking, so I came through the opening in the hedge and found her here."

"When was that?" Victoria asked.

"I'd just finished talking with the dispatcher," I offered. "As soon as Tim showed up, I heard the siren. You got here maybe two minutes later." Westham is such a small town, Victoria almost could have walked here faster.

"When was the last time either of you saw Mr. Lacey alive?"

I gestured for Tim to go first.

He shook his head. "Not in the last couple of days. On Sunday I was doing a training run along the water and I saw Jake with some woman. On the hill down near Westham Point."

"I saw him at the soup kitchen this afternoon," I said. "At around five o'clock."

"The one at the UU church?"

"Yes." The Unitarian-Universalist church where my father, Joseph Almeida, was minister-in-chief.

"And Mr. Lacey seemed well?" Victoria cocked her head, looking diagonally up at me since I was six inches taller than her.

"Yes." I thought back to the food line. "He seemed happy about something."

"What was that something?" She raised eyebrows so pale you could hardly see them.

I cleared my throat. "I'd told him I wouldn't pay him for the lousy job he did replacing some shingles on my house until he fixed them the right way, but he said that soon he wasn't going to need my money."

"Interesting. Sounds like you were angry with him."

"I wasn't angry, but I was curious about why he wasn't going to need what I owed him. Usually he was on my case about paying him promptly. I asked if he'd gotten a full-time job, and he said no, that it was better than a job. That it was 'wicked good.' His words."

She crossed her arms over her chest. "I don't suppose you got so mad you wanted to harm him, did you?"

"What? That's crazy! I told you I wasn't mad at him. I was unhappy about the quality of his work, but . . . wait." I stared at her. "Do you think someone killed Jake?" I rubbed the moisture off my inch-long curls. "On purpose?" Like what the dispatcher had alluded to when she asked if I felt safe.

She straightened, which really didn't give her much extra height at all. "Not necessarily. But it was an unattended death, and that makes it a suspicious one. The coroner will determine means of death in due time. My job is to ask the questions."

"Chief?" the kneeling officer called.

"You both stay right here," she instructed us before hurrying to his side. She knelt on one knee next to him. "What do you have?"

Tim extended a strong arm around my shoulders as I watched the bike officer turn Jake onto his back. My breath rushed in with a rasping sound and my hand involuntarily covered my mouth. Through the mist-laced light from the spotlights I could see a knife embedded to its hilt in the tender side of Jake's neck. I'd seen that knife before, with its four-inch carved wooden handle. I'd last seen it embedded in the guts of a striped bass. Held by my brother Derrick.

Chapter Three

Tim and I nestled on my two-person sofa an hour later. I'd tucked it in the nook under the sleeping loft. A tall narrow bookcase to our right was jammed three layers deep with cozy mysteries, and a low cabinet to my left held a lamp on top and storage underneath. A small coffee table in front of us also doubled as a bookcase, with a double-sided shelf below the table top. With only four hundred square feet, I had to make every inch count. Usually my cozy home gave me a warm fuzzy feeling inside. Not tonight.

"Cheers." He held up the glass of cabernet sauvignon he'd brought. "Even though it's not a cheery night."

I clinked and sipped before speaking. "No, it's not." The fog still filled the air outside and I was glad for the electric heater on the wall even though it was June. "Not cheery at all, in more ways than one." Victoria had kept us at the crime scene for another half hour, so it was already past nine thirty. She'd said a detective would want to talk to me tomorrow.

Belle, my African Gray parrot, hopped onto Tim's shoulder. "Gimme a kiss, handsome." She cocked her head, making a kissing sound. "Gimme a kiss, huh?"

Tim almost spilled his wine, he laughed so hard. "Did you teach her that?"

I giggled. "No, but I've said it to you before." Belle, the only pet I wasn't allergic to, had been with me since I moved back to Westham a year ago. I'd gotten her when I'd graduated from college. These birds lived for decades, and my parents had kept her during my years abroad. "Go on, she won't stop until you at least make the sound back."

Tim rolled his eyes but blew Belle a kiss.

"Mmm." The parrot nodded her head. "How about a treat? Gimme a peanut please."

"Belle," I scolded. "No treats before bed. Go get in your cage."

She gave me a wolf whistle but obeyed, hopping to the bookcase and then to her cage. In a compact space like this, she didn't have far to go.

"Oh, well." I swirled the wine in the glass, watching the red trail down the sides. But that reminded me too much of blood. When I shuddered, Tim squeezed my shoulder.

"Thinking about Jake?"

"Of course." I set the glass down and twisted to face him, wrapping my arms around my knees. "You saw the knife. That means he was murdered. Do you know of anybody who had it in for him? Except, I can't believe someone would go so far as to actually kill another person. Right here in Westham."

"Murders happen all the time. You read books about them every week."

"But those are fiction! They're made up. I read stories that come out of an author's imagination, Tim. They're not real life."

"Ever hear of the news?" He kept his voice gentle. "Dorchester, Chicago, LA, Miami. And it's not only big cities. Even in little towns people are murdered." He sipped from his own glass.

"I guess. Jake said he was going to be coming into some money soon. I wonder where he thought it was coming from."

"My first thought was blackmail."

My eyes went wide. "Blackmail? Like he knew dirt on somebody and was going to make them pay for not telling?"

Tim bobbed his head up and down once.

"Doesn't that happen only in books, too?"

"No. I read about a guy doing exactly that just last year. Got caught, finally. I guess he was lucky he didn't get killed for doing it."

I grimaced.

"So did I detect some tension between you and the police chief?" He nudged my foot with his knee.

I rolled my eyes. "Yeah. She never did like me. She thought we were rivals in high school."

"Were you?"

"We both got top grades. She was the top competitor on debate team. I was president of the Math Club. I didn't care, but she always had a thing about me." I lifted a shoulder and dropped it. "It was ages ago. I still don't care. As long as she doesn't accuse me of murder based on some imagined slight from decades past."

"She can't do that. They need evidence to make an arrest. They don't have any."

"I guess." I frowned. Should I tell him I thought the knife was Derrick's? Maybe it was a common haft. Maybe dozens of people on the Cape used them to gut fish. Just because I'd never seen one like that other than my brother's didn't mean his was the only one. I was going to keep that bit to myself for now.

Tim stroked my foot. "I bet you were cute in high school."

I'd met the hunky baker shortly after I'd opened the shop almost exactly a year ago. He'd been crazy about me from day one, wooing me in the bike shop with pastries and jokes until I consented to go out with him.

"I mean, in a different way than you're cute now," he hurried to add. "In a young girl way, not in a gorgeous woman way."

Gorgeous woman? Hardly. I was fit, almost wiry, with a speedy metabolism that meant I never had to worry about my weight. And I thought I was reasonably attractive. But not exactly model material. "I guess I was cute, if you think geeky is cute. I wore glasses and loved numbers. I read a lot. I didn't go on a date until college."

"Did you dance or play sports or anything?"

"I wasn't bad at softball, but I was really good at climbing." I gazed around my welcoming space, the framed blue Thai temple rubbing on the opposite wall, a colorful hand-painted Cape Verdean market scene next to it, the bright woven rug on the hardwood floor. Nowhere to climb in here except up to the sleeping loft.

"Like rock climbing?" he asked.

"Yes, and indoor, too. I'm kind of fearless that way."

"Honey, you wouldn't catch me going up a perpendicular wall for anything. I get nervous around heights."

I smiled. "That's because you're so tall."

"Did you ever fall off?"

"Only when I was learning, and I was wearing a harness. No harm done." My smile slid away. "I can't stop thinking about poor dead Jake. You told Victoria you saw him with a woman out near Westham Point the other day. Was it somebody from here in town?"

"I didn't recognize her, but I wasn't that close. Her profile looked sort of businessy, though. You know, blazer, heels, that kind of thing."

I nodded slowly. "She hadn't been into the bakery? Most out-of-towners stop in at some point, don't they?"

"Mac, half the time I'm in the back baking. I don't see all the customers who come through. You know that. And unlike you, I didn't grow up here. It's not a big town, but I've never set eyes on half the year-round residents. Not to mention summer folks."

"I know." This murder business was already frustrating. I'd have to find Derrick first thing tomorrow and make him look for his knife. Or ask him if he and Jake had had problems in the past. I didn't want to call him about it tonight, but I could see if the news had hit the local stations. I grabbed my tablet from the coffee table and clicked through to the news affiliate. A reporter with light-brown hair and a station jacket protecting her dress from the fog spoke dramatically to the camera.

"Our developing story tonight, from Westham on the Cape. A local businesswoman found a body on the

Shining Sea Bikeway. We're here in front of Mackenzie Almeida's bicycle shop on Main Street." The view zoomed onto the front of my shop, then back to the reporter. "The police suspect foul play."

I groaned. "Wonderful. Not exactly the kind of free publicity I'm looking for."

"Ms. Almeida was apparently walking home from a meeting when she literally stumbled over the body," the reporter went on. "Westham Police Chief Victoria Laitinen says her department is cooperating with both the State Police Detective Unit and the Barnstable County Bureau of Criminal Investigation on the case. Authorities are not releasing the victim's identity pending notification of next of kin, but one source says he was a handyman." The camera switched to a shot of the lights and police tape on the bikeway behind my house. Various personnel conferred, knelt on the trail, did whatever police did after a murder.

"Not a scene I want to relive." I pressed the Power button.

"You're going to be fine, Mac. Who knows, maybe you'll get an influx of customers from all this." Tim stroked my cheek. "Look on the bright side."

I wasn't sure how he could be so optimistic, but I was too tired to care. I yawned and extended my hand. "Take me to bed, handsome."

"Shh." He tilted his head toward Belle's cage. "We don't want her to learn that one."

Chapter Four

I dragged myself out of the covers at six thirty. Tim had left at his usual four o'clock to get the bakery going, and I was due to stop by Gin's Salty Taffy's candy shop at seven for our walk. Having found a body last night put a damper on my mood though, despite the morning sun shining through the wide, foot-high clerestory window at the end of the loft. At least the fog had burned off early today, or had blown through, more likely.

Standing on the steps, I made my bed, smoothing the multi-colored quilt my grandmother, Abo Reba, had made to welcome me back last year. She'd found cotton fabrics with prints representing many of my experiences and influences up to that point. Softballs flying, whimsical dollar signs, bicycles in all colors, a lighthouse, a Thai riverboat, even a stylized map of the Cape Verdean islands off the coast of West Africa. This morning the cheery coverlet didn't cheer me in the least. I zipped through a high-speed shower, put in my contacts, and wiped down the shower walls and sink. I threw on shorts and a long-sleeved t-shirt before lifting the cover from Belle's cage and opening her door.

She hopped onto my shoulder, her red tail rustling. "Good morning, Mac. I love you." She nipped my wet locks. "Hmm."

A little smile pulled itself onto my face despite how I was feeling. "Good morning, Belle. I love you, too." This bird with her eerily human voice could always lift my mood, even if only for a minute. "Can I have a kiss?" I pursed my lips and leaned my head toward her.

She made a kissing sound. Her curved beak moved but the sound came from farther down in her neck. "Can I have a kiss?" she echoed.

I smacked my lips again. "Now hop down, I have work to do." I threw a coffee pod into the machine. I usually didn't cut my departure this close, but I had to get that swig of caffeine into me before I left the house. Next up was to feed and water Belle, brace my bad knee, tie my sneakers, and add enough milk to the mug so I could down the java in record time.

Dark heart or not, I made sure everything was tidy before I left. I've been called a neat freak, but really I just like things to be in order. "A place for everything and everything in its place" is one of my favorite aphorisms. It's pretty much a requirement for living in a tiny house, anyway. My choice of residence is like living on a boat without the motion, and when one or two things are left lying around, the whole place looks messy.

Ten minutes later I set out on Westham's Main Street, arms swinging, water bottle in a waist pack, EpiPen bag across my chest. After a near-fatal encounter with a wasp a few years earlier, I never went anywhere without a double dose of the medicine. Since the little embroidered bag also held my phone, it was a handy accessory. In my pocket were my single house key and the tiny Swiss Army knife I never left the house without. You never knew when you might need one. I wasn't a girl scout, but I like to be prepared.

To the right of my shop was the Lobstah Shack, which was a mostly takeout seafood restaurant, not a lobster shack at all, and then both my father's white church and the red-doored Episcopal Church across from it.

Today I'd also tucked earbuds in my bag. During our first walk after a book group meeting, Gin and I each listened to the audio book of the mystery for the next week's book group meeting. After our first day of listening simultaneously, Gin and I finished either listening to or reading the mystery on our own so we could talk during our walk. But I wouldn't press Play on *Cracked to Death* until Gin and I hit the trail. And maybe not even then.

Across the street was Tim's bakery, Greta's Grains. He'd named it after his mother, even though the retired professor now lived on St. John Island in the Caribbean. He'd told me she'd taught him to bake and it was his way of saying thanks. Right now the alluring scent of fresh-baked baguettes, bâtards, and brioches floated out of Greta's open front door, but I didn't have time to pop in and say hi. I blew a kiss in that direction, earning me a puzzled look from the driver of a convertible who drove by at that exact moment. *Oops*.

The police department and fire department sat beyond the bakery. A good-sized man of about fifty in a square-hemmed short-sleeved shirt climbed out of a state police cruiser. Dark hair skirting his collar, he carried a cardboard holder of coffees into the police station. I'd never seen him before, and could only surmise he was working on Jake's death. Or maybe he was Victoria's husband delivering a dose of decent java. I'd heard she'd recently remarried but I didn't know the new spouse.

On my side of the street were more charming shops and the century-old red-brick and white-pillared Town Hall, which housed the library in a new addition to the right. The town green spread out in front of the municipal buildings. I hurried on, spying Salty Taffy's ahead. Gin stood on the sidewalk in front of her place. She had both hands on the brick wall and one leg extended behind her stretching her hamstring.

"Sorry I'm late," I called. I would have jogged to her, except the knee I'd blown out a couple of years ago in New Zealand made running pretty much of a prohibited activity. It also prevented me from biking, kind of ironic for a bike shop owner. Power walking was all I could manage, and even that I did with a black brace supporting the joint.

She waved and waited for me, switching to stretch her other leg. "You ever going to get that knee fixed?" she asked.

"I don't have time. And I don't want to have surgery. Too much could go wrong."

"You mean you're scared of it." She tied her thick, expertly colored chestnut hair back with a covered rubber band. Gin and I had met when I'd stopped into her candy shop on a visit home ten years ago when I was living in Boston. She was only two years older than me but already had a daughter and a divorce behind her. We somehow got to talking about reading mysteries and struck up a friendship. She now knew me well enough to gently rib me about my weaknesses.

"Maybe. A little." When she poked me with an elbow, I caved. "Okay, yeah, I'm scared. The prospect is too messy. Very disorderly, at least from a patient's point of view. IVs, anesthesia, blood, pain, narcotics, scars? Forget it."

"It's your body. As long as you can still walk with me, I don't care what you decide. Ready?"

I nodded and we set off past the two churches that bookended the other end of Westham's main drag, Catholic on the right, Quaker on the left. The former's ornate spires, stained glass set into complicated brick-work, and arched doorway contrasted sharply with the other building's simple design, silvered cedar shingles, and clear windows both tall and wide.

The cut-over to the bike trail at this end of town was next to the cemetery beyond the Friends Meeting-house. Gin hadn't mentioned Jake Lacey, so she must not have turned on the news.

When I saw her about to pop in her earbuds, I touched her arm. "Can we talk today instead of listening?"

"Sure. What's up?"

We turned onto the path in the direction of the lower Cape, or as we said, *Down Cape,* meaning toward the elbow. Cape Cod looked a lot like the classic bicep-flexing pose of the strong man. The upper Cape was the upper arm running west to east. The point of the elbow hit at Chatham, the forearm stretched north, and the hand curled around artsy colorful Provincetown. The appropriately named Westham sat near the west-ern reaches of the peninsula.

After we passed the log-body models of deer lining the path and the entirely realistic black dog sculpture, complete with red neckerchief, at the back of someone's property, I cleared my throat. "On my way home last night I found a dead person."

"Whoa, whoa, whoa." She stopped and faced me. "You did? Who was it?"

"Jake Lacey. I tripped over him on the trail behind my house. It was so foggy I didn't see him."

"And he was dead?" This time she whispered, her mouth pulled down in a horrified look.

"Definitely. I called 911. But it was awful, Gin."

"Geez, I'll say. He wasn't that old. Did he have a heart condition or something?" By unspoken agreement we resumed walking.

"No." I pictured Derrick's knife again. "Somebody had stabbed him."

"Right here in Westham? Crap."

A bike bell dinged behind us. "On your left," a voice called out a few seconds before three women pedaled by us on the other side of the yellow center line. They rode bright red Schwinn reproductions that looked like rentals, maybe from Joe's in North Falmouth. My seven-speed rentals were sunflower yellow and baby blue. Not a helmet among the ladies, but as long as they stayed off the roads, the trail was level enough that they were probably safe.

"But you shouldn't tell anyone about that particular detail," I said. "I probably shouldn't have revealed it, actually. The police asked me not to talk about the scene." *Oh, well.* What was done was done. Except, even though Gin and I had been friends for years, I decided not to tell her I'd thought it was my brother's fish-gutting tool. I trusted her completely, but the knife thing was just too personal. "I cleverly managed to tell Victoria that I'd had a disagreement with Jake at Our Neighbor's Table earlier in the day."

"You mean Chief Victoria Laitinen."

"Yep. She insinuated I might have killed Jake myself."

"You?" Gin hooted. "That seems pretty extreme. And talk about messy."

"I know. Tim said maybe Jake was blackmailing somebody, and that person got fed up and murdered him." The trail opened up to a marshy area, with a bridge leading over what looked like a pond but was really an inlet from Buzzard's Bay. A fragrant clump of coastal roses were in new bloom, and purple martins darted over the water, catching bugs mid-flight. I voiced the thought that had been top on my mind since last night. "I obviously didn't kill Jake. So the question is, who did?"

Gin stopped again, grabbing my hand. "You know what this means, don't you? We're going to be in the middle of our very own cozy mystery. You're the protagonist. Or we both are." Her eyes gleamed. "Maybe the book group can help us figure out who the murderer is."

"Gin, get real." I shook my head, hard. "That's why we have police, and real detectives. It's their job to solve crimes, not ours. What do we know about real-life murder? Nothing!"

Chapter Five

I took a moment before I left for the shop to call Derrick, but he didn't pick up. I'd see him at work soon enough but in case a lot of people were around, I wanted to talk with him about his knife in private first. No such luck.

By a little after nine I'd already set my OPEN flag in its holder, wheeled out two blue and two yellow rentals to the front, and paused to admire the shop I loved so much. I took great satisfaction in running my own business, a huge change from the stressful world of finance and working for a boss that I'd been immersed in previously. The left half of the shop was devoted to repairs, and the right half to rentals and retail, with shelves and displays full of bright biking jerseys, gloves, shorts, tune-up kits, and the bicycles themselves. Everything was in its place, just how I liked it. But now it was time for me to get to work.

Within minutes I'd returned a tuned-up recumbent

bike to a local lawyer, and rented bikes to a German family of four.

"No, we don't need helmets." The mother had pooh-poohed the idea in slightly accented English.

The European way.

"Children under sixteen have to wear them, though," I pointed out. "State law."

She agreed with a frown, and I had them sign the standard disclaimer.

"We heard about the crime." The father lowered his voice. "Will it be safe for us to ride on the Shining Sea trail?"

I winced inwardly. It seemed mercenary of me, but I hoped Jake's murder wouldn't turn people off biking. However, the path where I'd found Jake was still closed off with yellow police tape. "Yes. You can't use the closest access path, but you can get to the trail just down beyond the big white church." I pointed on the map.

A minute later I watched them pedal happily away, the adults' hair ruffling in the breeze. Last week a Danish couple had explained that because so many people in their country bicycled on lanes separated from auto traffic, helmets weren't necessary. I'd urged them to use extra caution on our streets and roads, since the only exclusive lanes here were the bike-and-pedestrian paths, and they were separate from where cars and trucks traveled.

Now where was my brand-new mechanic? I'd hired a local woman, Orlean Brown, to help me with the bike repairs. I'd realized last summer I couldn't handle running both sides of the business plus have anything like a personal life without help. Operating Mac's Bikes included ordering parts, buying new bicycles and accessories to sell, doing the books, keeping up the building, and dealing with the public besides the basic repair and maintenance work.

Derrick had agreed to work on the rental and retail side, but he hadn't shown up this morning, either. Where could he be? I really needed to talk with him about the knife. I texted him but my phone remained silent in return.

I stood still for a moment, gazing out the open door. Trees had leafed out and the swamp azalea was blooming, its pink-and-white blossoms fragrant. A salty breeze floated in, tangy and fresh. An oriole warbled from a branch. A carpenter hammered away at a project somewhere in the distance, and visitors in bright shorts and relaxed expressions moseyed toward Tim's bakery for a breakfast pastry. All up and down Main Street shopkeepers were opening doors, hanging out flags, expecting a profitable day. Westham, the town where I'd spent my childhood, appeared nothing short of an idyll.

Except this morning it was nowhere near idyllic. A man had been murdered. A killer wandered around free. And Gin was nuts if she thought we were going to solve this crime. Still, my brain was already in high gear trying to put the facts into some kind of order. The best way I could facilitate that was to put my hands to work and let my brain crank away on its own in the background.

The most urgent repair ticket was another tandem, and all it needed was a simple tune-up. I'd tied on a repair apron, hoisted the bike onto the arm of the workstand, and selected the wrench I needed from the blue cylindrical tool caddy on top of the stand. I was about to set about my checklist when Orlean hurried in. She was a taciturn woman with tired straw-colored hair peeking out of her Orleans Firebirds cap, the headgear worn by fans of the summer Cape Cod League baseball team. I'd never seen her flustered until now.

"Sorry I'm late, Mac. It's my . . ." She finished with a stream of swear words ending with "ex."

An ex. I knew nothing about her home life. As far as I knew, she lived alone. Nobody needed a rotten ex. I'd had a couple—not husbands, but long-term boyfriends—and was relieved to have finally found Tim, who was, at least so far, both easygoing and self-sufficient.

Orlean shook her head, eyes aflame. "I can't believe I ever married him. The no-good—" She cut herself off. "Well, you don't want to hear about that. Anyway, I'm here." She shoved a paper lunch bag in the little fridge in the corner and pulled a Mac's Bikes apron off the hook. She finally looked at me. "Hey, are you okay? I heard you found a dead guy last night."

"I did." I scrunched up my nose. "Yes, I'm all right. I—" A flushed-cheeks, hand-holding couple looking very much like newlyweds strolled through the door. "Tell you later," I murmured to Orlean, then approached the couple. "Can I help you folks?"

And they were only the beginning. A steady stream of tourists and cyclists of all sorts ambled in and wheeled out. The sun was shining and people wanted to see the sights by bicycle. I was glad we were that busy on a Thursday while school was still in session, but, man, did I ever need Derrick. Orlean was working as fast as she could, too. A woman who had rented for a week brought her bike in with a flat. A white-haired gent wanted to buy matching pink bikes for his six-year old granddaughters. A competitive cyclist needed a new tube and a CO_2 inflator cartridge.

I was working my way through a powdered-sugar donut during a brief customer lull when a big group of motorcyclists rumbled through town, most riding double, many trailing fringe. The sight made me wonder what the group adjective was, like a clutch of hens or a murder of crows. An assault of motorcycles? A rumble? A pack, a roar? After they passed I spied a van pulling up out front, a white van plastered with the local television affiliate's logo and call letters. *Uh-oh.* This day was about to get worse. A lot worse.

The reporter from last night's broadcast slid out of the van. A man holding a digital tablet fussed around her, and a tough-looking woman in black hoisted a big camera to her shoulder.

How I wished I could snatch away the OPEN flag, lock the door, and disappear. No such luck. But did I have to talk to these people? Maybe I should. It could be good visibility for my business. They wouldn't get much from me, though, since Victoria had said not to talk about the crime scene. I looked down. Store polo shirt, check. Reasonably clean blue Bermuda shorts, check. My usual Keens sandals. I could never do anything with my hair, which is why I wore it an inch long all over. I'd gotten my tight curls from my father, who was a light-skinned Cape Verdean-American, and my light green eyes from my mom, who had pretty much one hundred percent Celtic-European genes. I glanced at Orlean, brushing powdered sugar off my cheeks and shirt.

"Do I have food on my face?" I ran my tongue over my teeth.

"Only sugar on your nose." She pointed.

"Jeez. Can't take me anywhere." I brushed off my nose, too, and took a deep breath before heading to the open door. I kind of loved schmoozing with my customers, but didn't care a bit for public speaking. And if talking to a television reporter wasn't public, I didn't know what was. "Can I help you?"

The television interview hadn't lasted long, since I had to keep saying, "I'm not at liberty to talk about that," in response to the reporter's questions. I did say I had known Jake Lacey, and thought it was a terrible tragedy that he'd died so young. She'd left with a frustrated look on her face and I went back to work. What a relief. I loved breaking news as much as the next guy, but not when I was the subject of its crazy-intense focus. Thanks, but no thanks.

No sooner had the reporter and gang left when a beaming middle-aged man strolled in. He looked like he'd just gone down to his local Vineyard Vines store and commanded, "I'm going to the Cape. Clothe me." His lime-green shirt was tucked neatly into pressed light khakis, and his bare ankles peeked out from deck shoes. Above a thick gold chain around his neck, florid cheeks shone under a full head of pale hair. Well-outfitted he might be, but he didn't strike me as a bicycler. I'd been surprised before, though.

I smiled and stepped forward. "Welcome to Mac's Bikes. I'm Mac. How can I help you?"

He greeted me effusively. "In this get-up, miss, you

might think I was something of a sportsman." He swept his hands down his clothes. "But I'm afraid I haven't been on a bicycle in many years." He rubbed his hands together, flashing more than one gold ring. "I am looking to purchase property in the area, though, and thought talking to the shop owners might bring more leads than simply going to a real estate broker."

Really? Didn't real estate agents have a handle on all the properties before they even went on the market? I gave a little mental shrug. "I don't think I can help you, Mr . . ."

"Farnham. Wesley Farnham. Are you sure you haven't heard of an elderly aunt moving to a senior residence, or perhaps a family looking to get out from under coastal property taxes?"

I shook my head. "Not a one." I wasn't sure I'd let this man know about them if I did.

"Shame. Here's another question for you. I'm trying to find a man I knew growing up in the Providence area. I heard he was living around here somewhere. Lacey? Jacob Lacey?" Wesley Farnham's confident smile wavered just the slightest, his eyes narrowed a hair.

I opened my mouth and shut it again. Did I tell him Jake was dead, apparently murdered? Did this person never turn on a television or radio, not see news online anywhere? He was watching me. I had to say something.

"I don't know where you can find him, sir."

A boisterous foursome of young adults sauntered in. "We want bikes, we want bikes," two arm-in-arm guys chanted. The women with them grinned and murmured the same words.

"Excuse me, Mr. Farnham," I said. "Good luck with your property search."

"Nice to meet you, Mac," he said.

I turned to my customers, but after Farnham had left the shop I glanced out the door. He stood looking in at me, arms folded on his chest. What was that about?

Chapter Six

At noon I prodded Orlean to take a lunch break. She scrubbed her hands and removed the apron, then grabbed her lunch bag and disappeared out the back door. I kept a picnic table under the shade of a big old swamp oak for our break use, and sometimes for an after-work beer or three.

When Orlean was done and we swapped out, I sat munching on the same kind of sandwich I brought to work every day. Two slices of honey ham, one slice of white cheddar. Dijon on one piece of eight-grain bread, mayo on the other, never to be mixed. I also always brought a small bunch of grapes, and I kept a bag of small dark chocolates in my desk drawer. Why vary a good thing? And even though I lived only a few yards away, I always brought my lunch to the shop so I could eat on the premises in case a crowd came in that Orlean couldn't handle.

I texted Derrick again but he hadn't replied. I couldn't

imagine where he'd gotten himself to. Maybe my father would know, but he didn't like to text, so I either had to call him or drop by after work. Derrick was now a single dad to his little girl, Cokey, ever since her French mom had decided she didn't want to raise her daughter once she was no longer a baby. Our parents regularly helped out by taking care of Cokey. Dropping by the parsonage where my folks lived often turned into dinner, which was fine with me. Cooking was too much like work. I didn't get much joy out of preparing my body's fuel, even though I loved to eat the results of other people's efforts.

I pressed Pa's number and greeted him when he connected. Calling him "Pa" always sounded like something out of a Laura Ingalls Wilder story, but it was how you say "father" in Kriolu, the Cape Verdean creole my father still spoke when he called his dad's relatives back home on the islands off the coast of West Africa. I didn't grow up speaking the language, but I knew a few words.

"Is Derrick with you, by chance?" I asked. A bird of prey with striped tail feathers lit on the branch of a tall dead tree nearby. I watched as the snake in its talons stopped wriggling.

"No, Derrick's not here," Pa said. "He dropped off Cokey and I thought he was heading your way."

"He's not here, either. What time did he leave her?"

"Eight thirty. I assumed he was going to the shop next."

"He didn't. Did you hear what happened last night?" I asked.

"I certainly did. What a tragedy. And a shock for you, I daresay."

I started to tell him about it but he cut me off.

"I'm sorry, I'm late for a meeting. We'll talk later. *Txau, kretxeu.*" *Bye, sweetheart.*

I smiled, picturing the words written in Kriolu with its exotic spelling. We might write those words as *chao* and *creh-cheo.* But that spelling was the choice of the Cape Verdeans.

"*Txau,* Pa." I stopped smiling as the falcon tugged a long skinny piece of pink flesh up out of the snake and ate it with jerks of its head. I knew this was the way of the natural world, but it still made me shudder.

I peered out at the sidewalk. A slight young woman, almost a girl, with long smooth hair the shade of Cape sand, walked past with a heavy step. I'd never seen her before. She sniffed and swiped her eyes with the back of her hand, first one then the other, her gaze downcast. She finally grabbed a tissue out of a turquoise bag slung diagonally across her chest. Poor thing was upset about something. She disappeared behind the front of the shop.

My mouth was full of the last bite of sandwich when Florence Wolanski bustled through the back door, her boy-short white hair even spikier than usual.

"She said you were out here." She slid onto the bench facing me. "What's all this about murder?" Westham's head librarian's thin face and faded hazel eyes were focused so directly on my face they almost pulled her over the table. Violent death and my connection to it must be the topic of the day. "Only on Cape Cod." She shook her head.

I nodded and swallowed. "It's true."

"I heard you found that killcow Lacey stabbed to death on the path." She tapped the table for emphasis.

She was as much a Cape native as I was. It seemed a bit harsh to use a natives-only Cape word to say Jake didn't amount to much. What happened to *Speak no ill of the dead,* or whatever the phrase was? On the other hand, Flo wasn't one to mince words for any reason.

"I did. On the trail last night, on my way home from book group." *Wait a minute.* She said *stabbed.* Nobody knew that except me, Gin, and the police. And the killer, of course. "How do you know he was stabbed?" I asked, keeping my voice casual.

"Suzanne told me." Suzanne was Flo's adult daughter, who managed the bookstore in town. "So who did it? Too bad there's already so many tourists around. Did you recognize the knife?"

"Hang on a sec, Flo. How would I know who did it? And a flood of tourists happens to be good for business." I wasn't mentioning the knife to anybody before I talked to Derrick. If I ever found him. But I was curious about how Suzanne heard about the stabbing. "Um, the police asked me not to talk about the method of death, so please don't spread that around."

"Fine. But you're smart. You must have some ideas about the perpetrator. You found the—" Her mouth dropped open with an intake of air as she clapped age-spotted hands once. "They probably suspect you. Isn't the person who 'claims,'" she surrounded the word with finger quotes, "to find the body, the person who calls it in, aren't they always the first suspect?" Flo was a long-time member of the Cozy Capers.

"So what if they suspect me? I didn't kill Jake."

Now her tone dropped like we were planning a *coup d'état.* Her gaze darted right and left before settling on my eyes. "But Norland dropped by and said you'd had a fight with Jake. So maybe that'll throw the real killer off his game. Make him get careless. And then we can nail him."

"I didn't fight with him. And it's not 'we,' Flo. The police will be doing the investigation and the arresting."

She didn't react but just kept talking. "I think we need to have an emergency meeting of book group tonight. I'm going to let everyone know."

"Really? But we only met last night."

Orlean stuck her head out the door. "Got customers."

"I'll be in a couple of minutes, okay?" I called.

She rolled her eyes but headed back inside. She hadn't signed up for interfacing with the public, although I'd trained her on the basics of renting bikes and selling merchandise, and she didn't have any problem using the register and card reader to take payments. She wasn't much of a people person, though, and I hadn't thought I'd need to her to be anything more than an ace mechanic.

"Not to talk about a book, silly," Flo continued. "To discuss the Westham murder. We need to pool our resources. You'll come, right?"

"I guess." Pool our resources? What resources? "But Derrick might be busy tonight, so we'll have to meet somewhere else." I wasn't sure I wanted word getting around that Derrick seemed to have gone missing.

Flo waved off my concern. "My house, then. I have room. Seven o'clock sharp. We'll order out pizza." She stood. "See you there."

So much for dinner with the family. I shot Derrick a

quick text about the meeting. Maybe that would get him to appear.

"Mac?" Orlean called from the back door. "You got a visitor. You want I should send him out?"

"Who is it?" I didn't see anybody behind her.

"It's a detective? A Detective Haskins?" Her voice rose as if she expected me to recognize the name.

I didn't. And, while I'd been expecting more questioning, the whole situation suddenly seemed almost more real than it had last night. Flo's interest notwithstanding, this mystery wasn't a bit cozy.

Chapter Seven

"Please walk me through your evening again, Ms. Almeida, if you don't mind." Detective Haskins's voice was low and gentle, and he smiled when he asked questions, but his deep brown eyes never stopped watching me from behind dark-rimmed glasses.

He was the large man I'd spied taking a tray of coffee into the station early this morning. One tiny mystery solved. We'd been talking for half an hour since he joined me at the picnic table and Flo left. She'd clearly wanted to stick around but Haskins had made it equally clear this was going to be a private conversation.

Every once in a while Orlean stuck her head out the door with a semi-panicked look on her face, but I shook my head. I once again recounted leaving the lighthouse, making my way through the fog along the trail, looking for the gap in the hedge so I could slip into my yard.

"And you had no awareness of the body in the path."

The detective cocked his head. "Seems like it would have been hard to miss."

"Sounds like you don't believe me."

He folded his hands on the rough table and waited without speaking.

Up close I could see that his cotton shirt was of a muted floral print fabric. Beach community detectives must have permission to dress more casually than in the city. I'd figured him to be at least six foot six when he'd ducked through the back door of the shop. While he wasn't fat, he would never be described as thin, either. He had big bones and was bumping up to fifty, with gray shooting through dark hair.

I pressed my lips together for a minute, trying to figure how to keep my temper and explain how I missed seeing the body at the same time. "Sitting here in the sunshine makes it a little hard to picture. As I said, I was looking for the place in the hedge where there's a break. Where I take a shortcut into my backyard. It was super foggy at the time." I had a thought. "Weren't you out at all last night?"

"So you didn't see Mr. Lacey."

He wasn't going to answer me. *Fine.* "No, I didn't."

He glanced down at his notebook and picked up his pen. Maybe the state police refused to fork over the money for something a little more modern like a tablet. "After you determined he was deceased, you called 911." He looked at me for confirmation.

"Yes."

"Chief Laitinen seems to think you might have recognized the haft of the weapon in Mr. Lacey's chest. Did you?"

What? I hadn't said anything about that to Victoria. But I'd certainly gasped in surprise when I saw it. I must have given myself away. Could I stall until I found my darn brother? I hated to tell on him, but I knew from reading mysteries that it was very bad form to withhold information from the authorities. Especially when asked directly.

I mustered a little smile I didn't really feel. "You know, my assistant isn't used to handling the shop alone. It's a very busy day today and I really need to be getting back to my business." I half stood until he waved me down again.

"Please answer the question, Ms. Almeida." His tone left no way out.

I sat again, trying to suppress a sigh. "All right. I thought the knife looked a teensy bit like my brother's fish knife. But I'm sure it isn't. He didn't have any beef with Jake. Derrick wouldn't hurt a flea."

"Your brother's name, please?"

"Derrick Searle."

Haskins looked up from his scribbling. "You have different last names."

"He's actually my half-brother. My mom was married before. Derrick is her son by her previous husband, who was a Searle. After the divorce she took back her maiden name of MacKenzie, and used it for my first name, too, minus the capital K. It was quite a household growing up, with three last names."

"I see. So your mother is still a MacKenzie. First name of both your parents, please?"

Here we go. "My father is Joseph. He's the minister of the UU church. Mom goes by Astra." I saw him starting to ask about "goes by" and hurried to finish. "I mean, that's her legal name now, but it used to be Edna. She's an astrologer and always hated her birth name. Sorry, it's complicated." And probably way more than he wanted to know. But the guy seemed un-flappable.

"Any other siblings? A husband?"

"Me? I'm not married. I have another sibling, but she doesn't live around here."

"How about your brother? Your half-brother, I mean."

"He's divorced and has custody of his daughter, who's four."

"Where does Mr. Searle reside?"

"In the lighthouse." I twisted and pointed vaguely behind me and to the right. "He's the caretaker. It's pri-vately owned and isn't a working light anymore." De-spite the sunshine, I felt a sudden chill. Why was he asking about Derrick? Someone else at the scene must have recognized the knife.

"Your brother has not been responding to any con-tact information we've been able to locate. Do you have any idea how we might reach him?"

I swore silently. He hadn't been responding to me, either. Where was he? "No, I'm afraid not. He usually works here but didn't come in this morning. He must be indisposed." Where did I come up with that? The phrase made me sound like a character in a Miss Marple tale, or something out of one of Dorothy Say-ers's mysteries.

"I see. Now if you don't mind, run through your grievance with the victim again for me, please."

Yes, I minded. I gazed at my shop, at the tree, at anywhere but him. *No.* The sooner I got this over with, the sooner I could get back to work.

He cleared his throat. "Ms. Almeida? You were over-heard expressing your displeasure with the victim a few hours before you found his body."

"I was unhappy with some work I'd hired him to do

on my house." I told him about hiring Jake and the quality of the job. "It was just basic stuff."

He watched me. "Had you had other unhappy encounters with him?"

"No!" *Calm down, Mackenzie.* "Excuse me. No, I hadn't. I knew he was struggling financially—"

"How did you know that?"

"Everybody knows it. He lives, I mean lived in a crummy winter rental, and I don't even know where he moved to at the start of this month." Rents more than quadrupled once summer season hit, as in most resort towns. It left the low-income population to camp or live in their cars for the season. "He took free meals at the soup kitchen and food at the food bank. So that's why I hired him. I knew he needed the cash, and I needed the work done."

He checked his notes. "But he told you he wasn't going to need your money soon, correct?"

"That's right. I don't know what that was about." I sure was curious, though.

"Can you think of anything else? A fact, a bit of conversation, anything that might lead us to the person who killed Mr. Lacey?"

"Let's see." I frowned, thinking. "A man stopped in here this morning. An out-of-towner. He looked rich, and said he's looking for property to buy."

Haskins drummed the fingers of his left hand on the table. "Yes?"

"He also asked if I knew where Jacob Lacey was."

"Oh?" His fingers stopped tapping.

Now I had Haskins's attention. "Yes, said he knew Jake growing up in Providence." The Rhode Island city was some seventy miles west of here.

Haskins jotted notes. "Did you tell him about Lacey's death?"

"No. Not at all. I merely told the truth, that I didn't know where he could find Jake."

"Wise move. Know where the guy is staying?"

"No, sorry." I shook my head slowly. "I'm very sad Jake's dead. But I had nothing to do with it, Detective, and I have a business to run."

The detective lifted his leg over the bench and stood. Yep, six-six at least. I got up, too.

"I'll let you get back to work." He withdrew a card from his shirt pocket and handed it to me. He held out his hand, which bore a heavy signet ring on the next-to-last finger. "Please contact me without hesitation."

I'd recognize a Harvard class ring anywhere. *Interesting.* I shook his hand, astonished at the meaty size of it. "I will."

"I should have asked your employee's name. We might need to interview her, too."

"But she had nothing to do with Jake's death."

"If you don't mind?" He waited with pen to paper.

This was getting out of hand, but what else could I do? "Orlean Brown."

"Unusual name."

"She told me her parents figured with a last name like Brown, they needed to give her a unique first name. And since they lived in Orleans . . ." I flipped open my palms. Unique but not that creative. Orleans was the last town on the high-speed section of Route 6. The gateway to the outer Cape, the community sat in the crook of the Cape's elbow. The forearm of Cape Cod featured forty miles of sandy beaches, the Cape Cod National Seashore, which ended at Provincetown in the palm of the curled hand.

He nodded. "I'm off, then. And Ms. Almeida? We always hope to solve crimes with great dispatch, but right now Mr. Lacey's murderer is at large, possibly even nearby. Please watch your back." He ambled away toward the sidewalk.

I held up the card. Sergeant Lincoln Haskins, State Police Detective. I slid the card into my back pocket and headed to the shop. Watch my back? *Yikes.*

Chapter Eight

"Zane." I smiled at the slender distiller. He stood in the front door of my shop backlit by the afternoon sun. And he held a paper bag that looked suspiciously like it held a six-pack of beer.

He held his package aloft. "Got time for a cold one?" Zane ran Zane King's distillery and high-end liquor store, Cape King. He made rums and whiskeys to die for, and also stocked other fine local alcohol like Nor'easter bourbon from Nantucket as well as some eminently drinkable wines with price tags to match. Zane had been at book group last night with his husband, Stephen, Town Clerk for Westham. Both men loved reading mysteries, but I thought Zane was more into cozies than Stephen. The clerk was a brilliant cook, though, and we all loved it when it was the couple's turn to bring the food.

"My place is pretty quiet this afternoon, so I put my GONE FISHING sign on the door," he said.

"Fishing for information, you mean." I glanced at

the clock. Mac's Bikes was officially open until six, but it was after five and Orlean had left for the day. I wasn't expecting any rental returns. Why the heck not share an ale with my friend? Maybe it would take my mind off my increasing anxiety about Derrick. And since Zane loved gossiping about the town almost more than he loved Stephen, maybe I'd pick up some delicious tidbits of news. "Let's do it. I'll keep the doors open in case somebody drops in." If I sat in exactly the right spot at the picnic table, I could see all the way through the shop to the front door.

Two minutes later we were clinking bottles across the picnic table. An onshore breeze had set in, and I zipped up my hoodie to keep it out.

"Flo says we're meeting tonight to solve the mystery." Zane leaned toward me, eyes sparkling like the afternoon light on Buzzard's Bay. "So what do you know?"

"Wait a sec, Zane. We're going to talk about it, not solve it." *Geez.* First Gin, then Flo, now Zane.

"Of course." He flapped his hand, dismissing my concern. "Still, if we put our heads together, who knows what we'll come up with."

He might have a point. And if we did figure anything out, I'd simply pass it along to Detective Haskins.

Zane went on. "For example, I saw a new guy around town today who didn't look anything like a tourist. Tall hefty dude, dark hair with some silver in it, kind of ambled when he walked. But he was alone, not wearing shorts, no camera. Maybe he's somebody suspicious." He sipped his beer with eyes aglow.

"Flowered shirt, kind of comfortable body?"

"Yes. You saw him too?"

"Yeah, but no." I shook my head. "Sorry. He's the police detective."

His mouth dropped open. "No sir."

"His name is Lincoln Haskins. He interviewed me for a while earlier today."

"So much for that theory." He lowered his head as his posture deflated.

"The good thing is that he's on the case and he seems smart." And he told me to watch my back. I'd been so busy I hadn't even thought about the detective's words of caution since he'd left. But now? I glanced around. It was the same sunny coastal tourist town it had always been. How could it include murder?

"Earth to Mac." Zane waved a hand in front of my face.

"Oops. Brain wander." I laughed and sipped my beer. "So you haven't seen any other strangers around town?"

He frowned. "Lots, of course. Some actually interested in locally distilled beverages. Nobody looking like they just killed Jake." He tapped his bottle. "Not that I would know what that looks like, of course. But there was a girl who wandered in."

"A kid in a liquor store?"

"Sorry. Not a kid, a young woman. She wanted directions, but she looked lost in another kind of way, you know? Like emotionally lost or something."

"Light hair? Turquoise cross bag?"

"Sounds like you saw her, too."

"She walked by on the sidewalk while I was out here having lunch. I thought she'd been crying." My phone vibrated on the table where I'd set it. I checked it to see a text from Tim. "Excuse me a sec." I drew the phone onto my lap to read the message. *Rats*. He wanted me to come over for dinner, which I couldn't do tonight. I texted back that I had book group and wouldn't be home until nine or so, but I ended it with Xs and Os to soften my words. I looked up at Zane again.

"Have you seen Derrick anywhere?" I asked. "He didn't come to work today and isn't returning my texts."

"That's odd. Isn't it?"

"Of course it is. He's usually pretty reliable." Or was he? Since he'd come back from his two-year retreat in the Swiss monastery, Cokey in hand, he'd been a little flaky. Derrick was my big brother, but I often felt the older, more responsible one.

Zane drained his beer and stood. "Off I go. See you in a couple of hours."

"Thanks for the drink, my friend. Keep your eyes open."

He gave me a thumbs-up and sauntered away, leaving the rest of the six-pack on the table.

"Hey, take your beers," I called after him.

"Save them for next time." He waved.

I could do that, or I could bring them tonight instead. I took the beer inside, locking the back door once I was in. After I completed my shop-closing checklist, I locked up the front and took the beer to my house.

Except I didn't go home and relax. I had to find out where my brother was. If he was at home, he'd return my calls and texts, so I didn't head for his lighthouse.

I stuck the beer in the fridge, gave Belle a few grapes

in a bowl and a promise, and hurried down the road to the parsonage right beyond my father's church. I heard happy-girl squeals from the backyard, so I headed around the side of the shingled Greek revival house. Pa was pushing four-year-old Cokey in the rope swing hanging from a big old oak tree. It was a newer version of the same swing I'd played on for many happy hours as a kid. Cokey loved hanging out with my parents when Derrick was working or out socializing, and the love was mutual.

"Titi Mac," Cokey called, using her version of the Kriolu word for *auntie,* pronounced *tee-tee.* "Come and puth me," with "push" coming out in her trademark lisp. Her blond angel curls flew every which way in their ponytail as she swung. The late afternoon sunlight shining through the tree cast dappled shadows on her yellow t-shirt and shorts.

"I'd love to. How's my favorite niece?"

"Good." She was way too focused on the fun of pumping her legs, taking her higher and higher, to give much more of an answer than that.

I gave the tiny human pendulum a wide berth. "Hi, Pa." I kissed my dad's cheek and stood next to him behind the swing.

"Hey, sweetie." He put his arm around my shoulders and squeezed. He'd been six feet tall in his prime, but had lost an inch or two with aging. His kinky black hair was half silver but he wore it touching his collar as he always had. His arm was still strong from splitting wood for the winter wood stove and his hug provided comfort. "You're welcome to take over grandpop duty here."

"Sure, but don't go anywhere." I pushed Cokey next time she swung back, but as she went forward and up,

I murmured, "Where in heck is Derrie?" I rarely called my brother by my childhood name for him anymore.

He frowned as he turned to face the back of the property, which was rimmed with high grasses and reeds that bordered the salt marsh behind. "I don't know. He left her with us early this morning and said he'd be back tonight. You know we love having Cokey, but your brother usually checks in a few times during the day. He'd better keep his word tonight or he's going to have one upset little girl."

Derrick had had a few rocky years in high school and my father—well, our father—Pa and my mom had raised Derrick since he was a toddler and he was the only dad Derrick had ever known. Anyway, Pa had struggled to maintain a loving but firm discipline with him. I could hear some of that firmness in his voice now. But Derrick was in bigger trouble than with Pa if he didn't appear soon.

"He never came to work at the shop today," I told him. I wasn't sure if I was more angry with my brother for dropping out of sight or more worried about where he was and if he was all right. What if the murderer had targeted Derrick next?

Pa made a *tsking* sound.

"I told you about the murder." I spoke in a near whisper as I gave Cokey another boost.

"And of course it was on the news, too. I'm so sorry you had to have that shocking experience, honey."

"I'm all right." At least mostly all right. "What I didn't tell you on the phone was that the knife Jake was stabbed with looked exactly like Derrick's."

"What?" He whirled back to face me.

I glanced at Cokey but she hadn't heard. I pushed my hand down a couple of times to indicate he should speak softly. "And I'm sure at least one of the local police officers would have recognized it by now, too. You know, somebody who went fishing with him."

"Derrick wouldn't . . ."

"Of course not. But the detective on the case wants to talk with him and they can't find him, either."

"I know. Lincoln called here today."

"You know Detective Haskins?" I watched Cokey pump her strong little legs.

My father smiled. "Yes. He's a good man. A very good man."

"Maybe Derrie had a job elsewhere on the Cape and is coming straight to our Cozy Capers meeting tonight. Maybe he simply forgot to tell me. Or you." On the other hand, a murderer was out there. Someone who had stolen Derrick's knife. Was my brother even safe?

"Maybe."

A lean, athletic-looking man in his twenties rounded the corner of the house. His arms held an open laptop, arms so heavily tattooed I couldn't see a square millimeter of plain skin. "Father Joe?" he called out, studying the display.

"Who's that? And *Father* Joe? Does he think you're a priest or something?"

"That's Edwin. He's the church's new accountant. I'm over here," Pa called in return. "You haven't met him yet?"

The dude finally looked up and steered in our direction.

"I have not." I was frankly curious. The name Edwin matched the brainy occupation. But the arms, the green do-rag, even the cocky saunter—those didn't compute for me. Where had Pa found him? The clock on my musings ran out right about then, however.

"Edwin, meet my daughter, Mackenzie. Mac, this is Edwin Germain. He's a pretty serious cyclist."

I hoped Pa wasn't trying to fix us up, with our mutual devotion to bicycles likely the only middle ground. For one thing, the guy had to be at least ten years younger than me, and for another, I already had a boyfriend. I extended my hand. Edwin shook it with a firm touch, but not that knuckle-breaking clench some men seem to feel obliged to use with women.

"Glad to meet you," I said. "You're an accountant?"

"Yes, ma'am, a CPA. I decided it was a more reliable occupation than working as a repo man. Safer, anyway." The green in his do-rag picked up the green in his eyes but it contrasted with black hair that curled like mine out from under the scarf.

"I guess it would be." I glanced at the laptop. "Sorry, did you two have business to discuss?"

"Can it wait a few minutes, Edwin?" Pa asked.

"Abo Joe, I'm hungry." Cokey jumped off the swing. "Hi, Edwin."

"Hey, Miss Cokey." Edwin held out his fist for a bump.

"Then let's eat. Edwin and I have to do a little work together, too." Pa held out his hand for his granddaughter. "Does my seashell want a carrot or an apple?"

Cokey giggled at her nickname. Coquille, her actual name, meant seashell in French. Derrick and Cokey's mom had chosen to honor both the Cape and Derrick's ex's Gallic heritage in their choice of name for the girl.

"I want apple with cheese, please," she lisped. "Are you gonna have a snack, too, Titi Mac?"

"No, I have to go, sweetie. You have fun with Abo." I had to go look for her father.

She held up her arms for a hug. "Okay. Bye."

I bent over and embraced her, inhaling the sweet sweaty scent of her hair. I straightened, looking at Pa. "Call me if . . ." I held my thumb and pinkie to my ear.

"I will. You, too."

"Of course." I watched the tall, the tiny, and the tattooed start back to the house. Cokey began to skip, and Reverend Joseph Almeida skipped right along with her. Edwin Germain, CPA, did not skip.

Chapter Nine

Flo lived just far enough away to make it too far to walk. I didn't mind. Miss M, my convertible Miata, needed to be taken out for a spin, anyway. She was my one expensive indulgence. My house was ultra-small and super-efficient, and I didn't care about fancy clothes—or shoes and handbags, God forbid. But this red two-seater roadster made me happy, and I was glad I'd let myself buy sporty Miss M when I got back from my travels a year ago.

Before I aimed her at Flo's house, I steered for the lighthouse. I tried the breathe-in-breathe-out technique I'd learned in a meditation class to calm my worry about Derrick. Or was it anger I was feeling? Follow the breath, be aware of my surroundings, let thoughts float away. *Nah.* That wasn't working.

Only a few minutes later I bumped out along the long approach road to the lighthouse at the end. Pulling Miss M to a stop, I gazed up a hundred feet at the tapering cyl-

inder. The structure had formerly guided ships around
the promontory and warned them off the rocks with its
bright sweeping beam at the top. No lights shone through
the arched windows in the apartment now, though, and
Derrick's car wasn't parked in front of it. I swore and hit
the steering wheel with my hand. I took a moment to
e-mail Pa that Derrick wasn't home.

Turning around in the parking area, I drove with the
top down, sea breeze be damned. Despite the salt-
scented wind ruffling my hair, the drive wasn't making
me all that happy tonight. Maybe when I walked into
Flo's my brother would already be sitting with the
group, soda in hand, but I wasn't betting the shop on it.
If he was there, I couldn't decide if I was going to give
him a big hug of relief or wring his stupid neck.

I pulled over in back of the line of cars parked at the
curb in front of the house Flo shared with her daughter
Suzanne. I raised Miss M's top before I locked the car.
I knew from forgetting to do so in the past that I'd come
out to damp seats if I didn't. This way I also wasn't tempt-
ing car thieves partial to convertibles. My heart fell as I
walked past the line of cars. Derrick's beat-up Civic
was nowhere in sight.

I hurried into the house. My brother could have gotten a ride with someone, or even taken a long walk to
get here. But he wasn't inside, either. I delivered
Zane's beers to the drinks table.

"Is Derrick here, Flo?" I asked.

She glanced around the group. "No, haven't seen
him."

I swore silently, but plastered a smile on my face
and went around greeting people. I delivered a kiss on

each cheek to Stephen. A stocky man not much taller than me, he was the Jeff to Zane's taller, willowy Mutt. When I'd mentioned the comparison to them, I'd gotten puzzled looks. I can't help it if I have a weakness for vintage comic strips. I waved to Tulia Peters and gave a mock salute to Norland, who returned it.

I joined Gin where she was pouring a glass of Chardonnay for herself.

"Any news?" I asked, filling a glass for myself.

"Yes, but I'll share it with everybody once we get started."

"Sounds juicy."

"Maybe." She shrugged but held her finger to her lips like she knew a secret she couldn't tell.

"You haven't seen Derrick around anywhere, have you?"

"Not today, no. Why?"

"I'll tell you later." Or maybe I wouldn't.

The doorbell rang and Flo opened it to the delivery person. Soon we all sat with paper plates and slices of the best pizza south of Boston, short of homemade. Good thing nobody objected to having Italian pies two meetings in a row. Flo's living room was lined with floor-to-ceiling bookshelves, as befit a librarian's residence. An old-fashioned oval braided rug filled the center of the room, and the easy chairs and couch were upholstered in slipcovers. Flo preferred to spend her disposable income on books, not home furnishings. Managing a public library wasn't exactly a get-rich-quick scheme.

I swallowed a bite of my mushroom-goat cheese slice, turning to Norland on my right. I asked him how he was.

"Getting along." He nodded with a satisfied look on his lined face. "Loving retirement, although for some reason I'm busier now than when I was working. I volunteer here and there, got my twice-weekly golf games with the boys, babysit the grands after school most days, lead Men's Bible Breakfast on Mondays, and more. I don't even know where the time goes."

His wife had died the year before, and he'd initially retired to take care of her during her final illness. We'd all been a little concerned about how he'd do on his own, but he seemed to be thriving.

"Does having a homicide in town make you wish you were back on the force?"

He scrutinized me for a beat, then burst out laughing. "Are you kidding, Mac? Having to coordinate all the officers and being told what to do by statie detectives? Fielding calls from the public who swear they saw a suspicious character lurking when all it was was their regular garbage man?" He shook his head, his smile wide in his broad face. "No way. Makes me even gladder I'm out of it."

"But you came tonight." I took a sip of wine and continued. "You know Flo wants to talk about the crime. She's got some harebrained idea we can solve it ourselves."

"As long as any information shared here is also funneled to the detective on the case, it can't hurt to compare notes," Norland said.

We sat chatting a while longer, the delectable smells of baked crust, herbed tomato sauce, and melted cheese mixing with the tangy salty ones of olives and pepperoni.

A few minutes later Flo collected our plates and came back with a yellow legal pad and a pen. "Shall we get started? I think if each of us shares any suspicious behavior we've seen around town, we might come up with some, well, suspects in Jake's murder."

"Wait a second." Tulia held up a hand. "Before we get to that, how you doing, Mac? Finding a body must have been quite a shock." She was a hardy, no-nonsense native with ruddy cheeks and weathered hands. She ran the lobster shack, but had done her share of the lobstering itself on their boat alongside her husband in all kinds of weather.

"Thanks for asking, Tulia. I'm all right. I don't like all the attention, or the idea that whoever killed Jake is out wandering around somewhere, but I'm doing okay." I smiled at her.

"Good," she replied "Well, as for me, I haven't seen nothing goofy going on." She shrugged.

"What about Derrick?" Norland glanced at me, a smear of pizza sauce now adorning his white polo shirt. "Does he know about our meeting?"

I scrunched up my nose. "I don't know where he is. He hasn't answered my texts. My parents have Cokey with them and they haven't heard from him, either. I wouldn't hold my breath waiting."

Norland nodded slowly, gazing at me. I thought I saw sympathy in his eyes. Did he know about the knife? He might, with his police past. "I'll let you know if I see him around," he told me.

"I'd appreciate that."

"So." Flo poised the pen above the pad of paper. "Anything odd going on?"

"I have a man staying in my Airbnb," Gin said. "He's from New York City, and he's interested in buying a house on this part of the Cape."

"And that's suspicious how?" Stephen asked.

Gin shrugged. "It's probably not. But he's from off Cape and he's not a tourist. Seems to be loaded, too. Wears all kind of fancy gold jewelry and expensive clothes. And he arrived last weekend, so he was here on Tuesday."

"I met him this morning," I said. "He came into the shop looking for properties for sale. Expensive casual clothes, lots of gold."

"Name?" Flo asked.

"Wesley Farnham," Gin replied.

I nodded. "Right. Same guy. But he also asked me where he could find Jake, except he called him Jacob."

"Really?" Tulia asked. "That's gotta be important."

"I think so, too," I said. "He mentioned he knew him from when they both were younger near Providence."

Norland whistled. "Did you tell him about the body?"

"I said I didn't know where he could find Jake. Which is the truth."

"Interesting," Gin said. "He didn't ask me about Jake."

"Why wouldn't he have known the news, though?" Zane asked. "Between TV, radio, papers, and online, wouldn't he have heard about the murder?"

"I wondered that, too." I waited to see if Gin had an answer.

She frowned. "I don't provide television in the rooms. Some of my guests think that's a plus. And he went out early this morning somewhere, so maybe he was out of touch. Who knows?"

Flo finished scribbling notes on Wesley Farnham. "Good. What else?" She gazed around the circle.

Stephen tapped his fingers on the arm of his chair. "A couple of days ago I saw Jake and a young woman eating together at Yoshinoya." He looked at Zane next to him. "It was that day I got takeout sushi for dinner, remember?"

"Right. Monday," Zane said.

"And she wasn't from here, either," Stephen added.

"Had you seen her before?" I asked. "Like around town?"

Stephen shook his head. "But they both looked, I don't know, happy."

I didn't think Jake had the money to go out to eat. Maybe his guest was treating him, whoever she was. A young woman. My eyebrows went way up as I snapped my fingers.

"Was she sort of thin? Light hair?" I asked.

Stephen nodded. "You must have seen her, too."

"She walked by the bike shop when I was having lunch outside around twelve-thirty. I think she'd been crying."

Zane added, "And she came into the store today. She looked sad to me, too. Maybe she knew Jake and is upset he's dead."

"But she's not staying at your place." Flo directed her words to Gin.

"No. Since the rooms share a bath, if someone rents the bigger room, I keep the smaller one vacant. I only fill both when it's a family or other folks who are together."

"She could be with a friend, or in one of the motels," Tulia said. "It's not like we have any shortage of lodging around here."

"If anybody sees her again, try to figure out how to stop her and have a conversation." I gazed around the room, laughing inwardly at myself. It looked like I was getting into this amateur sleuth thing after all. "Figure out how she knew Jake, anyway."

Norland gave a thumbs-up, while Gin said, "Sure," and Zane tapped out a note on his phone.

Stephen raised his hand. "I was in Barnstable at the county courthouse for some town business and I saw Jake there. That was on Monday, as well."

"Was he alone?" Flo asked.

"I don't know. When I saw him he was talking with a woman in a blazer, but he might have just been asking directions."

"Oh!" I exclaimed. Heads turned in my direction. "Tim saw a woman in a blazer out on the point. Talking with Jake. He told the police, of course."

"I wonder if they've found her." Norland looked like his brain was on overdrive.

"Or if it's even the same person." I looked at our retired police chief. "Norland, question for you. Victoria responded to the scene after I called 911." I shifted my position on the couch, which had long since lost its comfy cushioning.

"As she would. As I would have."

"But a man named Lincoln Haskins interviewed me this afternoon. He's with the state police, and the news that night said the Barnstable criminal unit, or something like that, was also going to be investigating. How come the local police have these other departments working on the murder?"

"Ah, the curious workings of our criminal justice system. Big cities, like Boston and Worcester, have their own homicide detectives, crime scene techs, the works. But little towns like Westham? First of all, we simply don't get murders here. Well, almost never. Which leads to second," he ticked his points off on his fingers, "we don't have the resources to keep trained homicide investigators in the department. So we call in the big guns when a murder occurs within our boundaries."

"Is this Detective Haskins a good guy?" Zane asked. "Competent?"

"I can't speak to the competence, but I've known him since he was little," Tulia said. "He's a member of the Tribe, too."

"Wampanoag?" Zane asked.

"Yes. His mama isn't, but his daddy is. Linc is honest and a sweetheart. Had some grief in his past but he's dealt with it. You can trust him." She sipped her seltzer.

"I agree with Tulia," Norland said. "And I can vouch for his skill as a detective. He's busted some tough cases in the past. We're in good hands with Lincoln."

A click sounded from the hall. A moment later Suzanne Wolanski poked her head in. "Solved this week's 'cozy' murder yet?" She put quotes around the word cozy with her fingers. "Or, wait. You guys did that last night. Stepping up the pace of your reading, are you?" Her lip almost curled as she leaned against the doorjamb rubbing one earlobe.

Suzanne held a very low opinion of our chosen genre. I glanced at Flo, whose cheeks were red. Must be tough to have an adult daughter who insulted one of your favorite genres. Suzanne often scheduled big-name literary authors to speak at the Book Rack, but deliberately booked them on our book group night so none of us could attend. She did deign to order the paperbacks we planned to read if we gave her the list with enough advance notice, but the mystery section in the store consisted of only a couple of shelves of mostly hardcovers with names like Patterson, Cornwell, and Child on the spines, and cozies were so sparsely stocked as to be almost invisible. I had no idea why she treated cozies with such disdain, or why she still lived with her mother, for that matter.

"We're talking about the very real murder in town, Suze," her mother answered.

"Give me a break." Scorn poured from her face as she scanned the room. "You really think a bunch of rank amateurs can figure out who stabbed Jake Lacey?" She uttered an obscenity under her breath and turned away.

Footsteps clattered up the stairs. I gazed at the empty doorway. The news hadn't said anything about a stabbing, and Flo had said she'd heard it from Suzanne. So how did she know?

I surveyed the room. Stephen also focused on where Suzanne had stood. He looked at me.

"Stabbed? Is that true, Mac?" He wrinkled his nose. "Did you see the weapon?"

Norland caught my gaze and almost imperceptibly shook his head. So he knew, too.

"I was asked not to talk about the crime scene. I'm sorry, Stephen. I'm sure it will all be in the news soon." My answer didn't seem to please him, but I couldn't help it. I just hoped my brother's name wasn't going to be in the news along with pictures of the knife.

Chapter Ten

Finally I was home. I'd had two fly-by stops here, the second between talking to Pa and heading to Flo's, and they'd been exactly that. Feed the bird, use the facilities, and change out of work clothes. Now at nearly nine o'clock I made myself a wine spritzer with seltzer, Cape Cod Winery Pinot Grigio, sweetened cranberry juice, a dash of Grenadine, and a squeeze of lime juice, and sank down on the couch with my phone. Belle, as always, hopped onto my shoulder and asked for a kiss, so I obliged. She scooted into my lap.

"Give Belle a cuddle."

I stroked the soft feathers on her head and neck, but my brain was bursting with questions. Who was the young woman several of us had seen, and what was her connection with Jake? How about the woman Stephen saw with Jake at the county courthouse, and the one Tim spied with him out on the point? Were they the same? Who was Wesley Farnham and how did he know Jake was here? And how did Suzanne know Jake had been stabbed?

But my primary concern was Derrick's whereabouts. I'd muted my phone during the meeting and had missed a call from Pa. I didn't waste time with the message and decided to phone my brother directly. Much to my surprise he answered and greeted me in a subdued voice.

"Derrie, where have you been?" Why go subtle when you can cut straight to what's important?

"Nice to talk with you, too." His already deep voice was a pitch lower and his words came out slow and tired.

"Are you home?" I asked.

"Yes."

I waited for more but it didn't come. "With Cokey?"

"She's sleeping over at the parsonage."

"You know we were all worried about you. And I needed you in the shop."

"Yes, and sorry." He cleared his throat. "Mac, I need to get some sleep."

"But Derrick, you have to—" The call went dead. I held my phone out, staring at it. He hung up on me. I shook my head, but let it go. I supposed I could drive over there right now and demand to know where he'd been and if the knife I'd seen was his. But I was tired too and I knew from experience when Derrick needed sleep, waking him never went well. The Mystery of the Disappearing Brother was going to have to wait until tomorrow to be solved.

"Are you home?" Belle squawked. "Are you home?"

"I'm home, Belle. Derrick is too. No worries." Not really, but a bird wasn't going to solve my problems for me.

"Gimme a kiss, Cokey."

"Later, Belle, later." Smart bird. She knew the words Derrick and Cokey were linked.

I sipped the cool fizzy spritzer and frowned, picturing Suzanne's scorn for our genre. She was younger than I was by eight or ten years. I didn't really care if she liked cozies or not, except that she barely stocked them and special ordered what we wanted only reluctantly. More important, why did she have such an important position in the bookstore? I realized I didn't know the current owner. The old lady who had owned it when I was a kid had to have died some time ago. Certainly Suzanne herself wouldn't have had the resources to buy a thriving business. Or would she?

I plugged Suzanne Wolanski into Google and peered at the display. She'd won swimming trophies in high school. Graduated from U Mass Dartmouth, the campus of the state university about an hour away on the way to Rhode Island. After that I couldn't find much about her. She was thanked in a quote from an article about the time she'd brought Elizabeth Strout to the bookstore for a reading, quite a coup for a small town like ours. Maybe she'd inherited a chunk of money and had bought the store. I kept digging but didn't see a transfer of property to her. Or maybe the owner didn't want to have any part in running the store and handed all the responsibility to Suzanne.

The more pressing question was how she knew Jake was stabbed. I was pretty sure that information hadn't been made public. Surely Suzanne wasn't our murderer. Flo's own daughter? *No.* Could she have some in with the police department? I dug into Google. Nope, at least nothing the world's biggest search engine knew anything about. No part-time job with the Westham

Police, no internship with the state police. Nothing. On the other hand, she could have a friend in the police department who blabbed the details.

Time to move on to the other people we'd discussed at the meeting. I didn't know Sad Young Woman's name, or Blazer's. I tapped in Wesley Farnham instead. Sure enough, he owned a number of buildings in New York City, and several apartment complexes in Hoboken, New Jersey, across the river from the Big Apple. I hoped he wasn't thinking of building a McMansion here in Westham, or a developing a resort. We prided ourselves on still being a small and mostly tasteful Cape Cod village.

The "tasteful" part had led to conflict in the past, when summer people complained about the smells coming from the lobster pier, for example. Hey, you want a seacoast vacation, you have to take the smelly with the delicious, the junk with the scenic. It was like people inland who bought houses next to a decades-established pig farm and then griped about the stink of the pigs. I shook my head. Back to Mr. Farnham. I couldn't find any link with Jake Lacey nor any sordid criminal past. A Wes Farnham did graduate from North Providence High School, with a Yale acceptance in hand. Jake or Jacob Lacey didn't appear to be on the list of graduates, though. Maybe he'd dropped out before finishing.

An incoming text vibrated the little computer in my hand. Finally something to smile about. I pressed Tim's speed dial button and said, "Guess who?"

We chatted for a couple of minutes about his day, which had included the success of his new cranberry-orange-nut bread recipe and a ten-mile afternoon run.

"But what about you?" he asked. "How'd book

group go? And why are you meeting twice in one week?"

Tim barely read any fiction, and had no interest in cozy mysteries, so he'd never been part of the group. I explained about the gathering of so-called sleuths.

He laughed. "Really? Florence thinks you guys can figure out the murderer yourselves?"

"I know, it's crazy. But they all seem excited about the prospect."

"Mac, you need to be careful." The laugh was gone from his voice. "This is real crime. A real killer."

"I know, Tim. Don't worry, I'm watching my step, locking my doors. My only goal is making sure that if one of us learns something, we turn it over to Detective Haskins. Like ASAP."

"Good."

"One person you could keep an eye out for, though, is that woman you saw on the point with Jake. Let me know if she comes into the bakery, okay?"

"I guess. But why?" His voice went up as if he was puzzled.

"Because she might be a link to Jake. I mean, she's a stranger, and you saw them together. None of us knows who she is."

"And you think she killed him? Seems like a stretch, hon."

"I don't know." I stroked Belle's smooth head. "I think we need to learn what her connection with him was, that's all."

"Okay. I'll keep my eyes open. I didn't see her on my run today, though, as a point of information for you."

"Thanks." I fell silent, thinking about somebody I hadn't seen.

"Earth to Mac. Penny for your thoughts?"

"Sorry. It's my absent brother who's still something of a mystery. Derrick went missing all day today. He's home tonight but he wouldn't explain. I hope I can get him to talk tomorrow." And I hoped he'd come to work, too.

"For sure I'll give you a buzz if he comes into the bakery. Let me know if there's any other way I can help you with him. You know, have a little man to man. I like the dude. I'd ask him out for a beer, except . . ."

"He doesn't drink. And good for him." Derrick had struggled with an addiction to alcohol, but he'd been sober for six years now. As far as I knew, anyway. "By now he's comfortable having a soda at a bar. You could still ask him."

"Maybe I will. So," he lowered his voice to sexy husky, "can I get you to come over for dinner tomorrow, Ms. Almeida?" The audible smile was back.

"Twist my arm, Mr. Brunelle. Or actually, don't. Just tell me what time." I couldn't wait.

Chapter Eleven

At our usual seven o'clock meetup the next morning, Gin and I once again were walking the bikeway *sans* earbuds. The investigation was too urgent to ignore.

"I googled your Mr. Farnham last night," I said.

"Yeah? And?"

"And nothing, unfortunately. The guy is a real estate magnate. But no ties to crime that I could dig up, no past murders, and no link to Jake. That I could find, anyway." I pulled my sleeve cuffs down over my hands. It was supposed to warm up later but for now the air still held the nip of late spring, not the heat of summer.

Gin, in a sensible windbreaker and cotton gloves, shrugged. "I guess he's simply a paying guest who loves the Cape as much as millions of others. Nothing wrong with that. Although it's kind of funny he wanted to rent a room above a candy shop and not somewhere swankier."

"I hadn't thought of that. I learned he graduated from a high school in Providence, but I couldn't find Jake in the list of graduates. Maybe they were childhood playmates or something. But how did he hear Jake was living here?"

"Dunno. He must have heard by now about the murder. If he hasn't, I'll tell him when I put out the breakfast."

"I'll send Haskins a text and tell him Farnham has a room in your bed and breakfast, if that's okay." A text I probably should have sent last night.

"Sure."

We strode in silence for a couple of minutes, swinging our arms, inhaling the fresh air, and thinking. Except my thinking didn't get me any further than it had last night. A woodpecker hammering away on a dead cedar tapped at my memory.

"Gin, what do you know about Suzanne?"

"Besides that she doesn't like cozies, and that she runs a successful bookstore?"

"Right."

"She's enough older than my daughter that Lucy didn't know her in school. I think Suzanne got a degree in library science thinking she'd follow in her mom's footsteps, but then the bookstore job opened up and she took it."

"So she doesn't own the store?"

"Own it? I don't think so. But I guess I don't know for sure." Gin stopped walking. "Hang on, have to retie my shoe."

I took the time to lean on a tree and stretch my calves. "Have you seen or heard anything in the news about Jake being stabbed?"

She straightened. "No, I don't think so."

"And you didn't tell anyone about that?" I asked as we resumed walking.

"No. You asked me not to. Why?"

We arrived at a small cross street and waited to be sure an approaching car would stop for us before continuing. "Last night Suzanne mentioned that he was stabbed. I wondered how she knew."

Gin sucked in a noisy breath and clapped a hand to her chest. "Suzanne killed Jake. That's the only way she'd know, Mac!"

"Hey, relax." I gently elbowed her. "I know that's how it goes in the books we read. But this is real life."

"But how else would she find out?"

"That's the thing. She must have a friend in the police department who leaked the news. I tried to see if she'd ever worked for them in the past. If she did, it's not public knowledge."

Gin snapped her fingers. "Alibis. We haven't been talking about alibis. All we have to do is find out where Suzanne was when Jake was killed. That should be easy, right?"

"Maybe. She wasn't at book group with us, of course. I don't know exactly what time Jake died, but it had to be after the fog came in. Otherwise somebody else using the path would have come across him. But nobody was out once the pea soup descended."

"I don't remember about the fog, but I'll ask around, see what time Suzanne closed the bookstore."

"And I'll figure out the fog bank. I don't remember watching it come in from the lighthouse. Somebody in the group will know."

"What about the woman Stephen and Tim saw?" Gin asked. "How can we find out more about her? If we had a picture of her, we could search on that."

"But we don't have one." I thought. "Maybe she'll come in to get some candy from you, or hit up Tim's bakery. I told him last night to look out for her and he said he would."

Ahead the trail took a gentle curve where it led out toward Westham Point. Our normal route was to stride to where the Point extension branched off and head out on the branch. The extension ran first on a boardwalk over the marsh and then up the sloping Point Hill. We normally spent a few minutes stretching at the bay overlook before retracing our steps. A road led to the Point, too, and there was a parking area for a dozen cars. It was a perfect vantage point from which to watch the sun set over water.

The boardwalk over the marsh in the morning was also a perfect vantage spot for bird watching, and this morning didn't disappoint. A clutch of teals paddled serenely until one at a time they darted underwater, while a marsh hawk tilted above and red-winged blackbirds buzzed a *twee* call. A great blue heron stalked a fishy prey, which reminded me that a human murderer might be stalking his—or her—next victim, too. Even though I wanted the crime solved and the criminal locked up for life, part of me wished the killer would just get out of town and never come back.

Gin pointed to the tall, long-necked bird. "Do you think that's what Jake's killer is doing? Looking for the next victim?"

"I was thinking the exact same thing." I shivered and hugged myself. "Come on. Race you to the top." I started up my best speed walking form, rolling my hips, pumping my arms.

For Gin's part, she just walked faster in her usual gait, and swung her arms high, forward and back. When our race ended in a tie at the end of the path where it opened up to the vista and an empty parking lot, I pointed.

"Looks like rain later." Thick clouds were massing in the west, and the wind came from that direction, too. "I bet it'll be a quiet day at the bike shop, at least on the rental and retail side. Which is good, because I have a big touring group of Dutch riders bringing their bikes in for a quick mid-ride tune-up while they take the day off."

As we stretched, a sleek silver sedan pulled into the lot. First a pair of black three-inch heels slid out of the driver's seat, then the woman they belonged to, phone in her hand. The car dinged to signal that the keys were in the ignition while the door was open. The woman strolled to the edge of the lot overlooking the bluff to our left. She held the phone in front of her and apparently hadn't seen us, since she didn't lower her voice. The onshore breeze carried everything she said straight to us. More important was her outfit.

"Blazer," I whispered.

"Heels," Gin murmured.

"Mystery woman," we said in unison under our breath.

* * *

"The deed checked out. And I've handled the other matter," Blazer said. Her narrow skirt was black, and she wore a red scarf draped around her neck.

A tinny voice came out of her phone's speaker but I couldn't make out any of the words. Gin also strained to hear but shook her head in frustration.

"Yes, Mr. Wu." The woman sounded impatient.

Deeds. Mr. Wu.

"I told you, things are moving apace," she went on. "I foresee no issues moving forward. The only obstacle has been . . ." The wind shifted and a gust of air took her last words out to sea.

I fixed my gaze on my friend. "An obstacle," I whispered.

"Was Jake the obstacle?" Gin murmured in return.

When the tinny voice resumed I grabbed Gin's elbow. We edged sideways a few paces to get closer. "Keep stretching so it doesn't look like we're listening." I kept my voice to the quietest whisper I could manage. I got close enough to see a small decal on the back window that read, "Cape Luxury," which was a luxury car rental place in Bourne.

Gin nodded and reached for her feet. I set my legs wide and tilted an arm over my head in a side stretch. My eyes pointed toward the water, my lungs inhaled the salty air, but I kept my ears tuned to the stranger.

"I'll contact you as soon as things are settled," Blazer said to her phone. "You'll be staying in the country until we can sign papers?"

Staying in the country.

A moment later she said, "Fine. Talk to you then."

In my peripheral vision I saw her jab at the phone

and turn. She stopped in her tracks when she saw us. Her nostrils flared.

"Were you—" she said at the same time as a smiling Gin called, "Good morning."

I looked over, abandoning my pose. The woman stood about my height and wore the streaked reddish hair of a mature woman who had it professionally tended. She had small eyes and a thin nose. Her profile was thin, too.

"Nice spot, isn't it?" I asked in a cheery voice. "Do you come to the Point often?"

"Yes, it's very scenic." She shook her head slowly. "But no, I don't come here often." She glanced at the phone in her hand and slid it into the jacket pocket, then took a few steps toward us. "So it's called the Point, is it?"

I nodded. *Funny.* I knew the sign at the beginning of the road clearly said Westham Point Road. Maybe she'd missed it.

She drummed her fingers at her side like she was impatient to be somewhere other than trapped by a couple of talkative women in a parking lot. "Do you live around here?" she finally asked.

If she wanted to leave, why continue the conversation? It was fine with me, though. The longer we kept her, the more we might learn.

"You bet," Gin said. "Best town on the Cape. I'm Gin Malloy, owner of Salty Taffy's, and this is Mackenzie Almeida." She waved a hand toward me.

"But please call me Mac." I extended my hand to the woman. "I run the local bike shop."

Blazer hesitated that brief second that indicates distrust of either people or germs, but finally shook my hand. "Katherine Deloit. Nice to meet you both." Her red-painted smile was perfunctory. She shook Gin's hand after mine.

"Is this your first time to Westham, Katherine?" I asked as a gull lit on the bluff with a plaintive cry.

"Yes. Well, I arrived a few days ago. It's a charming town. Little shops and restaurant. Lovely. It must be popular with tourists starting about now."

"It is, as long as it doesn't rain too much," I said.

The woman cleared her throat. "You people hit the news hard this week. Do you get many murders around here?"

Gin laughed. "Thank goodness, no. First one I've ever heard of, and I've lived here for years."

I watched the woman. I don't know what I was expecting, but she acted perfectly normal. The distant thrum of a fishing boat's engine floated on the air before another gust of wind swept it away.

Gin wiped the smile off her face. "And the killing was a terrible thing to have happen. Jake was a good man. He didn't deserve to die."

"Very sad indeed." Katherine knit her brow and shook her head a little.

"Had you ever met him?" I asked. Stephen thought he'd seen this woman and Jake together at the courthouse. "Jake Lacey?"

She stared at me as if I'd recently been released from the loony bin. "Did I ever meet someone from here named Lacey? Why would you even ask? I've only been here three days."

I shrugged. "Just wondering. It's a small town. Where are you visiting from?" I asked, shoving my hands in my shorts pockets. I'd worked up enough of a sweat speed walking that I was getting cold standing around in a sea breeze.

"Actually, I'm located in Westwood. California."

"From Westwood to Westham," Gin said. "That's a long trip."

"It is, but I'm here to visit an old college friend, and to do a bit of business, too. Now, if you ladies will excuse me?"

Gin nodded. I waved. Katherine Deloit walked briskly back to her car, her heels tapping on the pavement. We watched her drive off.

"What do you think?" Gin asked. "She said she's here on business."

"Right. But notice she didn't say what kind of business. I think she was about to ask if we'd been eavesdropping when you greeted her. She looked upset, or angry, more so."

"And then she covered it up and got polite in a superficial kind of way."

"Stephen must have been wrong about seeing her with Jake at the courthouse," I said. "Maybe she was only asking a random stranger for directions. Although, why would Jake be at the courthouse? Unless . . ."

"Unless what?"

I tilted my head. "What if Jake owned land somewhere? That nobody knew about, that she wanted to buy for her client."

"Jake Lacey?" Gin's voice went way up on the question. "If he owned land around here he'd be a rich man. He wouldn't be eating at the soup kitchen and living in a flea-bag room or a campground."

"You're right, of course. Or maybe this Deloit

woman was lying. Right? Suspects in our books lie about everything."

Gin pointed a finger at me. "True. Too bad we couldn't ask her what the obstacle had been, and what happened to it." She gazed down the now-empty road.

"Or who Mr. Wu is."

Chapter Twelve

If I'd thought I would have some time to think about murder this morning, I was wrong. Actually, all I could think about was murdering my brother.

Twenty touring bikes showed up at nine o'clock sharp as I was unlocking the front door. Today I had no moment to pause and enjoy my shop before the rush hit. The visit was by prearrangement, but once again Derrick hadn't showed for his shift. Where was he now, and why wouldn't he talk to me last night? I'd both texted and called him after my walk with no response. Orlean was late again, too, and also unresponsive to my text, so I had to do everything on both sides of the shop. I pasted on a smile.

"Good morning." I swiped back through my hair with one hand, not sure I'd even combed it after my shower. "Let's bring the bikes around the side and I'll check them all in."

The tour leader and his helper wheeled the first four bikes out of the back of the trailer. The European riders were taking a day to be walk-around tourists in town before hitting the next leg of their trip. The bikes, which had been on the road for a week, were in for light tune-ups, tire checks, and general cleanup. Why the riders themselves weren't responsible for wiping down their own bikes I couldn't say. If they wanted to pay me to do it, more power to them. I was often amazed at how much so-called disposable income some people had. Back in my biking days I more than once rode a few hundred miles with no support vehicle. I hauled my own tent, gear, food, and toolkit in the zippered panniers slung across the back of my bike. I guessed it was good that these older folks from across the pond wanted to get out on bikes, see the sights of the Cape, and spend some considerable number of dollars along the way. I was sure the tour company facilitating the trip didn't mind, either.

The men were gone fifteen minutes later, with a promise to return by four-thirty. I finished my shop-opening procedure, grumbling at both Derrick and Orlean under my breath as I did. The weather was staying breezy and cool, but when I peered to the west it looked like the rain clouds had tracked south of us. I'd bet on not getting too many new rental customers today, although sometimes I was surprised. After I found Haskins's card in my desk, I sent him a text about Farnham staying with Gin. Responsibility to pass on information accomplished.

Once the flag was snapping in the breeze, I parked the sample rentals out front, watching as four big motorcycles putted loudly down the main drag. They were the kind of bikes where the driver had to stretch out his or her arms to hold the wide high handlebars. If they were on a bicycle they'd be called hi-rise apehangers. I didn't see how holding onto them could possibly be comfortable, but hey, I didn't have to ride a bike like that, motorized or not. I restocked the register with starting cash and took a minute to press Derrick's number, with no expectation of him actually answering. Sure enough, he didn't, so I phoned Pa.

"Hey, querida," he greeted me.

"Hi, Pa. I'm going to be quick, since the shop is open, but—"

"But you're wondering if I've talked to your brother."

"Yeah, pretty much. He answered his phone last night and was home, but he wouldn't say a word to me. And he's not here working. What did he tell you? Anything?"

My dad kept silent for a too-long moment. "Honey, it's his story to tell. I'm sorry."

Rats. "What about Cokey? Do you have her again today?"

"We kept her overnight, and today is her morning at preschool. Your mother has committed to take Cokey for the afternoon, because I have pastoral calls to make."

"Sheesh. Can you at least tell me if Derrick talked to the police?"

"I don't believe he has yet, no."

"Does he know they're looking for him?" I was the one who had told the detective about the knife kinda sorta looking like Derrick's. My brother avoiding the police would only make him look guilty. Which he couldn't be. No way. A half-dozen college-age-looking women in shorts and windbreakers or hoodies approached my store. "Customers are here. Gotta run."

"I'll try to arrange some help for you this afternoon," Pa said. "I know somebody who might be interested."

"Really? Thanks. I'll owe you."

He disconnected. Who could he shanghai at such short notice? Did the UU congregation harbor spare bike mechanics? I shook my head. I'd meet that bridge when I crossed it.

What I really wanted to do was go to the courthouse and see what I could learn about Jake. But I had a business to run and not a spare minute to drive across the peninsula and spend a few hours in the files. I didn't even have a minute to spare to let Mr. Google help me.

I fixed up the six young women, who were Boston College undergrads, with a rental each. After I lowered the seat for a petite girl wearing two chestnut-colored braids, she peered at the bike.

"How can it be a seven-speed with no gears?"

I pointed to the thick hub on the rear wheel. "It has internal gears in the hub. That way nobody gets grease on their right leg, and the gears don't get sand in them."

"Cool." She clicked her helmet straps together and slid onto the thick, comfy seat. "Thanks."

I watched them ride off, pleased with the women's smiles and excitement at being on vacation on Cape Cod. I slipped on a store apron, and wheeled in the nearest tour bike. I lifted it onto the workstand that supported the bike on an arm at a comfortable working height but still let the wheels spin free. I had a checklist for this procedure, too, one specific to the requests of the tour agency. But I hadn't even gotten through the first item when Orlean hurried in. I glanced at the clock. Almost an hour had passed since the touring bikes were dropped off.

"Sorry, again, Mac." She rolled her eyes. "You're going to think I'm chronically late."

"You weren't late at all last week. But in full season—"

"Which hasn't even started yet, I know." She had the grace to hunch sheepish shoulders and wince.

"Right. I'm going to need you here promptly." I set my hands on my waist but I cushioned my words with a smile. "Are you sure you want to work full-time? Maybe I should look for a part-timer to help out."

She gave a quick, alarmed-eyes shake to her head. "No, I'm good. I need the hours, and I won't be late again—barring an act of God, that is. I promise."

"Good. Right now we have twenty bikes needing a full check-over before four-thirty."

Orlean might have been late a couple of times, but when she did work, she was orderly and thorough. She worked reasonably fast without cutting corners, too.

"Can I leave them to you?" I asked.

"You got it, boss."

An hour later my cell phone buzzed as I spoke on the store phone with a family wanting to reserve ten bikes for the Fourth of July weekend. Yes, they could, and yes, I had trailers for small children. No, I didn't give discounts for multiple rentals. Yes, I provided helmets and yes, I sanitized them between users. No, they shouldn't take the bikes on the ferry to Martha's Vineyard. Yes, they had to return the bikes by closing time or I charged a late fee. All my policies were written clearly on the rental agreement, of course, including the final item: IF YOU'RE THE KIND OF PERSON WHO BLAMES EVERYTHING THAT HAPPENS IN THEIR LIFE ON SOMEONE ELSE, DON'T RENT THIS BIKE. OUR INTENT IS

FOR YOU TO HAVE FUN WHILE RIDING. TO THAT END WEAR A HELMET, ENJOY YOURSELF, AND PLEASE BE CAREFUL.

It was ten minutes before I could pay any attention to the cell call. Tim had left a message, saying the woman from the Point was in the bakery. A text from him two minutes later said she'd already left, coffee in hand. So much for surveillance. Anyway, she was probably a regular person here in Westham for a few days doing exactly the business and visiting she'd come to the Cape for.

And it would behoove me to quit thinking I was some sort of private investigator all of a sudden. Hadn't I told three different friends a day or two ago that this wasn't a cozy mystery, that we weren't living in a book? We had no business pretending to be Sarah Winston from the Garage Sale Mysteries, a woman who paid her bills by organizing yard sales and solved crimes on the side. We weren't even Kinsey Milhone from Sue Grafton's long-running series, although at least that character was actually a licensed PI, not some amateur.

My stomach wasn't only growling, it was yelling at me. After my walk with Gin and our encounter with Ms. Deloit early this morning, I'd run out of time to make my lunch, and the eleven o'clock energy bar from my emergency snack stash was no longer making it. Orlean and I were too busy for me to even dash home and assemble a sandwich so I was just grinning and bearing my hunger pangs. And not even grinning that much.

But when my mom, Astra MacKenzie, walked in the front door at one o'clock carrying a paper bag smelling suspiciously like lobster rolls, I knew I was saved.

"Mom, you're an angel."

"You know better than that, Mackenzie." She tilted her head diagonally, half down and half to the side, as was her habit, and raised her light eyebrows. "However, I haven't seen you in a few days, and your father says you're a little stressed. Plus, Neptune is in Pisces right now and I figured you'd be extra hungry for seafood."

Keeping my face immobile, I figuratively rolled my eyes. Stressed, I was. Affected by Neptune being in Pisces, I hadn't signed up for.

"So here I am." Mom beamed, her flyaway graying curls and equally flyaway rainbow-colored scarves creating an aura around her face. "You have time for lunch?"

"You bet I do. Thanks." It was all I could do not to snatch the bag from her hands and stuff the whole sandwich into my mouth with two hands. I exercised admirable restraint, however, both with the food and with her astrological predictions, and followed her toward the back door.

Orlean was on her way in from her own lunch break— today taken not at the picnic table but elsewhere—so I grabbed two water bottles from the mini-fridge and told her I was taking my lunch.

"Hey, Edna." She greeted my mom.

Ooh. Was this going to cause fireworks? Far as I knew, Mom didn't let anybody call her Edna anymore. Why change your name to Astra when people refuse to relinquish the first name they knew you by?

Instead, Mom stiffened a little but waved on her way out. Maybe she was used to it by now. Or maybe not.

"I hate Edna," she muttered under her breath once we were outside. "Why does she insist on calling me that name?"

"It's okay, Mom," I whispered. "It's only a name."

I was ten when she'd gotten sick of being a wife of the cloth and had taken a couple of classes in astrology. Later I realized she'd been lucky to have a UU minister as a husband—and my dad, in particular—instead of, say, a more conservative preacher who might demand a lot more hostessing from his woman. Dad knew Mom didn't care for being his support person in that way, and he was all for her following her dream.

It wasn't long before she hung a literal shingle outside the den of the parsonage, which had a separate entrance, painted with the words, "Astra MacKenzie, Astrological Services." It had caused a few rumblings among the more conservative members of the church as well as three minor defections to the United Church of Christ.

After a couple of years, though, between word of mouth and some low-key advertising, Mom was actually making money in her new field, and the UUs were still thriving despite her departure. My mother drew up natal charts and interpreted them, consulted on auspicious dates on which to hold weddings or make major decisions, and rented a table at farmers' markets and craft fairs on the Cape all summer long. Mom was very nearly a modern fortune-teller, but she insisted her practice was not mumbo-jumbo. She used century-old astrological principles, telling people their natal chart might be their path of least resistance but also that they could do whatever they chose with their lives. A certain path might be more difficult for a double Scorpio, for example, than for someone with both sun and moon in the sign of Taurus, but she'd advise it didn't mean that path was impossible.

Once we were settled under the shade at the picnic table out back and I'd swallowed my first gigantic bite of the best lobster roll on the East Coast, I relaxed a little.

Mom glanced toward the shop. "How's she working out?"

"Orlean?"

"Who else?"

"Remind me where you know her from." I chomped into another rich, mayonnaisey, delectable chunk of lobster meat on a white hot dog roll.

"We're both from Orleans."

"Back when you were Edna."

She groaned. "Exactly. Orlean doesn't see the sense of accepting a name change when, as she says, I had a perfectly good one. Anyway, she and Derrick were in a playgroup together when they were little. I've known her ever since."

"I didn't realize she was close to Derrick's age." I leaned over the table and lowered my voice. "She looks almost as old as you, Mom. Of course, you don't look sixty-three." Mom had the loveliest skin, almost ivory. The only lines in her face were fine ones, and her skin wasn't spotted from sun damage like many women's. She was always careful to slather on sunscreen, and she wore hats to keep her face unblemished.

"Thanks." She twisted her head to gaze at the shop. "I know, Orlean has a face to match her experiences. She's been through some pretty tough times, which is why I was so happy to see you hire her. Thanks for doing that, sweetie. Orlean means well. She's stubborn as heck, but a good egg."

I hoped she'd get a better egg timer soon, but I didn't say so. "She's good with bikes, I can say that. Knows what they need, is careful with the parts, has a light hand with a wrench. She keeps things in order in the shop, too."

"Liking things in order. That's your sun in Virgo talking. But you need to watch it a little, Mackenzie. You should make sure wanting your life orderly doesn't become an obsession. You're prone to those, you know."

"Whatever." I could almost recite the "sun in Virgo" traits from the four thousand and twenty-three times she'd described them. Now four thousand and twenty-four. "I'm only saying I couldn't ask for more in a mechanic." Except arriving on time. But surely Derrick would be back on the rental/retail side soon and I could fill in on the mechanic side when we were overloaded with repairs. That was how my business model, my plan, was supposed to work. Or would he be back?

I finished eating my heavenly lunch without speaking. Mom seemed to be of the same mind, because she didn't say anything, either. Gazing at the street beyond the shop, I peered at a man making his way slowly past on the sidewalk. Despite being at least as old as my mom, he wore his pants as low on his rear end as any teenager's. His gait wasn't that of a young person, though. He hauled his right leg along like it wouldn't bend and kept his eyes on the pavement. In one hand he grasped a beat-up gym duffle, or maybe it was a bowling bag. And in the other he clutched a bunch of mixed cut flowers in a cellophane sleeve.

Who was he? Where was he dragging off to? Maybe

to a job? He definitely wasn't a tourist. And who were the flowers for? A sweetheart, perhaps. Or maybe his mom. I thought he passed by here most weekdays, but I'd never seen him with flowers before.

My own mom cleared her throat. "Uh, honey, about Derrick?"

My attention went *boing*. Suddenly I couldn't care less about a random man taking flowers somewhere to someone. "What about Derrick?"

"He seems to be deeply troubled. Perhaps it's his Venus transiting Saturn."

My nostrils flared of their own accord. "Or maybe it's the fact that he's not telling the truth to his family or anybody else! And he's not coming to work, either. Listen. The police want to talk with him, Mom. The knife I saw in Jake Lacey's neck?" I waited a beat. I needed to be sure I had her full attention. "It looked exactly like Derrick's."

She fast-blinked those light green eyes at me, orbs identical to mine. She craned her head in my direction. "His fish knife?" she whispered.

I nodded slowly. She had to understand how important this was.

"Did you tell the police that?" She still whispered.

Rats. I now wished I hadn't revealed that bit to the detective, but I'd been so sure of my brother's innocence that I'd told Haskins about the knife. I took a deep breath. "Yes. But you can't tell anyone. The police asked me to keep it quiet." Although I'd told Gin, and with Suzanne talking about stabbing, by now the news had to be getting around,

She gasped and brought her hand to her mouth.

"Mom. I know Derrick didn't kill Jake. The murderer has to have stolen Derrick's knife. But the longer

Derrick keeps hiding and hanging out in the Valley of Denial, the worse it looks for him." I reached out for her other hand.

"It was a custom knife." Mom's voice shook. "Nobody owns one identical to his."

I pursed my lips. "Really? How do you know?"

"I special ordered it for him. I gave it to him for his birthday. It's one-of-a-kind in the material universe." She squeezed my hand and reclaimed hers, knitting and rubbing hers together on the table.

That sounded bad. But I didn't want to worry Mom. "So what? We figure out who wanted Jake dead and who could have stolen the knife, and voilà. We tell Detective Haskins." We find that fool brother of mine, too, and make him talk.

At the name a fond smile crept across her face. "Oh, Linc. He's a sweetheart if I've ever seen one."

So Pa wasn't the only one who knew him. And by the look of that smile, my mom wasn't only mildly acquainted with him. "What, did you used to date him?"

"No, honey. I'm nearly old enough to be his mama." She gazed over my shoulder at a memory. "But he came to a charity gala once when he was a young officer. He was the dreamiest dancer in the whole place. I felt like I was Ginger Rogers dancing with Lincoln Haskins." The fear was gone from her voice. "You know your father, for all his fine qualities, has two left lead feet. We barely even danced at our wedding." She kept that dreamy look in her eyes.

"Daughter to Mom." I waved a hand in front of her face. "Back to real life for just a little minute? Did you talk to Derrick today?"

"Only for a minute on the phone. He asked if I'd . . ." Her voice trailed off as she checked her wristwatch.

"Oh, for . . . crab sake. I was supposed to pick up Cokey five minutes ago." She stood and rushed toward the street. "See you, darling." Both her voice and her scarves trailed after her, plus the end of her lobster roll lay abandoned on its paper wrapper.

I picked it up and munched. She was my mom, after all. I didn't care about her germs, and it was criminal to waste such a perfect food. My life today wasn't perfect at all, though. Derrick a hundred percent incommunicado. His own knife the murder weapon. A strange woman popping up here and there. A girl who seemed to know Jake, first happy, then sad. Why did I feel like I was stranded in the eye of a coastal hurricane? It might seem calm for the moment, but all around me whirled boiling motives, with information and conversations obscured by a rotating cone of windblown sea spray. And quite possibly additional malice.

Chapter Thirteen

"**A**bo Ree!" I smiled at my little grandmother, who bustled into the shop a few minutes after Mom left. I came out from behind the rental counter and leaned down to hug her. "Out for your afternoon walk?"

"No. I'm here to work. That son of mine says you need help, and I happen to be free." Reba Almeida was nothing if not forthright, despite being barely five feet tall and eighty years old. She tugged off the hat she always wore outdoors, a multi-colored cross between a beret and a Rastafarian cap, and stuffed it into her huge handbag. "I can't help whatever your brother is up to, but I can surely assist you. Set me up with the rentals price list and information, show me how to use the cash register and what not, and you can go about whatever else you need to do."

I knew she'd suffered, growing up African-American in Boston during and after World War II, despite her skin being the color of milky café au lait. But I'd never heard her complain about anything. She'd married my

Cape Verdean grandfather and happily become part of his family. They'd raised my dad and four other children not far from here. Her optimism carried enough energy to light up an entire village, or at least my mood.

I gave her proposal two point six seconds of consideration. "You've got a job. It's pretty easy, and either Orlean or I can help with any questions you can't answer. Thank you for coming."

"Well, you know. I was sitting home with my spyglass minding everybody else's business when Joseph called. I might as well do it out here in public." Her laugh was an infectious tinkling sound, and her cheeks pinkened to match her signature hot pink tracksuit.

I laughed, too. We'd given her the spyglass as a gag Christmas gift a few years ago because she was such a keen chronicler of the town's goings-on. She kept it next to her easy chair by the window of her senior living apartment a quarter mile down Main Street. And used it daily. My grandma, the village Peeping Reba.

After I got her set up with the system, I checked in with Orlean. The tour bike tune-ups seemed to be going right along.

"Think you'll make the four-thirty pick-up, or do you want me to help?" I asked.

"Should be good. I only have five left."

I glanced at the clock. It wasn't even two o'clock. "Awesome. Thanks." I slid back to the other side of the shop, where Abo Ree perched on the high stool behind the counter, peering at her smart phone. This was an octogenarian who kept up with technology. She swore mildly under her breath.

"What?" I asked.

"Oh, you know, our fool politicians. Say, I saw Jake Lacey with some young girl last week, don't you know. They were walking down by the pier. Looked happy."

"Really? Somebody else mentioned seeing him with a young woman. She wasn't from around here, was she?"

My grandma fixed keen brown eyes on me. "Wouldn't I have used her name if she was?"

"Of course. I wonder who she was. I saw a young woman yesterday, too, walking along the sidewalk. Didn't look a bit happy."

"Maybe she was related to Jake and is sad he died."

I frowned. "I didn't think he had a family. But come to think of it, I didn't really know anything about his personal life." All these sighting of Jake with strangers. What had he been up to shortly before he died? Of course, he'd had every right to hang out with whomever he pleased. Followed by his brutal murder, though? One of them might be important. How could I find out which?

A hand-holding couple wandered in wanting to rent bicycles through the weekend. I puttered around the merchandise shelves, straightening and dusting, and let Abo Ree handle the transaction, but I stayed nearby in case she needed help. Which she didn't. She pulled off the deal as if she'd worked here forever. She answered their questions, gave them the bike trails map, and swiped their card through the reader like a pro.

"Now, you lovebirds be sure to wear those helmets, you hear me?" she called after them from the doorway.

I came up behind her to see the customers clip on their helmets. They pedaled off, the woman waving at us.

"What? Somebody's got to be sure they don't hit their heads." She lifted her chin as if anticipating a criticism.

"It's fine, don't worry. It's simply that I usually leave wearing head protection up to the adult customer. I do make them take the helmet, but I have no idea if they go and drop it off in their room before heading out to ride."

"Got it. So, am I hired?" she asked.

"At full pay."

"Good. Now go do whatever you need to do. The books, the repairs, a nap. I can stay until five thirty."

I thought for a minute. A respite from the shop was just what I needed to start following up on some of the questions surrounding Jake's death. And try once more to find Derrick, too. "I do need to talk to somebody in town, and I should hit the bank, too. Are you sure?"

"Of course." She gazed down the street. "But hang on a second. Who's that man?"

A fireplug of a man hurried down the sidewalk toward us.

"I don't know," I said. "A potential customer?"

"The way he's huffing and puffing, I bet he's not looking to rent one of your bicycles for a leisurely ride somewhere. He's not dressed like a tourist, either."

The round, squat man wore a loosely knotted tie with a blue dress shirt, its sleeves haphazardly rolled up, and dark cotton trousers that strained at the waist. He must have seen us looking, because he lifted one hand in a wave when he was still two shops away.

I exchanged a glance and a shrug with my grandma. "Might as well see what he wants before I go."

He arrived blotting his high round forehead with a handkerchief. "Good afternoon." He swiped the cloth over the top of his balding head, leaving a few strands of a brown comb-over in serious disarray. "Just the ladies I wanted to see."

Huh? My heart sank. He must be another reporter. "Hello," I said.

Abo Reba smiled at him. "I'm Reba Almeida and this is my granddaughter, Mackenzie Almcida."

He held up a meaty hand. "I know, I know." He gave her a little bow. "Your reputation precedes you, Mrs. Almeida."

"But we don't believe we know you," my grandmother said.

He whipped a couple of business cards out of his shirt pocket and handed them to us. "Billy Crump, Private Investigator. I wondered if I could have a word with you both."

Chapter Fourteen

I squinted at the PI. "About what?" I asked simultaneously with Abo Reba's, "Of course, young man."

Crump threw his head back and laughed. When he calmed down, he said, "Isn't that human nature for you? Same question, two different answers." His smile revealed a considerable gap between his top front teeth, which gave him a goofy, boyish look despite his thick stature and thin hair.

I nodded to my grandmother, ceding to my elder, as I had been brought up to do.

"We're happy to help," she said. "I assume this is in regard to the murder in our town?" She clasped her hands in front of her waist and waited with sparkling eyes and mouth partly open in anticipation of whatever exciting development was coming next.

"That it is, ma'am. I've been hired to look into his death by an interested party."

"Who hired you?" I blurted before Abo Reba said anything more.

"I'm not at liberty to say." He narrowed his eyes almost imperceptibly.

"But it's not the police you're working for," I pressed him.

"No, indeed it is not." He addressed his next remarks to Abo Reba. "I must say I have heard others mention that you would be the go-to woman for information in Westham, ma'am. I'm glad to have found you here with your granddaughter."

Was it safe to talk to this guy? Or if safe, was it prudent? Obviously I couldn't stop my strong-willed grandmother from doing she wanted, but that didn't mean I had to speak with a private investigator who hadn't even shown us his license.

He glanced around. "Can we can sit down somewhere?"

I didn't have any place to sit and chat inside, and there was nowhere out front here, either. We could sit at the picnic table, but either Abo Reba or I should really be inside ready to welcome new rentees. Orlean was too busy to saddle her with welcoming customers right now. Rats. Despite not wanting to divulge anything, I was dying to hear how the conversation would go, and whether Billy Crump would leak a speck of information or two. I wasn't interested in leaving my grandmother alone with him.

Two older couples sauntered up. Older than me, younger than my grandmother. "We'd like to rent bikes for a week," one of the women offered.

"Sorry, sonny," Abo Reba said to Crump as she shook her head. "Our chat will have to wait." She ushered the customers into the shop, saying, "Come along with me."

I could have protested that I'd help them, instead. But I didn't.

"I'd love to have a word with you, too, Ms. Almeida," Crump said, plastering on a hopeful look.

I gave my head a little shake. "I'm sorry. I'm otherwise engaged and already late for an appointment. Maybe another time." *Maybe.* I turned my back on him. Unless he wanted to tell me who had employed him, my lips were zipped. I couldn't avoid talking to the actual police if they asked. But PIs of questionable provenance? That was another pot of chowder entirely.

Once inside the shop I snuck a quick look through the front window. Crump stood rooted in place with a notebook, madly scribbling. Recording direct quotes? Casing out the layout of the shop? Jotting down the questions he didn't get to ask? Maybe I'd judged him too fast. Or maybe he was a reporter in disguise. I'd nearly crumpled his card in my hand. Now I smoothed it out on my palm.

Billy Crump, Private Investigator was all it read, with a telephone number in the bottom right corner. The other side was blank. No website, no license number. I'd made the right decision. I was dying to know who'd hired him and why, but he didn't seem willing to share that information. I entered his name and phone number in my phone Contacts, just in case.

I grabbed yesterday's profits in their zippered envelope of out my small safe and poked my head into the repair side. "I'm heading to the bank and a few other errands. Give my grandma a hand if she needs it, okay?"

Orlean nodded without looking up from spinning a wheel to check its truing. I sidled through to the other side.

"I'm going out for an hour. You good?" I asked Abo Reba.

She gave me a thumbs-up.

"Get you anything?"

She made a shooing motion with both hands. "Go, Mac," she said, and turned her back on me.

I went, slipping out the back door with my EpiPen bag. First I made a quick stop home to use the facilities, then took a minute to Google Billy Crump, private investigator. Not a hit came up. Really? He didn't appear to be legit at all. To avoid whoever he was if he still loitered in front of my shop, I headed out on a side street toward the other end of town instead of back through the shop. Billy Crump could go bug somebody else for a while.

Chapter Fifteen

After I made my deposit at the bank, I popped into Salty Taffy's next door, but Gin was busy with a line of customers, so I grabbed a free taffy sample, waved at her, and moved on.

Where to next? I gazed up and down the main drag. School must be over for the day, because small clumps of students big and not so big were hanging out, buying a soda, throwing a fluorescent green disk around on the green in front of Town Hall. The sidewalks were also nicely full of tourists. Seeing so many of them boded well for the summer if the trend kept up.

I snapped my fingers. I was invited to Tim's for dinner and I should pick up a bottle of wine to go with the meal. Zane sold wine as well as liquors, his own and others', and his shop was right beyond the library. Maybe he'd seen the sad young woman again. I could stop in and say hi to Flo on my way, too. She'd been so organized at the meeting last night, with her pad of paper and her questions about suspicious behavior. I wondered if the reputed private investigator had been in to quiz her, too. But when I turned down the lane leading to the library, a Westham police cruiser drove toward me. It pulled to a stop and Victoria climbed out.

"Hi, Vickie."

She blew a breath out from between clenched jaws. "Mac, you know I hate that nickname. Why do you even try?"

I didn't know. It was perverse of me. And not a bit nice. Abo Reba would have scolded me up one side and down the next. "Sorry about that. How's the case going? Did you all find Jake's killer yet?" I used my sweetest voice.

"Innocence has never become you, Mackenzie Almeida. No, we haven't found the murderer. That is, Detective Haskins hasn't. Don't you think you would have heard if we had?"

Of course I would have. Hard to keep news from leaking in a town the size of ours. Although more folks than usual seemed to be keeping secrets this week. "Are there any developments you can share?"

"I'm not at liberty to say. You do know that police work is for the police, not for amateurs."

"Of course."

She set her fists on her slim hips. "I've heard your mystery book group has some crazy notion you can solve this case. That could be very, very dangerous."

"That's what I told them." I went for the innocent look again, but this time she didn't comment on it.

"I hope you'll dissuade them from even trying. However, I do have a request for you personally," Victoria continued. "The detective very much wants to speak to your brother. Do you know where he might be?" She ducked just in time to avoid getting a haircut from the flying green disk. It clattered to the pavement behind her.

"Sorry, Chief Laitinen," a boy's voice called. Boy becoming a man, since the voice started out deep and cracked through to a higher pitch by the end of her name. The speaker, a slender young teen, dashed past the police car, scooped up the disk, and threw it back over our heads.

"Stay out of the street, will you?" Victoria replied, but her tone was more friendly than harsh. She watched him run off before speaking again. "Well, do you know how we can reach Derrick?" She crossed her arms and looked up into my face, which had even more altitude than usual, since she stood in the street and I was on the curb.

I stepped down to minimize the difference. "Frankly, I don't know where my brother is. He hasn't come to work for two days." Should I at least tell her that I'd talked to him last night? I decided I had an obligation to. "I did speak with him by phone last night and he said he was home. But he wouldn't talk about anything. In fact he hung up on me."

She shook her head, looking thoroughly exasperated.

"I have a question for you." I lowered my voice. "A guy named Billy Crump stopped by the shop a little while ago. He said he's a private investigator and he wanted to talk to both my grandmother and me. He gave us a card, but the only contact info is a phone number. Maybe PIs don't advertise with a website, but he also didn't show us a license or anything. Should I worry? Have you seen him?"

"Do you still have the card?"

I pulled it out of my pocket and handed it over.

"What does he look like?"

"Fireplug, thin dark hair, balding." I looked across the street, thinking. "He might have had one more identifying feature. I can't think of it now."

She handed back the card. "Never heard of him. I'll ask around the station, though. You could do a search on his name, you know."

"I did, and nothing came up."

"Did you talk to this Crump about the murder?" she asked.

I shook my head. "No, I told him I wouldn't talk to him at all. I also didn't like that he wouldn't say who had hired him. Only that it was an interested party, as he put it."

"Good. You know not to reveal details of the crime scene, correct?"

"Yes. Detective Haskins also told me that." I thought again of Suzanne referring to the stabbing. Where had she learned that?

"Probably better not to talk with this so-called PI at all," Victoria advised.

"I won't. Abo Reba was willing have a conversation with the guy, but then customers came in and she got busy."

Victoria cocked her head. "You got your grand-mother filling in for your brother?"

"Actually, yes. She's a natural, and I needed the help." I extended Billy Crump's card to her. "I saved the number. Keep it, if you want. Otherwise I was going recycle it. And I'm going to encourage my grandma not to talk with him either, but of course I can't control what she docs."

"Too bad." Victoria slid the card into her uniform shirt pocket and thanked me. A radio crackle came from the open window of the cruiser. She stuck her head in the passenger side and listened, then straightened.

"Gotta run. And please, if you—"

"I know. If I find Derrick, urge him to contact you. Of course I will."

Florence wasn't in her office or at the library's main desk when I arrived, so I signed in for a half hour at one of the computers. Obviously I could extend my search for Billy Crump on my phone, but it was so much easier to use a full-size keyboard and a big screen.

Searching the Internet wasn't my friend today, though. All the permutations of Billy/Bill/William/Will Crump plus the words "private investigator" yielded exactly nothing. I swore silently. Why couldn't I find mention of him somewhere if he was a genuine PI? He must have been lying. But if he was a reporter, wouldn't he get in trouble for using a false name to interview someone? Maybe the entire name was false, including Crump. I typed the phone number into the search bar to no avail.

I poked around looking for other information about Jake's death. For news stories about the killing. For anything, really. When that search proved unsatisfactory, too, I typed in Katherine Deloit. Now here was a person who appeared to be exactly who she said she was. Real estate agent in Westwood, California. When I looked up Westwood, it appeared to be a town where stars lived and shopped. Where rich Chinese investors were snapping up property right and left. Where filmmakers rubbed elbows with venture capitalists, politicians, and the occasional UCLA professor, but only professors in lucrative fields of study like engineering and business. That pocket of Los Angeles sounded almost as elite as what I'd heard about Beverly Hills.

And Ms. Deloit was earning her share of the wealth, one property at a time according to the past sales listed on her website. Not a criminal act, however. Neither was looking for a property for one Mr. Wu. I tried to search on Mr. Wu, but the name was way too common to get anything useful without a first name, even specifying Westwood. I slumped, staring at the screen. This was going nowhere. I probably should get back to the shop and see if my grandma needed bailing out.

"Mac, find anything good?" Flo asked, having approached me from behind.

I exclaimed and sat up straight. "You startled me. No, I didn't find anything good. Or much of anything at all. You?"

She sank down at the next station over. "I've been working all day. Head librarian is a great job, don't get me wrong. But I also have to 'interface' with the town, the Friends of the Library, and sometimes even the Fire Department chief. I spend much of my day dealing with people instead of books and information. Only on Cape Cod." She lifted a shoulder and dropped it. "Oh, well."

"Then help me find some information. A man calling himself Billy Crump told my grandmother and me this afternoon he's a private investigator." I repeated what I'd told Victoria about us not talking to him, and him not saying who had hired him. "I can't find a trace of him on the Internet. Which, these days, kind of makes you wonder."

Flo stood, crooking her index finger in a come-hither gesture. "Ve haf our methods."

I grinned, logged off the public system, and followed her to her office. Flo always left the door open, but at least she had walls around her space. Other than the restrooms, it was one of the only private rooms in the building. She pulled the visitor chair over behind the desk and patted the seat.

"So you can follow what I'm doing," she said.

Except she typed so fast and the screen changed so often I couldn't follow a thing. As I waited, I pulled out the file blade on my little Swiss Army knife and smoothed off a rough edge on my thumbnail that kept catching on everything.

Two minutes later, thanks to the specialized databases Flo could access, we had our answer.

She pointed to a head shot. "Is that him?"

I nodded. "It is." This picture was from his slightly slimmer days but it was him all right, gap between the front teeth and all. That was the bit I'd forgotten to tell Victoria.

"His driver's license is under the name Wilhelm Krumpf, and his PI license, too." Flo kept typing. "He's a German national, apparently. Hang on. Let me follow that thread a little longer."

"So maybe he had to use his passport to get his license?"

"Wait. Almost got it." Her fingers flew over the keyboard. "Voilà." She sat back. "He's lived in the States since he came here for college, but never became a citizen."

"And the reason I couldn't find Billy Crump on the Internets?"

"All his official dealings, any record keeping about him, it's all as Wilhelm Krumpf. Not Billy Crump, which he must have Americanized himself."

"Like what immigrants have done for years, Ameri-

canizing or simplifying their names to fit in," I said.
"Schwartz to Black, or Honghui to Henry." I'd met a
banker in Boston who'd done just that. Even when I
was interested in his Chinese name, he'd insisted on
being called Henry.

"Exactly." Flo bobbed her head but kept her gaze on
the screen.

"Does it say where he lives?"

More rapid fire typing. A crew of early-teen girls bustled by, all whispers and giggles, one of them glancing
behind her at a couple of boys. A man in a wheelchair
rolled by us toward the checkout desk, five books
stacked in his lap. The elevator dinged its arrival
across the spacious room, and a toddler wailed to her
mom about wanting more stories, now.

"Looks like Crump, aka Krumpf, lives up Cape in
Plymouth," Flo declared. "Not that Plymouth is really
Cape Cod at all, being north of the canal."

The seven-mile long Cape Cod Canal, completed a
hundred years earlier, sliced the upper arm of the peninsula in half. The cut greatly facilitated boat travel, both
commercial and recreational, from Cape Cod Bay to
Buzzard's Bay, from Sandwich to Bourne and back.

I sat back. "Now that we know he's actually a PI, do
you think I should call him, talk to him?"

Flo turned to look at me. "What do you think?"

"Actually, doesn't much matter what I think. Victoria advised me not to."

"You already told her about him?"

"Ran into her out front." I gestured vaguely in the
direction of the street.

"Ah. Well, as long as you don't reveal stuff to him
she doesn't want you to, can it hurt?"

"What I'd prefer is getting information from him

rather than the reverse." I scrunched up my nose. "Have you heard anything from Norland about the murder, or from Tulia? I know they were going to be keeping their ears and eyes open, too."

"Not a thing."

"I'll drop by the Lobstah Shack when I get a chance and ask her."

"How are you doing with next week's book?" Flo asked.

"Terrible. I haven't even started it. Gin and I usually listen during our morning walks, but we've been talking about murder instead." And I'd volunteered to check something this morning. What had it been? Ah. The fog bank. "I need to figure out when the fog rolled in on Tuesday. Do you remember? Was it before we started the book group meeting?"

Flo tugged at her earlobe, a habit she had when she was thinking. "I think it was right about that time. Yes, it was around six. I remember because I was driving over from my house, which is a bit inland, and by the time I got to the lighthouse it was socked in."

Her tugging her at her ear made me think of Suzanne. She'd done the same after she arrived home last night. Right before describing Jake as having been stabbed.

"Flo, have you heard anyone talking about how Jake was murdered? Read it anywhere?"

She shook her head slowly. "I don't think so. You didn't say, did you?'"

"No."

"I only know what Suzanne told me." Flo turned back to her desk and resumed typing. After a couple of minutes, she said, "Can't find a single mention."

I waited, but she clearly didn't remember what her daughter had said last night. I wasn't about to bring it up, but I couldn't deny that Suzanne's knowing worried me. A lot.

Bottle of Shiraz in hand, I browsed the shelves at Cape King Liquors while I waited for Zane to finish with his current customer. King's Bounty Rum was one of Zane's specialties, along with Z&S Bourbon, which he'd created after he and Stephen became husband and husband. I didn't care much for hard liquor. Clearly plenty of people did or Zane's business wouldn't be the success it was. On my way here I'd wanted to pop into Greta's Grains across the street and say hi to Tim, but I'd missed my window. He closed the bakery at 3 P.M.

The door shut after the customer. "Hey, Mac. That's all you want?" Zane smiled and waved from the register.

"In the wine department? Yes, for now." I set the bottle on the counter.

"I'll bet you're like me, wanting to know who killed Jake."

"Of course. I was talking to Victoria Laitinen a little while ago."

"Chief Laitinen." A ding sounded from the register. "That'll be fourteen ninety-nine."

I dug a twenty out of my pocket and handed it to him. "She wants to be sure our book group knows we aren't supposed to be trying to investigate this thing. That it could be, in her words, *very, very dangerous*."

He handed me my change. "Sure, if we actually start chasing after a criminal or something. But I don't have any intention of doing that. Do you?" He rapped his long narrow fingers on the counter.

"No, of course not. But you know, sometimes in the books we read the killer gets suspicious of the amateur sleuth asking too many questions, right?"

Zane nodded slowly, sliding the bottle into a narrow paper bag and handing it to me.

"And the sleuth gets in big trouble because of it," I went on. "So we have to keep real quiet about this around town. And any information has to go directly to the detective."

"Haskins, you said his name was. The big guy I saw."

"Exactly." But was I actually following Victoria's directive myself? Had I discovered anything I was neglecting to pass on to Haskins? Something to ponder.

"I promise. Scout's honor." He held up three fingers. "Now, have you learned anything?" He rubbed his hands together, looking eager.

"Not much." I told him about how Gin and I met Katherine Deloit, and the conversation we'd overheard. "She must be the person Stephen saw with Jake at the courthouse."

"Could be." His eyes lit up. "Did you ask her about Jake?"

"Yes. After she brought up the murder in conversation, I asked if she'd ever met him. But she looked at me like I was nuts."

"Maybe Jake and this woman simply ran into each other in the hallway."

"That's what I was thinking, too. I wish I had time to go to the courthouse myself and see if Jake conducted any business there recently, but that's at least a half-day commitment. A half-day I don't happen to have free." I switched the wine from one arm to the other. "You haven't seen my brother in here, have you? Or anywhere around?"

Zane gazed out the window and then back at me, frowning. "Jeez, Mac. What do I say? He asked me not to tell you."

"What? You saw him? You talked with him? Did he say where he'd been?" Light dawned over Marblehead. "Wait a minute. He came in *here*?"

"I'm afraid he did. He rushed in as soon as I opened at eleven and bought a bottle of bourbon. He seemed shaky."

My heart plummeted. Derrick was drinking. After years of sobriety. "That's bad. Really, really bad." A terrible doubt washed cold through me. What would drive him to drink again, and whiskey at that? Was he involved in Jake's death, after all? I was as sure as I could be that my brother hadn't hurt Jake on purpose. But what if they'd fought? What if—

Zane's words interrupted my thoughts.

"I shouldn't have sold it to him. I'm so sorry." He shook his head.

I took a deep breath and let it out. "It's not your fault. He would have gone to the next closest liquor store instead." I looked down. My feet, the sandals, the floor, it all looked so normal. Derrick's life was suddenly not normal, and really, none of our lives were. Murder in Westham. Suspicions running rampant. Detectives and investigators everywhere. I looked at Zane again. "Did he happen to say where he's been hiding out? Did you talk to him at any length?"

"No. I tried, but he was antsy, like he wanted to get out of here."

"To go start drinking before anyone else saw him, I

bet." Or to keep drinking. Maybe he'd been at a bar all day yesterday. Cape Cod offered no shortage of dimly lit bars for the locals with no questions asked, usually located away from the cheery tourist areas.

"Probably. He nearly threw the money at me, told me not to mention his purchase to you, and hurried out."

"Thanks for telling me, Zane. Really." I cursed under my breath. "I gotta go find him." Right this minute.

Chapter Sixteen

Except I couldn't go find Derrick right that minute, of course. If nothing else, I was a responsible person, and that included being a responsible business owner. It was both my primary strength and my main weakness. I'd always known I had to follow through on commitments, even though it meant I rarely let myself act spontaneously.

So I trudged back across the street and down the block to my shop. I'd told both Abo Reba and Orlean I'd be gone about an hour and it had been almost two. That was irresponsible enough. At least neither of them had called with a question or, God forbid, an emergency. And if I was lucky, the tour leader wouldn't have returned for the bikes yet. It was this outfit's first time using my services and I hoped for return bookings. I also preferred for me to be the interface with customers rather than Orlean.

No such luck. The repair side of the shop was clear

of bikes. Orlean was wiping down tools and putting them away.

"Did I miss the pick-up?" I asked.

"Yep. Came early. But I was all done."

"And you settled up with them?"

"Yep. Needed a few extra parts and whatnot. Slip's in the draw."

Despite being born and raised here, I'd trained myself as an adult to pronounce Rs where they were written and not where they weren't. Most locals left off the last consonant of *drawer* entirely.

"Thanks," I said. "Sorry I didn't get back sooner. Take off for home any time you want." One of these days I ought to offer her a beer, see if she wanted to talk about her personal situation, the rotten ex, or whatever. I hated to pry if she didn't want to talk, but I wanted her to know I cared. "I'll cover until closing."

In response I got a nod absent of eye contact, Orlean's *modus operandus.*

"Got to clean up first," she answered.

I headed through to the rental/retail side. My grandmother sat behind the counter on the high stool perusing her phone, exactly like she had been earlier. I delivered a kiss to her papery cheek. She'd found the radio and tuned it to the classical station, so strains of calming music filled the space.

"You've been gone a while," she said, lifting a single eyebrow. "Out sleuthing, were you?" Nothing escaped Abo Reba, even when she couldn't see it.

"Maybe a little." Could I hide Zane's news about Derrick from her? I was determined to try, at least until I located him and talked some sense into the idiot. "How did things go here?"

She handed me four rental slips and three retail re-

ceipts. "Absolutely fine. Not too busy, not too quiet."
She slid off the stool. "I've got to go. Millie's picking
me up for bridge at five thirty sharp."

"Thank you so much for filling in. I'm sure Derrick
will be back tomorrow."

She pulled her hat on and paused at the door. "No
sign of your wayward brother around town, I suppose?"

I unnecessarily straightened the slips, and lined up
three pencils and two pens in perfect order as if my future depended on it. I cleared my throat. "I didn't see
him anywhere."

She gave me one long look, the same look I'd gotten
when I was eight and she knew full well I was lying
about breaking Mrs. Somerville's window with an er-
rant baseball. I fully expected my Abo to come back in
and start grilling me, but she trundled out, instead.

"Tell him hello when you find him," she called
back.

Close one. I busied myself tidying up. I rearranged a
couple of shirts and put a pair of gloves back where
they belonged. I checked the schedule for tomorrow.
One major tune-up, five reserved rentals, and a tandem
repair. Nothing we couldn't handle, as long as my
brother wasn't drunk in a ditch somewhere. Or worse.

Orlean left a few minutes before five and I locked
the back door. I had to admit she was good at leaving
things orderly. The repair area was clean with everything in its place, ready for the next day. Exactly how I
liked it. I added up the day's till and credit card re-
ceipts, and locked the cash in the small safe in my office. At loose ends, since the store stayed open until
six, I paced a little, but all I could think about was the
murder. The people acting oddly. The missing one—

my dear brother. And the ones we hadn't even seen yet. The least I could do was write it all down in some organized fashion.

My next choice was paper or digital file. I ended up fishing a piece of clean white paper out of the printer and taking it to the rental counter. Maybe typing information into a file where I could find it again was wiser. But something about the flow of a good gel pen on a nice, smooth unblemished sheet of eight-and-a-half by eleven made my mind function differently.

I started by writing a big question mark on the left side and drawing a line under it. What didn't I know? *Derrick's location* went first. Next I jotted down, *Was Jake blackmailing somebody? Who? Why?* I added, *Who is happy/sad girl?* Abo Reba had told me this morning about seeing the young woman with Jake. Happy when he was alive. I'd seen her after he was killed, as had Zane. Definitely sad. How to find out who she was, though? *What does Katherine Deloit want?* was next. Then I added, *What is Wes Farnham up to?* I doubted he was involved, but in business, creativity brainstorming always meant allowing all ideas to be in the running at the beginning of a project, no matter how corny or impractical they sounded on the surface. I included *Who is Mr. Wu?* and *Why was Jake at courthouse?*

On the other side of the sheet I wrote Truth and underlined that. What was truth? I wrote, *Jake's death by stabbing with fish knife.* But what else? I added *Suzanne knows about stabbing.* Did I know anything else for sure?

I wasn't sure this was a good exercise. My foot tapped the rung of the stool like it was a metronome. The list of what we didn't know was going to stretch way longer than what we did know. I blew out a noisy frustrated breath and hopped off my seat. I paced to the exit and back.

The sign on the door said we closed at six. But I was dying to get out of here, which was not responsible behavior at all. What if a rental needed an emergency repair? Or a Provincetown-bound rider needed a quick tire fix. Or . . . Sighing, I wheeled in the rental bikes one by one from out front. The heck with it. I couldn't stay any longer. I decided to play copycat and use Zane's trick. I lettered another sheet of printer paper. I grabbed the wine and my list and locked up, my expression grim as I taped my sign to the front door.

GONE FISHING

"Belle, where's Derrick?" I asked my parrot after I fed her a few minutes later. It was all well and good to leave work early, but I still didn't have a clue where my brother was holed up. And now he had his own bottle of whiskey. Pa had left a message that Derrick wasn't there. I could go driving around town looking for him, but that didn't seem like the best use of my time. Not that asking a bird was.

"Derrick's going home. Gimme a grape, please." She whistled, then did one of my least-favorite tricks, the car alarm. Which she reproduced with the din of all its shrieking whoops.

"Hey, we're not even outside. Stop it, Belle." Thankfully, she did, so I doled out a few frozen grapes, one of her favorite treats.

"Belle's a bad bird. Give Belle a kiss. Derrick's going home."

Maybe she was onto something. I gave her a kiss

and a few peanuts, then looked down at my work clothes. I was due for dinner at Tim's at six thirty. In case I didn't get back here, I'd better change now. I washed up and threw on a short-sleeved dress and leggings.

I took a minute to sit and tap the items from my paper list into a notes app on my phone so I'd be able to access it without hauling around a piece of paper. Then the wine went into a cloth bag with a shoulder strap. I slung on my EpiPen bag and grabbed a sweater. Leaving a light on inside for the bird and one outside for myself, I went out and turned toward the trail to the lighthouse. But, no. If ever it was the right time to lock one's door, it was when a murderer was at large. Once I had my hand on the door, I thought about my destination tonight. I went back in and coaxed Belle into her cage.

"Sorry, my friend," I told her. "I probably won't be back tonight."

"Sorry, Mac. Sorry, Mac."

"We'll play tomorrow, okay?" I smiled and stroked her head, then gave her a couple of chunks of carrot. I kept a bag ready in the fridge for Belle treats, since she loved them almost as much as grapes.

Door and bird secured, I set out again. Derrick hadn't been home at all yesterday until last night. My dad had checked. But maybe he was in his house today despite his lack of response. It was worth giving the lighthouse a shot, anyway. Mom had texted that Cokey was still with her and Pa was working. This retrieval was up to me. I hoped it wasn't going to turn into an intervention, if he was even home, but I was afraid it might.

I cut through the hedge to see the police tape had been removed from the path to the bike trail. It was the shortest way to the lighthouse and I was determined not to let the memory of finding Jake's body keep me off it. I hadn't gone more than a couple of yards when I spied something glinting in a bit of late afternoon sunlight. I squatted to see that it was a button lying at the edge of the path almost hidden by the *Rosa Rugosa*.

An inch in diameter, the button was black and unremarkable, and looked like it belonged on a coat of some kind, except that it was clean. It could have popped off anyone's garment. If the person now wearing a jacket short a button had lost it weeks, months, a year ago, though, the button would be dusty. Soiled. Muddy, even. Dirt might have been ground in from a passing bicycle or sneaker sole. This one looked as fresh as the day the tailor sewed it on.

And it was right about where Jake had been killed. Maybe it was a clue to his murderer. My heart pounded. Because I'd read about an amateur sleuth doing it, I fished a tissue out of my bag and picked up the disc, feeling a bit like Nancy Drew. The tissue was supposed to protect the button from acquiring my fingerprints or even my DNA, I supposed. I would drop it by the police station tomorrow. I didn't know how they would go about searching for a coat missing a button, but that was their job, not mine. I carefully folded the tissue around the button and slid it into my bag. Before I stood, it occurred to me that the police might need to know where I'd found the button. I glanced around and found three small rocks. I laid them in a triangle around the spot where the button had been, hoping that was good enough.

Ten minutes later I was knocking up a storm on the lighthouse door. No answer. I rang the bell and got the same lack of response. I cupped my hands around my mouth. "Derrick," I called in my best outdoor voice. "Are you home?" But I might as well have been a giant hunk of breakwater boulder for all the good it did. Either he wasn't home or he was stonewalling me. His car was parked in the drive, though. That was one blessing. At least he hadn't taken his bottle of hooch out on the road and endangered others as well as himself.

"Derrick!" I gave it one more shot. I didn't have to worry about bothering neighbors with my yelling. The lighthouse perched at the end of a road, built on a rock promontory. I'd seen pictures from a century earlier when water had crashed on three sides of the ledge, but over the decades sand had shifted and filled in, with vegetation following. The barrier island nature of the Cape, one of the biggest in the world, meant its geography was always changing. Inlets opened. Passageways closed. People had no business attempting to control the contours of the land, although that didn't keep them from wanting and trying to. These days one side of this promontory was mostly scrubby dune plants and the other was a bracken marsh, with only a thirty-foot point sticking into the water beyond the land.

I walked out behind the tall sloping cylinder that went up almost a hundred feet. Wind blew straight across the promontory. A small shed sat a couple of yards behind the lighthouse, but I knew it was crammed full of gardening tools, discarded furniture, a broken lobster trap, and other detritus of a coastal residence. When the wind let up for a moment, I cocked my head. Was that whistling I heard? The wind picked up again and I lost it. Odd. Usually wind caused whistling, not the other way around. *Wait*.

Pressing my lips together, I stalked around to the

other side of the shed. My brother, whistling an unrecognizable tune, sprawled in an old lawn chair facing the water, legs spread wide. His flax-colored hair flew all which way and his face was flushed. From the open, mostly empty fifth of bourbon in his right hand, no doubt.

"If it isn't my sweet baby sister." His words came out slow and lazy but pronounced clearly. "Have a seat, Mackie. Isn't the view pretty?"

The nickname slapped me with nostalgia. He hadn't called me Mackie since I was twelve. My anger and worry overrode the sweet memories. "What are you doing out here, Derrie? Don't you know everybody's looking for you?" I swallowed when I heard myself screeching. "You're letting everybody down. Pa, me, the police, not to mention your own daughter."

"I'm sorry." He focused on his knees.

"And what's up with this?" I snatched the bottle from his hand and held it in front of his face. "Are you trying to ruin your life?" I used my still-strong high school softball arm to fling the bottle as hard and far as I could. It landed in the waves with a splash and a plunk.

"Aw, Mac." He looked after the liquor and shook his head. "Now why'd you go and do that? That was some really nice whiskey." He squinted up at me, his eyes bleary. "My life's over, anyway. And now I'll have to be sober to face it."

I stood in front of him. The breeze whipped my skirt around. "What do you mean, your life is over? You have work, you have family, you have friends." What could he mean? The horrible doubt pierced me again. Had my brother, through some awful accident, killed Jake?

"You don't understand." He choked out a sob.

I knelt in front of him and took his face in my hands, both my heart and my voice softening. "Then make me understand. I'm your sister, remember? Please? We all want to help you."

"They'll never believe me," he croaked. "Never."

"Believe you about what? About your knife?"

He groaned and turned away, hanging his head over the side of the chair, swearing. He vomited onto the ground, but the heaves took him and the lightweight chair right over sideways. His head hit a protrusion on the ledge. He lay still.

Chapter Seventeen

"**D**errick!" I scrambled to his side. "Derrie, talk to me."

My brother lay half on his stomach with his face against the rock. I turned him gently onto his back and gasped. A gash in his forehead seeped blood over his brow and down behind his ear. He reeked of vomit, and his eyes were closed. This time the sob came out, but I swallowed it down. He needed my help.

As fast as I could I unslung my cloth carrying bag and grabbed the wine bottle out of it. I pressed the bag against the cut with one hand, feeling his neck with the other. He had to be all right. He had to. His heartbeat was fast and strong. *Good.* I watched his chest rise and fall. Also good. The cloth bag wasn't particularly clean, but it would suffice for now.

I flashed on a memory. We'd been playing in an old tree out back when we were kids. Derrick, always the risk taker, had ventured out on a limb that wasn't strong enough for his chunky preteen weight. The branch cracked and broke, tossing him to the ground. The limb hadn't been too high off the ground, and he hadn't broken any bones. But, boy, had his scalp ever bled where it nicked a shard of splintered branch on his way down.

I lifted the cloth and watch new blood come to the surface, but it wasn't as much as before. Maybe, with any luck, this was the same kind of superficial scalp wound. When I pressed down on it again, with more pressure this time, he squirmed.

"Hey, that hurts," he mumbled. His eyes flickered open and he mustered a wan smile. "Hi, Mackie. What's shakin'?"

Conscious was good, too. Very good. "You fell over and hit your head. Now be a good boy and lie still. It's only a cut in your forehead."

"Oh, I've been cut before. Bad ones. I'm gonna take a little nap for a minute and let my guardian angel, I mean sister, take care of it." He closed his eyes again.

It probably wouldn't hurt for him to rest for a bit. What should I do now, though? That gash was going to need both cleaning and stitches. I sat back on my heels. I could call an ambulance, but that seemed like overkill. I decided on the next best thing.

"Hi, gorgeous." Tim's deep baritone greeted me through the phone. "On your way over?"

"I'm afraid not. I have a situation here, and I need your help." I stood and walked a few paces away, but not so far I couldn't keep an eye on the drunk patient. I explained about Derrick, Zane's tale of a bourbon sale, and what had happened after I arrived out here.

"That's a situation, all right." He softened his voice. "And you said he's blotto, too?"

"He's totally smashed. But he has to go get this wound cleaned, and have somebody stitch it up, too."

"And he's a big guy and you need me. Hang on a sec." The sound of a pot scraping on a burner came through. "Okay, I can put dinner on hold. It'll be fine. Give me five. I'll drive over, all right?"

"Please. I walked, and your station wagon has more room than his car, not that I know where his keys are." My Miss M was out of the running, of course, being a two-seater.

"Gotcha."

"Tim?"

"Yes, ma'am?"

"You're the best."

"I plan to extract appropriate payment later tonight." He disconnected.

Despite this mess, I'd heard the smile in his voice. That was enough. I went back to Derrick's side. He was a big guy. Mom was about an inch shorter than I was, so he didn't get height from her side, particularly. But Derrick's dad had apparently been six-three with a large frame, not that I'd ever met him. Derrick himself had ended up taller than Pa and had a tendency to carry weight. I'd never be able to safely hoist him up and help him walk to the car. Thank goodness for a boyfriend who was both tall and well-muscled.

What I really wanted was to get Derrick sewed up, cleaned up, and sobered up before either my parents or Cokey had any contact with him. Cokey had no experience of a father out of control and I didn't want her to. It was bad enough her mother had essentially abandoned her. She didn't deserve a daddy who did that, too. .

I gazed out at the water. A red-breasted merganser bobbed by, the shaggy feathers pointing back off its head making them look windblown, except they were like that even on a still day. When the bird dove under looking for dinner, a small clutch of common gallinules swam into view, the red of their beaks extending up their faces like a Halloween mask. A herring gull lit on top of the lighthouse with a shrill cry. Derrick still rested with his eyes closed, but his breathing was regular and he had almost as much color in his cheeks as the gallinules's bills, so I didn't worry.

At a crunching of the shells that paved the drive, I glanced behind me. Tim backed up his blue 1970 Volvo wagon as far as he could. He kept the vintage vehicle in pristine condition, even massaging leather cream into the cream-colored seats. He also used the back for bread deliveries to restaurants twice a week.

"We're back here," I called after he climbed out and gazed up at the lighthouse.

He hurried toward me, a first aid kit in his hand, and put his arm around my shoulders as we gazed down at my silly, stupid, stinky, soused brother. "Shall we?"

It was ten o'clock before Tim and I finished dinner. The emergency department at Falmouth Hospital had been amazingly under-subscribed this evening, so Derrick was treated promptly. Still, it was a drive to get to the hospital and back, and we hadn't left until almost six, what with getting my brother up off the ground, clad in a clean shirt, and into the car, where he promptly fell back asleep. I'd put a clean dressing on the wound, too.

On the way to the hospital, I'd texted my parents that I'd found Derrick and he'd cut his head, and that Tim and I were taking him to get stitches. I added that we would all spend the night at Tim's, which Tim had offered after my brother fell asleep. I omitted mention of the whiskey. Derrick could tell them that himself if he wanted to.

His inebriation hadn't gone unnoticed at the hospital. After the tests, tetanus shot, and stitching, the doctor had beckoned Tim and me into Derrick's bay.

"I've told him he should not have any additional alcohol tonight. Can you help keep track of that?"

"Of course," I replied. "He, um, has been sober for about six years, so I'm sure this is a temporary slip-up."

"I can hear you, you know." Derrick waved his hand from the bed.

The doctor nodded. "You were on private property and not behind the wheel of a motor vehicle when you fell, correct?"

"Correct."

"That's right," I confirmed. "I was there."

"Can one of you keep a good eye on him tonight for signs of concussion?" The doctor handed Derrick a discharge sheet. "They're on this sheet."

"We will," Tim said. "You're going to stay with us tonight, dude," he said to Derrick.

"Good," the doctor said. "I'd like a note of that location, please." He took down the address and made sure he had my cell phone recorded, too. He frowned at my brother. "An alert came up when we recorded your injury in the accident database. The state police asked us to let them know if you came in for any reason. They're apparently interested in talking to you."

"I know all about it," Derrick said in a low voice.

"I know, too," I said. "We'll be in touch with them."

"Fine. You are free to leave, Mr. Searle. Be well."

The doctor shook hands with Derrick and with each of us.

I echoed the doc's lovely farewell back to him. "Be well."

Derrick was listless on the ride back to Westham, staring out the window, answering our few questions in monosyllables. When we arrived at Tim's modest house on the hill behind downtown, Tim showed Derrick the guest room and the bathroom, told him to make himself comfortable, and then join us for dinner. Instead, when we were ready to sit down to eat at the table in the kitchen, which doubled as a dining room, I could hear Derrick's snoring.

"We'll save him a plate," Tim said as he lit two tapers in glass candlesticks.

"The wine!" I exclaimed. I'd completely forgotten to pick up the bottle out on the promontory.

"Good thing I have a couple of cases in my wine cellar."

"Wait. You don't have a wine cellar," I pointed out. He owned the two-bedroom cottage, which he kept clean and in good repair. And I knew he didn't have a custom-designed temperature-controlled wine cellar.

"It's a cellar, and it has wine in it." He shrugged with a wicked grin and reappeared three minutes later with both a cool Oregon Pinot Gris and an Australian Shiraz. He poured white for both of us and we tucked into our dinner. He'd already mostly cooked the shallow dish of cheesy, creamy potatoes and assembled the salad before my call earlier, so by the time he'd seared the scallops, the potatoes were ready, too.

I pushed my chair back a little when my plate was empty. All we'd had at the hospital were bottles of water and a bag of chips each, and I'd been famished. A lone piece of arugula decorated the rim of my square white plate, and a tiny sprig of dill was the only evidence of the scrumptious scallops, which he'd quick-seared in olive oil, butter, and garlic, with a wine de-glaze at the end.

"That was perfect, Tim. Thank you. And especially thank you for helping me with Derrick. I couldn't have gotten him to the hospital without you." I drained the last drop from my glass of wine, but capped it with my hand when Tim lifted the bottle to pour more. "That's enough for me for tonight."

"You could have called an ambulance. He would have had good care. But anyway, your needs are my needs. Got it?" He squeezed my hand.

"Got it."

"Do you think he's going to be able to get sober again?" Tim asked softly after glancing at the door to the hall.

"I sure hope so. I think he'd stopped going to AA meetings lately. He'll need to start that up again." I ran a finger around the rim of the glass. "Who knew the hospitals had an accident database?"

"It makes sense, I guess. And that way if the authorities are looking for someone, they have a way to check with the hospitals."

I shuddered. "If the police had had a warrant for Derrick's arrest, they probably would've come right to Falmouth and taken him away. A small blessing, I suppose, that they only want to talk to him."

"Good point."

I stood and cleared the plates while Tim put away the rest of the food. I'd finished rinsing the dishes when my phone emitted its incoming-text double beeps. I groaned when I read the message.

"What is it?" Tim asked.

I looked into his baby blues. "Detective Haskins says he's on the porch. And he wants to talk to Derrick." So much for snuggling with my sweetheart.

"Now?"

"Now."

Tim frowned and tapped his index finger on the table. "How did he know you and Derrick both were here?"

I thought for a second. "Because we gave the doc your address. So what do I do?"

"What do you want to do? And what do you think you should do?" He stroked my hand.

I let out a sigh worthy of a nine-point-nine in the Olympics. "I want to go to bed with you five minutes ago. But I should go talk to him." I stood. "So I guess I will." I pushed back my chair and headed toward the hall.

"Ask him in if you need to," Tim called after me.

I nodded, pulling open the front door a moment later. "Good evening Detective," I said in the glow of the front porch light. "I'm afraid my brother is sleeping. He injured his head tonight."

"Yes, I know. And you know we need to speak with him on some matters of great importance. I can talk to him here or I can bring him to the station. But given how elusive he's been, I'm not leaving until one of those two things happens." He cleared his throat and pushed his glasses up the bridge of his nose. "I'm sorry to disturb you and Mr. Brunelle at such a late hour."

Tim's presence was warm behind me even though he

hadn't spoken. "Why don't you come in, then?" I twisted my head up and back. "All right, Tim?" I asked, even though he'd already given me the answer.

"Of course," Tim said. "Right this way, sir."

I added, "I'll see if I can get Derrick up."

Chapter Eighteen

I'd barely been able to wake Derrick, which made me feel bad that I hadn't checked him for signs of concussion since we'd been home. I finally convinced him to get up and splash water on his face, avoiding the bandage on his brow.

"And put some toothpaste on your finger to brush your teeth, okay?" I added. "We'll put coffee on."

The house didn't have any doors to the outside in the back or I'd have been afraid Derrick would make a run for it. Still, after I started coffee I returned to stand outside the bathroom door to make sure he didn't go anywhere. I wasn't positive if he was awake enough to register that a police officer was waiting for him, but if he was, I was determined to deliver my charge without him slipping away into the night. How odd it felt to be the younger sibling and have to take care of my big brother this way.

When he emerged, he pulled me into a hug. "I'm sorry, Mac. I was just so afraid," he whispered.

I rubbed his cheek. "What were you afraid of?"

He gave a little shake of his head. "I'm still afraid, but I'm going to face what I have to face."

Moments later we sat in the small living room. Table lamps cast warm light into the room. Artwork featuring West Coast beaches and surfers decorated the walls and bright Central American cloth covered the comfortable chairs where Derrick and the detective sat. A small fireplace was covered by a screen, with an antique clock ticking away on the mantel above. I loved the way Tim had decorated his home. It reflected his tastes and likes, but wasn't a man cave.

Tim brought mugs of coffee for the men, then settled onto the sofa next to me. The detective thanked him, and Derrick sipped his brew like he hadn't had any in a year. I was about to offer to fix him a sandwich when Haskins began. He asked Derrick's permission to record the session, then clicked something on a tablet and got the preliminaries of identification out of the way.

"Wait. Do I need a lawyer?" Derrick asked.

"At this time I'm merely gathering information," Haskins said. "You may call one if you'd like."

"But he's not being accused of anything?" I inserted myself in the process.

"Not at this time, no," the detective said. "Mr. Searle, we have reason to believe the murder weapon in the death of Jake Lacey on Tuesday June second was your rather unique fish knife. When was the last time you know of it being in your possession?"

Derrick shook his head, clutching his mug in both hands, gazing at the floor.

"Excuse me, sir. You need to answer out loud for the record."

"I don't remember."

I pictured Derrick's fish-gutting implement. "Can I say something about the knife?"

Haskins nodded, so I went on. "Mackenzie Almeida, Westham. I'm Derrick Searle's half-sister. I remember him using the knife to gut and clean a twenty-pound striper on Saturday. The thirtieth of May."

Derrick finally raised his eyes.

"Would that be correct, Mr. Searle?"

"Yes, I think so."

"Who lives in the lighthouse for which you are caretaker?" the detective asked.

"Only my daughter Cokey and me. She's four."

"Had anyone besides the two of you been in your home between May thirtieth and the evening of June second?"

"Yes," Derrick said, but offered nothing more.

"Who?" Haskins checked the same paper notebook he'd had when he interviewed me.

"That Tuesday night most of the Cozy Capers were there, like they are every week."

"I can give you those names later," I offered.

"Fine," Haskins said.

"On Sunday a couple of small tours came through," Derrick continued. "That's part of the caretaker deal, that I lead tours of the lighthouse on weekends during the summer season, which only started this week."

"Do you have the names of the people who took the tours?" Detective Haskins asked.

"At home I do." Derrick nodded. "If they signed the guest book, that is. I'm supposed to get their names and addresses so the owners can hit them up for restoration funds. But as long as the people pay their ten dollars for the tour, I let the sign-in thing slide if they object." His eyes were gradually becoming clear, but his slumped shoulders and the big honking bandage on his forehead gave away his ordeal of the afternoon.

"We'll pick up that book tomorrow. Now let's talk about how you knew Jake Lacey," Haskins said. "Had you had any dealings with him here in Westham, interacted with him?"

I watched my brother. Of course I wasn't with him all the time, but as far as I knew he hadn't. No, I was wrong about that. Once, when Jake was repairing my house, he'd come into the shop to ask me something while Derrick was working the rentals. The two men hadn't spoken, but I'd picked up on a funny dynamic. Jake had smirked when he'd seen Derrick, and Derrick had turned his back, busying himself with the files behind the counter.

"Any contact at all, of any kind?" Haskins pressed when my brother didn't answer.

"Yes." Derrick lifted his chin. He looked straight at the detective.

"Please describe that contact."

"Every month I gave him money. Not much, but some."

"Why?" I blurted out, then muttered, "Sorry," when the detective shot me a quick glare.

"He was blackmailing me." Derrick's voice was level, calm.

My eyes couldn't have gotten wider. I glanced at

Tim, who gave a little shake of his head, then back at Derrick. *Blackmail? About what?* This time I kept my mouth shut and waited.

The detective's voice dropped softly into the silence. "He was blackmailing you about the time you spent in prison with him?"

"Yes."

Chapter Nineteen

I stared at the detective. *"Prison*? Derrick? But when? And why?"

Tim covered my hand with his. He looked surprised too.

Haskins consulted his notebook. "For two years. You were released on March first a year ago."

"That's right." Derrick finally looked at me. "I told you I'd been living with monks in Switzerland, trying to stay sober and get my act together. But I wasn't. I did go to Europe to pick up Cokey after I was released, when her mom, my ex, said she didn't want her."

"You came back to live in Westham about the same time I did last spring." I nodded slowly. "At least being in prison explains how you could have left Cokey for two years. That had always seemed wrong for a father so devoted to his little girl."

"I'm sorry, Mac." My brother clasped his hands in his lap. "I'm sorry for all of it. But especially for not telling you."

Haskins cleared his throat. "How did you pay Mr. Lacey?" he asked Derrick. "And what did he threaten you with if you didn't pay?"

"He gave me deposit slips to his bank account. I put the money in every month. I didn't want to see him if I could help it, so I insisted on that method."

"That's why you turned your back when Jake came into the shop," I said, leaning forward.

Derrick gave a single nod in return.

"And the threat?" the detective reminded him.

"He said he'd make it public that I'd been incarcerated. I felt ashamed about it. Dirty. And I didn't want my only daughter thinking I was a criminal. Or you, Mac." Derrick's eyes pleaded with me.

"Where were you on Tuesday after five thirty?" Haskins asked.

Would my brother tell the truth? I was still reeling from learning he'd been in prison. My world felt like it had been caught in a big wave, tossed and tumbled in all directions.

Derrick squared his shoulders but studied his hands for a moment. "I went to tell Jake I wasn't going to pay him any more money. I was sick of hiding behind him, owing him. We'd arranged to meet outside the food pantry at six after the free dinner. But he never showed. I waited and waited. The fog had already come in and it was damp and miserable, plus I had the book group showing up. So I headed for home on the path near your yard, Mac. And there he was."

"You didn't report the body." The detective adjusted his glasses as he gazed at Derrick.

"No. I panicked. I didn't think anyone would believe me because of my past with him. I ran all the way home." His voice shook.

I cocked my head. "That explains why you were late to book group and why you were breathing heavily when you arrived. Now your being nervous that night makes sense."

"It also explains your absence the last two days, with a bottle of bourbon to top it off," Tim added.

"I'm sorry, sis. I know I acted irresponsibly. I let you down. Again." Derrick shook his head, then winced and squeezed his eyes shut.

It looked as if his head was hurting. I wasn't surprised. Derrick would have a major headache even if he hadn't fallen and cut his temple.

"If you'd called it in, stayed with him, Mr. Lacey's life might have been saved." Haskins lifted his eyebrows.

"Oh, no." Derrick opened his eyes. "He was already dead. No question about that."

The detective checked his notebook. "Do you know of any other people in the area who might have had grievances with the victim? Anyone you've seen around town, any other acquaintances from your incarceration who might have showed up?"

Derrick tented his fingers. "No. I can't help you with that. Like I said, I avoided Jake wherever possible. And I haven't seen anyone I recognize from that time. But Lacey wasn't an easy man. He liked to get under people's skin. I wouldn't be surprised if he had plenty of enemies wherever he went."

The clock on the mantel chimed eleven times. Derrick drained his coffee, while Tim and I sat together, silent. Was Haskins going to arrest my brother? My palms grew sweaty as I waited.

The detective studied us, then stored his pen in his shirt pocket, clicked off the recording, and stood. "Thank you for your time, all of you. I expect we'll find your fingerprints on your knife, Mr. Searle, since it was your knife, after all. But I can't arrest you without hard evidence." His expression grew grave. "Believe me when I say we'll be looking for it. I'd appreciate you staying close to home until you hear otherwise from me."

Derrick rose, too. "I'm not going anywhere. As my sister reminded me earlier today, I have work here, and friends. But most important, I have family members who need me."

"You might want to avoid the liquor stores, too," Haskins advised.

"Yes, sir. You can count on that."

I knew from Derrick's experience how hard that truly was, and hoped he would get the help he needed, from AA if not from other sources. A person of interest in a homicide couldn't afford to get into even more trouble.

My gaze drifted onto my bag on a side table where I'd laid it. "Detective, before you go, I have a clue for you." I stood and went to my bag, then handed him the button. "I saw this by the side of the path earlier today. It was right where I found Jake's body, and it's clean. It has to have fallen off someone's coat recently. I picked it up with the tissue, and I marked the spot. That was the right thing to do, wasn't it?"

Haskins frowned and held out his hand for the tissue-wrapped button. A heavy sigh slid out of him. "I'm glad you didn't touch it directly, Ms. Almeida. But next time, just call us." He glanced at Tim. "Got a clean plastic bag I can have?"

Tim hurried into the kitchen. Why hadn't Haskins even thanked me? "Is there something wrong, Detective?" I asked.

"We need to be the ones to retrieve pieces of evidence. We have procedure to follow so that items like this will be admissible in court. It's a done deal now, but in the future please don't move anything you think might be important to the case. Let us handle it."

My excitement at finding what might be a real clue turned to a bad taste in my mouth. What if I'd just spoiled the case against Jake's killer?

Chapter Twenty

The front door clicked shut. Tim, who had seen the detective out, popped his head into the living room.

"I'm going to tidy up the kitchen." He couldn't hide a yawn. "You hungry, man?" he asked Derrick.

Derrick started to shake his head but thought the better of it. "Actually I'm starving. Just realized." He made as if to stand.

Tim waved him down. "I'll heat you up a plate. You slept through dinner."

And Derrick had had a liquid lunch, too.

"Thanks, dude."

I smiled my gratitude, as well, then gazed at my brother. "I feel like my world got thrown up into the air and everything came down different." I kept my voice gentle. But I did want some answers. The hurt of it split my heart, that he'd never told me. If my parents knew, they hadn't let me in on the secret, either. My world had gotten stood on end.

"And I feel like I'm going to be saying I'm sorry a

lot. But I am, truly. What I did was stupid, from Tuesday right through this afternoon. I'm forty-effing-one, Mac. You'd think I'd learn." He pounded his fist into the palm of the other hand, over and over.

"We always have time in our lives to learn, don't we? You shouldn't beat yourself up about it."

"I guess."

I waited but he didn't offer any more information so I kept talking. "I want to know where the prison was, why you were in, all of that. But it's even more urgent now that we figure out who killed Jake. I know it wasn't you."

"That's the truth. I hope you believe me."

"I do, of course. We need to convince Detective Haskins of that before somebody makes up some evidence simply so they can show an arrest."

Derrick rubbed the cuff of his right sleeve with the fingers of his left hand. "I don't think I should be part of this 'we,' sis."

"Well, I'll find the killer, then. But the question is, who was it? I have to find him." I straightened the coasters on the coffee table that had started to slide off their stack.

"Or her." Derrick raised his eyebrows. "Equal opportunity murder."

Tim returned and set a plate, fork, and paper napkin on the side table next to Derrick. "Get you anything, Mac?"

Now I wanted that second glass of wine, but despite what I'd said to Tim earlier about Derrick not minding if others drank alcohol in front of him, I didn't think now was the best time for that. "I'd love a glass of seltzer, please."

Derrick dug into the scallops and potatoes. Tim

brought back a glass of clear bubbly for each of us a minute later, plus a plate of oatmeal chocolate-chip cookies. We all ate in silence for a bit.

I swallowed the last of my cookie. "Were you telling Haskins the truth, Derrick, that you don't know of anybody in town who'd rubbed Jake the wrong way? And you really haven't seen anyone who you knew during your incarceration?" I had trouble even pronouncing *your* and *incarceration* in the same breath, but I was obviously going to have to get used to it.

"Truth. I haven't seen anyone in town I knew there except Jake. Or anywhere on the Cape, even, but I haven't been looking. You know me since I've been back, Mac. I mind my own business. Hang out with Cokey and the family. Work in your shop. Play trivia on Thursdays. I lead a pretty quiet life. However, I think Jake followed me here, or came here because this is where I was returning. We were released on the same day."

"Really?" Tim asked.

"Really. Didn't he show up about the same time I did last year?" Derrick asked.

"Actually, he got to Westham before you did," I said. "I recall because we served a Saint Patrick's Day dinner at the soup kitchen and Jake introduced himself to me. I'm pretty sure it was last year's dinner, not this year's."

"The little rat." At a glance from me, Derrick added, "May he rest in peace."

"And you didn't roll into town until Mother's Day," I added. "Remember how happy Mom was?"

Derrick nodded. "Right, because I went to France to get Cokey. I had to hang around a while so she got to know me again, trusted me enough to take her." He set his demolished plate on the table, and reached for a cookie. "Seriously, Mac. I think he had planned to blackmail me all along, as soon as he found out I was from here. He had some notion everybody on the Cape is rich and has limitless pockets."

"What was Jake in for?" I cocked my head.

"Low-level embezzlement."

Tim yawned again. He kissed my cheek and stood. "I'm sorry, I have to hit the sack. That four o'clock alarm is going to bust my ass. A bakery's a bakery, though, and it's mine." He extended a hand to Derrick, who shook it. "Make yourself at home, man. A robe hangs on a hook on the back of the door in your room, and you'll find clean towels in the bathroom cabinet."

"I really appreciate it." Derrick extended his hand and shook Tim's. "Appreciate everything you did for me today, both of you, and I owe you. I'll be out of your hair tomorrow."

"Hey, bro. Any brother of Mac's is a brother of mine. Even though she's definitely not my sister." Tim shot me a wicked grin, blew another kiss my way, and headed down the hall.

"You got a good man there, Mackie," Derrick said after a moment. "He didn't have to trust me. Give me his guest room. Say that about being his brother. Lots of guys wouldn't have."

I nodded slowly. "He's a keeper, all right." I flashed on what our father had said this morning when I called him. I'd asked if Derrick had said where he'd been the day before, and Pa had said that was Derrick's story to tell. Was it a bigger story than I'd suspected? I sat back against the sofa arm and tucked my feet up on the cushion. I was tired, too, but I had to see this conversation through. "Pa knew you were in prison."

Derrick eyebrows went way up. "How did you know?"

"I didn't. But I picked up on something he said. Mind you, he didn't tell me a thing. He didn't reveal a single confidence."

"Yeah. When I was accused and convicted, I really needed his help. He said he couldn't keep it from Mom, but I pulled the confession card on the minister, frankly, and made him promise not to tell you. I felt crappy about hiding it from you, Mackie. What did you pick up on?"

"It was what he said this morning when I asked if he knew where you'd been yesterday. He said it was your story to tell. Now I realize the story was bigger than only where you'd been yesterday."

"You're right." He rolled his eyes.

"Where were you yesterday, anyway?"

He examined a frayed corner of his chair. "Working my way through a dozen beers at a seedy bar in Bourne. After the first one, my conscience took a really long nap, and my higher power said, 'You want to screw yourself, be my guest.' Or at least that's what I told myself." He looked up.

"Aw, Derrie. You know you can always call me if you get tempted like that again."

"Of course I know. But you're not an addict. I've seen that. You don't understand what a demon it is. Simply making that call is the hard part."

"Well, the offer stands." I sipped my water. "So Mom knows you were in prison?"

"Yes, but she thinks I'm some sort of golden boy anyway because of all the blah-blah-blah in my chart. Delusional, as usual, but I know she means well."

"It is a bit hard to take if you don't believe in astrology. But hey, enough people do, plus they pay her for her interpretations. And it makes her happy." I laughed. "Maybe I should consult with the great Astra about who around here might have had their stars and planets in a murderous position Tuesday."

He laughed, too. "As long as she doesn't say it was my Aries in Scorpio conjunct Saturn." He rolled his eyes.

"Or Jake's left foot in Pisces in aspect to Province-town." I couldn't help myself from giggling.

"Maybe Westham trine the house of Aquarius with tourists rising." Derrick snorted, then dissolved in laughter.

Which made two of us. We'd been doing this fake horoscope routine ever since Mom converted to the religion of Astrologism. We never cracked irreverent lines in her presence, of course, but to see my brother once again sober, relaxed, and joking comforted me. He was going to be all right. We'd be all right. Once I removed him from the house of suspects, that is.

Chapter Twenty-one

My own alarm came at six, a scant two hours after Tim's the next morning. I'd roused ever so slightly when he climbed out of bed. I asked him to look in on Derrick, since we'd both completely forgotten the doctor's caution to check my brother for signs of concussion. Tim came back in and said Derrick had good color and was breathing regularly, so I kissed my man and rolled over to two more hours of oblivion, missing the sunrise completely.

Now, though, I had a bird to attend to, a walk with Gin to squeeze in, and a shop to operate. I splashed water on my face and threw on my dress and leggings in a hurry. Why hadn't I thought to bring a change of clothes? I hated putting on last night's outfit in the morning. Oh, well. I'd be home and in my walking togs soon enough.

My own check of my brother had the same results as Tim's—sound asleep, with normal color in his face and regular breathing. I let him sleep. The man needed his rest, and it was only six o'clock, after all. I headed into the kitchen where Tim, the angel, had left me a cup's worth of coffee in the French press. While I heated the brew in the microwave I read the note he'd left me next to a small ring with a key on it.

> *Left my car in case you need it. See you at*
> *Brews and Breads, I hope.*
> *XXX OOO*
> *T*

He'd ridden his bike to work as he always did on non-delivery days, but made sure I had the car key. Sweet of him. But, nah. I'd walk home. It wasn't far. I pocketed the note, poured my coffee, and sat at the table to write a message to my brother. Normally I would text him, but I didn't even know if he had his phone.

> *Derrick—Hope you're feeling better. Am off*
> *home and to the shop. You should spend time*
> *w/Cokey, but come into work later if you can.*
> *Text me.*
> *love,*
> *Mackie*

There. I gazed at the key as I breathed in Tim's comforting kitchen scents of java, something yeasty, and a trace of cardamom and cinnamon. He must have baked at home recently.

Did I want to leave Tim's car for Derrick? No. As long as he stayed sober, I'd trust him with my life. But seeing him smashed with a bottle in his hand yesterday had eroded my faith in his judgment just a teensy bit.

An underlayment of sadness colored my mood. Derrie had worked so hard to get sober in the first place, and I believed this was his first screw-up. I hoped it wouldn't repeat any time soon, and preferably never.

I slid the key back into the drawer where Tim kept it, drained my coffee, and washed out the cup. Before I left I wiped down the kitchen counter, too. What a blessing that Tim also liked a pretty clean kitchen, but then a cook would have to. Nobody was as devoted to—or as both Gin and my mom would say, obsessed about—a tidy environment as I was, but I knew from experience, a relationship with a messy man was doomed from the start.

I headed out into the morning, glad for my sweater as I walked down the hill. The sun peeked over the buildings of Westham's main drag but the air still had a nip to it. I cut across Main Street to the bikeway, my brain full of all this new information. I wrinkled my nose, imagining Derrick in prison. He was a good man. Generous, gentle, and fun. Wasn't prison a dangerous, hard-edged place, with gangs and violence despite the guards? Or maybe from the guards themselves? I had not a scrap of personal experience or knowledge of incarceration. But I'd read stories in the news, and fictional accounts, too.

And I'd seen TV shows and movies about incarceration, although I'd never liked criminal investigation kinds of shows. I'd rather get my police intrigues through the written word. And these days the only TV I watched was via the Internet, anyway. I stopped in my tracks. Speaking of the Internet, I'd never even run a search on my own brother. I supposed I never thought I needed to. I almost pulled out my phone to do it then and there, but I was almost home. It could wait.

* * *

I'd changed into my walking clothes and was hanging out with Belle by six thirty. "How's my best bird?" I asked her, feeding her bits of a seed cookie. "Did you party all night, Belle?"

"Did Belle party?" She cocked her head and eyed me as if she'd been partying so much she couldn't remember. "Did Belle party?"

I laughed. "I don't know. Did you? Maybe you did."

She whistled. "What a party!"

I swapped out the newspapers on the floor of her daytime roost cage with clean ones. African Greys didn't soil the place where they slept—another proof of how smart they were—so I had fit two cages in my little living room. I sat at my laptop at the table, with Belle standing next to me peering at the screen. A minute later I frowned at a news article from the *Dallas News*. The headline read, DA STRIKES WHITE COLLAR CRIME CASE PLEA BARGAIN. The story began, *Derrick Searle to serve two years in minimum security, says the Dallas County District Attorney's office. Plea for reduced sentence accepted in exchange for information about company management.*

Sitting back, I searched my memory. I'd almost forgotten that my brother had lived and worked in Texas. I shouldn't have. It was where my only niece was born. Derrick had been working at a tech company doing IT work. He'd met Genevieve at work, the brilliant but disturbed French mother of his daughter. They hadn't gotten married when she'd announced the pregnancy, and all I knew was that she'd left him and taken the baby home to Grenoble.

But where had I been three-four years ago? If, as

we'd discussed, Derrick got home from his reputed monastery retreat a few months after me, and if he'd served all two years of the sentence, he'd have gone into prison during my second year abroad. I'd cashed out of the high-power job I hated in Boston's financial district and had joined the Peace Corps. I didn't even want to think about the slob of a boyfriend I'd also abandoned at the same time. So I'd been living in a Thai village when my brother had gone in. When my Peace Corps stint was over, I'd headed for Australia and New Zealand. I'd had a glorious year touristing, bicycling, and enjoying the attentions of a high-energy Kiwi cyclist until my knee blew out at the same time the New Zealander blew me off. I'd decided it was time to go home.

I checked the article again then went back to the search, where I saw only a couple more links, and most regarded the misdeeds of the company execs, not a low-level IT worker. I returned to the article again, the only one mentioning Derrick by name. I was surprised how little coverage there had been, even out West. I'd be willing to bet the news of the case never made it to the Cape newspapers, or the *Boston Globe*, either. I read the article through and saw no mention of Derrick's hometown. That must be why it wasn't public knowledge in these parts. Maybe keeping his name off the Internet was part of his bargain. My poor beleaguered brother.

But what about Jake Lacey? Derrick had said he'd been in for low-level embezzlement. But who had he embezzled from, and was that his first crime? Googling Jake's name wasn't anywhere near as easy as Derrick's. In fact, it was impossible, whether I switched to Jacob or not. The dead Jake was not a baseball player, a musician, or a marketing whiz. As far as I knew he wasn't a Rubik's Cube master nor an economist, and he definitely wasn't a star cross-country runner at a Catholic college. I had too many possibilities to pore over. I gave up on that line of inquiry right away. I assumed Detective Haskins and his team would already have pursued it, anyway. Probably should have thought of that before I started.

Leaving Jake to the side, I still needed to talk with Derrick in detail about his own past. But he was injured and sleeping, so that wasn't going to happen now. In the meantime, I knew exactly the person to call. Pa was an early riser. He wouldn't mind.

He answered on the second ring and wished me a good morning. "How's your brother?" His voice was even deeper than usual, and more gravelly. "Cokey's up and asking," he added softly.

She was probably nearby, playing or watching a PBS cartoon. "He's going to be fine," I said. "I think he'll be over to your place this morning sometime. Can you keep her until then?"

He wait a moment before speaking. "I can, of course. I'm pondering Sunday's sermon, and sometimes she's less a hindrance than an inspiration. But doesn't Derrick need to work at your shop?"

"He was still asleep when I left this morning. I left him a message to go get his girl, and come in this afternoon if he can." I heard the tinny sound of a laugh track in the distance, then the unmistakable reedy tones of *Sesame Street*'s Bert chastising, "Ernie, Ernie. That's not how it's spelled." Yep, Cokey was watching her favorite show.

"Mackenzie, was your brother inebriated yesterday?" my father asked. "Is that how he fell?"

"You're using big words so she won't understand, right?"

"Very perceptive. Please answer the question."

"Yes. He was very much inebriated. In fact he was stinking drunk for the second day in a row, apparently. But Pa, after Derrick was checked into the hospital, his name triggered an alert in an accident database. The police had informed hospitals they were looking for him, and Detective Haskins came to Tim's place late last night." I told him about the questioning, about Haskins's suspicions. "Derrick told us about his incarceration and about Jake threatening to expose him."

"Mmm."

"He said you knew all along." I waited. When Pa didn't respond, I asked, "Why did you keep it from me?"

"He must have told you he'd asked me not to reveal his experiences. Mac, many troubled people have asked me to keep their secrets. I have no choice but to agree, as long as it won't result in anyone being harmed by my silence."

I sighed. "I wish he'd told me, too."

"I know, honey." Pa cleared his throat. "And I ask for your forgiveness."

"You don't have to do that. It's part of your life, your calling."

"I will say I had gently encouraged your brother to stand up to the scoundrel."

In the background I heard a tiny high-pitched voice lisp, "Abo Joe, what's a scoundrel?"

"It means a bad guy, Coquille."

I smiled. Pa was one of the few who called Cokey by her full name. "Derrick said he was going to confront Jake," I said. "But Jake didn't show up, and when Derrick saw him on the path, Jake was already dead." I glanced at the time display on my mini-microwave. "Shoot. I'm late for my walk. Talk to you later, Pa. Love to Coke."

"Love you, sweetheart."

"Thanks for talking. For being there for all of us. You're the best."

I could tell by the way Gin was stretching in front of her shop that she was figuratively tapping her foot at my being late.

"I'm sorry," I said, breathless from rushing over. "I lost track of time. Ready?"

"I've been ready for ten minutes, girlfriend." She raised one eyebrow at me. "It's not like you to lose track of time. What were you doing, anyway?"

We set off toward the walking-biking-running trail as I thought about how much to tell her. I didn't want to fill her in about Derrick's past. As my father had said, that was his story to tell. But she might hear about his accident around town, so I wanted to give her some kind of explanation. "I was checking up on Derrick. He had a little accident yesterday. Tim and I took him to the hospital to get stitches and I wanted to be sure he was doing all right this morning." That would have to do.

She gazed at me. "That's terrible. Was it a car accident?"

"No, he was being careless. He's fine." I winced inwardly at the lie of omission, but it couldn't be helped. And if—or rather, when—his past came out, she'd understand about my not breaking his confidence.

"I'm glad. He's a nice guy."

A little wheel started rolling in my brain after we

turned onto the path proper and passed the first tenth-mile marker set into the pavement, this one recording MILE 4.2. Derrick was a nice guy. He was a great guy, when he wasn't relapsing. Gin was single. He was single. They were close to the same age and I loved them both. Maybe I should work on the tiniest bit of matchmaking. The thought made me smile. On the other hand, Gin's daughter was out of the home. Would she even want to get involved with the single dad of a four-year-old? Or with a recovering alcoholic? I mentally scolded myself for that leap. They weren't even dating. Yet.

"Have you started reading *Cracked to Death* for next week?" she asked.

"No. I'm too busy trying to learn stuff about Jake's murder." And my brother's criminal past, I didn't add. "Have you?"

"Not a word." She laughed. "I did poke around downtown. Suzanne closed the Book Nook early that day, at five thirty. And not because she had a special event scheduled for the evening, either. She easily could have killed Jake."

"That would explain how she knew he was stabbed. But how would Suzanne have gotten Derrick's knife? And more important, why would she kill Jake?"

Gin pulled her mouth to the side. "That's the tricky part. I'll see what else I can find out about her past. Maybe she knew Jake from somewhere else."

Like from prison? Like Jake and my brother. My brain was full of what I'd learned about Derrick's crime and his sentence, so I walked in silence for a few minutes. I barely saw MILE 4.3 and MILE 4.4 disappear under my feet, and I jumped a little when Gin spoke.

"Did you find out about the fog bank?" She smiled. "Or as Lucy used to say, the frog bank?"

"I did. Flo said the lighthouse was already socked in when she arrived for book group at around six. Funny I didn't remember that."

"We're so used to it, we probably don't even notice." She didn't speak again until we'd walked over the section crossing the marsh. "So I've been watching Wes, the rich guy from New York. The one staying at my place."

I elbowed her. "And we're on a first-name basis with the guests now, are we?"

She rolled her eyes. "Mac, I always tell my guests to call me Gin, and they always reciprocate. So yeah, I don't address him as Mr. Farnham."

"And what have you learned from watching him?"

"Not much, to tell the truth. I keep expecting him to act suspiciously, but I've only seen one odd thing."

I raised my eyebrows and waited.

"I was freshening up his room. And I saw a brochure for custom-made fish-gutting knives on the floor next to the wastebasket. As if he threw it away but missed."

"Custom-made? Like somebody could have copied Derrick's? That's creepy." The thought was almost as creepy as the thick vines twisting down from the trees we passed, looking like an alien being was trying to choke the life out of the arboreal specimen. Other trees featured gray-green scales on their trunks, a color matched by the hairy tufts of *usnea* lichen lining the branches of their neighbors. The lichen looked for all the world like disembodied gnome goatees.

"He's not exactly the fisherman type. At least not that I've seen." Gin pursed her lips.

"Was the place that makes the knives somewhere here in town?"

"I think it was a shop in Chatham called Sharp Stuff. The name was something like that."

"Maybe he bought a knife from the shop." If he did, Wes Farnham might have been faking it about asking where he could find Jake. He might be the killer with a knife identical to Derrick's. That would prove my brother's innocence. "We should call them and ask."

"Good idea. I'll do that when I get home. After I saw the brochure, I asked Wes if he wanted information about going out on a fishing boat for the day. I thought there was a chance he might be interested, especially since he seems to want to buy property here."

"And?" I asked.

"He kind of looked at me funny. And—"

The telltale whir of a well-tuned bicycle in motion approached behind us. It was getting louder way too fast. I twisted my head.

"Hey, careful," I yelled, pulling Gin to the side of the path. A lean person in black and orange, including helmet, shades, and gloves, whizzed by us head down on our side of the yellow line. The rider was astride a Cannondale CAAD 12. He or she—I couldn't tell which it was—would have knocked Gin over if I hadn't grabbed her.

Gin swore. "He cut that way too close."

I shook my head. "Some riders think they're better than us mere pedestrians. Didn't even call out or ring a bell to warn us." I shivered and couldn't help but wonder if the close call hadn't been accidental. Maybe it wasn't just Rude Rob from Revere. Maybe somebody was out to get us on purpose.

Gin gazed down the path after the cyclist, too, until the bike and rider disappeared around a bend. "Too bad bikes aren't required to have license plates," she muttered. "I'd have called it in."

"Agree. I mean, the rules of the road are posted at every entrance to the trail, right? And they include *Audible signal before passing* as well as, *Keep right, pass left.* On the right is exactly where we were." I flipped the rider disappearing into the distance an obscure Thai hand gesture that no American would recognize but was a definite insult in East Asia. "Back to your Mr. Wes. He had information about custom knives and you asked him . . . what did you say you asked him?"

"I asked if he wanted to know about going out fishing for a day. He looked at me like I suddenly had a purple horn growing out of my head. I guess he doesn't like fishing."

"Not everybody does. Or maybe he gets seasick. You haven't seen him doing anything else suspicious, have you? Other than being in possession of a brochure, that is."

"No. I feel something odd about him, but I can't put my finger on it," she said.

"He looked at me oddly when he left my shop after asking about Jake, too. Almost as if he knew I wasn't telling the truth about Jake being dead. I didn't lie, but I didn't say, 'Don't you know he was killed last night?' Gin, you know what we should do?"

"What?"

"I want to share information with book group, but I don't have time to have another meeting in person. We could start a group text. Each of us could add what we've learned."

She tilted her head. "That's a good idea, Mac. But maybe a group e-mail would work better. Do you think everybody texts?"

I pictured each member of the group. "Does Norland?"

"Sure. He's texted me since he retired. I gave him a ride to his car once when it was in the shop."

"Otherwise Flo is the oldest in the group, and she certainly texts," I said. "I think texting would be better. With e-mail, if you forget to hit Reply All, it only goes back to the sender. With a group text, it's automatic."

Gin nodded. "But what about Suzanne? What if she picks up her mom's phone and reads the text?"

"We'd have the same issue with e-mail," I pointed out. "We'll have to leave our thoughts about Suzanne out of the discussion. We're the only two who know she shouldn't have been aware of the stabbing."

"You're right. Group text it is."

Chapter Twenty-two

Today was turning out to be a Fine Weather Friday. At a few minutes before nine I hung out the OPEN flag at Mac's Bikes. I wheeled a few rentals to the front, then examined my flowering annuals in their window boxes. Judging from the limp look of the pansies and geraniums, watering was my first task of the day. That accomplished, I leaned on the wall next to them for a moment, enjoying the morning sunshine and the prospect of a profitable weekend, no matter what was going on in the fraternal and criminal departments.

My mood was almost unreasonably optimistic, due largely to finding Derrick and our clearing of the air yesterday. Even Detective Haskins's threat of detaining my brother couldn't dampen my mood. A cardinal chirped happily in one of the many maples that lined Main Street, and I was determined to have an equally positive day. When I saw the slow-walking man with the lame leg head by across the street, I raised my hand in greeting, and got a nod of recognition in return. He wasn't carrying flowers today. Maybe one of these days we'd actually exchange a few words.

After Gin and I had agreed that I'd start the group text, I told her I had to get home a bit early. I craved a long shower and had to put in more bonding time with Belle. African Greys were very social creatures and needed a lot of interaction or they'd pluck their own feathers. I'd neglected my own Grey far too much this week. I also needed a decent breakfast. Before heading to the shop, I'd composed and sent a text to all of the Cozy Capers except Derrick, listing some of the questions we still needed answers for. I'd encouraged others to add their own questions—and answers.

Now, much revived with bacon, a bran muffin, a delicious ripe pear, and two scrambled eggs in my belly, I headed inside, ready for whatever this glorious day might bring. But I apparently had that thought too soon. Way, way too soon. Five minutes later Orlean texted me that she was sick and wouldn't be in. No other explanation, no prognosis for the future. Being my grandmother's progeny I cursed her under my breath, but only after I'd made sure nobody had wandered into the shop.

Derrick's text was next.

Thanks for offer of late arrival, Sis. Now back home with the Coke. Feeling pretty good. In to work after lunch. Love you.

Okay. I'd offered, he'd taken. Except I'd counted on Orlean being here. I knew I couldn't handle the shop solo. It was worth a try to see if my grandmother could help out again. I didn't know what I'd do otherwise. One of yesterday's rental customers had gushed over what great service Mrs. Almeida had provided, and how delightful it was to have senior citizens in the work force. All true, and I had smiled and agreed, of course, but I knew Abo Reba had plenty of other things going on in her life. Senior yoga, water aerobics, her bridge group, and a tutoring gig for starters.

Today was apparently one of her busy days. She didn't pick up her phone, so I left a message asking if she could possibly work for me again this morning, as soon as possible, and that of course I'd pay her. Double if she wanted. I finished the message and clicked off. I knew she didn't need the money. My Abo, Pa's dad, had left his wife well provided for, plus she had an annuity from some deceased cousin and her pension from being a public school teacher for forty years. She was set financially, not that she flaunted it.

I'd just have to manage until the afternoon. I reread the schedule that I'd checked yesterday, since a few other events had shoved it out of mind. I gulped. A major tune-up, five reserved rentals, and a tandem repair, plus I always had lots of walk-ins. One thing at a time, I told myself. One thing at a time. And, I reminded myself, I was living my dream. I was a successful solo businesswoman in the most beautiful place on Earth, with family nearby and a man who loved me. So what if things got a little hectic at work now and then?

The five rentals bundled through the door about thirty seconds later. Two high-energy athletic mothers and three sullen sleepy children made up the group. They turned out to be homeschoolers from Rhode Island up for a weekend of enforced history lessons while exercising. My words, not the moms'. I tried to talk up how fun it was to bike the trails with no cars around. The kids did not look convinced. Finally, after

I fitted them all with maps, helmets, and bikes of the right sizes, I watched the quintet pedal away.

The store phone rang. "Mac's Bikes, Mac speaking. How can I help you?" I wrinkled my nose as I listened. A family staying all the way down in Woods Hole wanted drop-off.

"I'm sorry, but bike delivery is not a service we offer." I would need a store van to drop off and pick up bikes, and a paid employee to drive it. So far I hadn't laid out the money for either.

The customer let me know quite clearly how unhappy she was with me and where she planned to take her business instead. I hung up and pondered changing my business model. I was doing all right the way things were now. I could pay all my bills, including payroll, and deposit a paycheck for myself every month, too. It wasn't a big one, but was enough for my personal expenses. Buying a van and figuring out if I was going to drive it or hire another person to do the job should be in my future. If I wanted to serve tourists who weren't staying within walking distance of the shop, that is. I wasn't going to decide right now, though. I'd see how things went this season.

The scheduled tandem repair appeared next. The riders were tandem, too. Identical twin men, by the looks of it, in matching blue shorts, green shirts, and greased-over boyish haircuts despite them being on the far side of fifty.

As I was filling out the top part of their repair slip, one of the two leaned both elbows on the counter. "Heard you found the murder victim on the bikeway a couple of days ago. What was that like?" His dark eyebrows, a perfect reflection of his brother's, pulled together in the middle and his gaze unsettled me with its intensity.

I pulled back. What a thing to ask. "It was sad and upsetting, that's how it was. It still is." What I wanted to do was rant, "What did you think it was like?!" But I didn't, in the interest of keeping my shop open and in the black. The customer was always right, no matter how gross, bizarre, or unattractive they were. These two were going for the trifecta. But the bottom line was that I would take customers' money and be polite to them as long as they didn't harm themselves, anyone else, or the rental equipment.

"We write horror novels, so it's a research question," Twin Two chimed in, beady eyes bright. "We're always trying to deepen our characters' reactions."

"Make them real." Twin One's voice spoke with more drama than a voice-over artist's in a movie trailer.

"Show how death cuts into their emotional core." Twin Two nodded.

"How lovely for you," I said. My mouth curved into a faint smile but the rest of my face stayed in place. How could I get rid of these guys?

"Could you tell if his death was peaceful or anguished?" Twin Two pressed.

"Were you afraid?" Twin One leaned closer. "It was dark and foggy, wasn't it?"

Ick. Now I had ghouls for customers. I kept the fake smile on, leaning back as far as I could. "Now, what seems to be wrong with the tandem?" I should probably text Stephen King and warn him about the competition.

The Adams brothers—their real name—finally left after explaining in the most disjointed way why they thought their shared steel steed was making funny noises. I heaved a sigh of relief deserving of a Presidential Medal of Honor with Distinction. People like them were the down side of serving the public. Luckily, they were the exception rather than the rule.

But by nine thirty I was still by myself. And swamped. Slammed. Sunk. How had a man's murder so messed up my life? Before this week I'd loved my job. The store ran smoothly with Derrick's help, and I'd thought hiring Orlean would let me feel less harried about getting everything done. Instead, here I was flying solo and more harried than ever. Well, Derrick would be back soon, and surely Orlean's absence was short-term.

Four white-haired couples were perusing their rental options with much discussion. A preschooler was throwing a tantrum outside where his father had taken him after I'd asked him to please keep his child from climbing on any of our display bikes, yes, even the adult tricycle. And the major tune-up job had turned out to be a major pain in the you-know-where, but I'd finished it and its very nice owner had paid and left a few minutes ago.

I perked up when Norland Gifford wandered in. He was not wheeling a broken bike, which was already a plus. I hailed him from the repair bench.

"I'm back here." I gave a wave. "But I should be out front, and over on the rental side, too. Problem is I'm alone in the shop this morning. Personnel problems. What can I do for you, Chief?"

He chuckled. "No need for that title any longer, thank the good Lord. No, I was passing by and thought I'd drop in, see . . ." His voice trailed off as he glanced from side to side. He came closer. "To see if you learned anything useful about, you know, our friend's demise."

"I'm not sure if I have or not." I kept my voice low, too.

The group considering rentals came toward us. "We've decided. Can you help us now?" one of the men asked, his silver hair perfectly combed, his sportswear perfectly co-ordinated with his wife's.

"Sorry, Norland." I blew out a breath. "Can you wait a couple of minutes?"

"Of course. Better yet, I can shadow you. Maybe I can fill in for an hour or two. Give you a hand."

He was a friend sent from heaven, it looked like. I blew him a kiss. And shadow me, he did. He watched how I helped these well-heeled seniors select the right size of bicycles and choose helmets. They were easy, pleasant, cooperative people, the best kind of customers. Norland observed the paper work we filled out. Saw where I kept all the supplies. By the time the helmeted seniors left with locks, maps, and their copies of signed waivers, Norland was a fully trained employee.

"You really want to do this?" I asked. "I mean, why, when you just retired from a job?"

He laughed, an infectious throaty sound. "Mac, this is about as far from police work as you can get. I have to get my grandkids off the bus at two thirty, but until then, I make my own schedule. That's the best thing about retirement. Nobody tells me where to go or what to do. I'm my own boss and I'm loving it." His clothes looked like he was his own boss, too. His well-worn striped cotton shirt included a frayed collar and looked like an old friend, as did faded blue jeans and sneakers, one laced with hot pink and the other with fluorescent green.

He saw me checking out the shoelaces and smiled. "My granddaughter's handiwork."

"I love it. And you're hired." I held out my hand for a good firm handshake.

"It seems like a pretty straightforward job," Norland said. "But I thought your brother was handling the rental and retail business for you?"

"He is. He's been taking a couple of personal days. He'll be in this afternoon." I hoped. I beckoned for the former chief to follow me. "Know anything about bike repair?" During the rental transaction, the father and wailing child had taken themselves elsewhere, to my immense relief.

"Not a thing."

I resumed my work. Norland folded his arms and leaned against the only bare stretch of wall.

"I got the group text," he said, measuring his words.

Uh-oh. I glanced at him. "You know we only want to help Detective Haskins. Really, none of us is interested in getting into trouble or going all maverick on him. Nobody's going to go off into a dark cellar with a murderer at large or do some kind of vigilante stunt."

He laughed, this time a soft gentle sound that reminded me of a low engine rumble. "Mac, I'm not here to chastise you or any of the group. I've been thinking about how I could help."

"Really? That's awesome." I straightened and bent the crick in my back the other way.

"I mean, I do have a little expertise to lend. A few years of experience up and down Cod's Cape." Now his smile was wistful. "Maybe I do miss the work. But not enough to go back to a full-time position."

"Would they take you on as a consultant?"

"Maybe. But what if I was hot on the trail of a killer? Could I still grab my coat at two o'clock and tell them so long, I have a date with a school bus?" He shook his head. "I don't think so. I know the way departments work." He fixed his kindly gaze on me. "An amateur effort, though? That's a different story entirely."

"Let's talk while I work." I focused on the tune-up while the shop was quiet. Finally I could do the straightforward work I was good at instead of all this disorderly people stuff I couldn't control.

"I particularly was interested in what you said in the text about this guy, Billy Crump." Norland folded his arms and leaned against the wall. "He's a PI, you said."

"Right. Flo and I looked him up in her secret librarian databases yesterday."

Norland laughed at that.

"Well, not secret to other librarians, obviously. But not commonly available to regular people like me."

"I know what you mean. Police have their own secret databases, too, or maybe they're the same as Florence's. I'd have to check."

"Anyway, we learned that Billy Crump is a German national." I filled him in on the German name and the rest of what we'd discovered. "I didn't talk to him when he approached me because I didn't know him from anybody."

"It might not hurt for me to give him a call, see what else he knows."

"Could you?" I looked at him, eyes wide.

"Of course."

"Part of the reason I didn't want to deal with him was because he said he was hired to look into the death by an interested party, but he refused to tell me who'd employed him."

"Hmm. SOP, I'd say." Norland pursed his lips.

"SOP?"

"Standard operating procedure."

"Oh." I thought for a second. "Man, it feels like a week ago when he stopped by here. But I guess it was only yesterday."

Norland fell silent. I looked up from my work to see him gazing at me.

He cleared his throat before speaking. "A lot happened yesterday, didn't it? No wonder it seems like a week."

Crap. He knew about Derrick. "You mean with my brother?"

Once again he kept his voice gentle. "Yes. I don't mean to pry, but I heard it from the old boys' network. Old police boys, that is."

I sighed. "So you know Haskins came by Tim's and questioned Derrick. And you must know that earlier yesterday I found my brother totally drunk and watched him keel over into a rock, resulting in a scalp injury and possible concussion. And that we took him to the hospital to get stitched up." I blurted the words to get them over with.

He nodded.

"And you also know about his past conviction, his prison time?" I asked.

Norland nodded again, then held up both hands. "I'm not here to accuse him of anything. Just so you know."

I blinked at him. Finally I spoke. "Okay. I hear you. But you have to know *this*." I punctuated my words with pointing at him. "I do not think Derrick had anything to do with Jake's murder. I believe my brother when he says he came across Jake dead on the path and panicked, because of their shared past."

"That part I didn't know. He found the body and didn't report it?"

I spread my hands. "I think he was just really afraid. He has a daughter, and Jake was blackmailing him."

"I hear you. And I want to work with you on this," he said. "I've heard of this Crump character. Or Krumpf, as the case may be."

I tilted my head. Why hadn't he said so a few minutes earlier when we'd first talked about him? As if he'd heard my thoughts, Norland laughed.

"What's so funny?" I tightened a loose nut and spun the front wheel.

"I didn't mention it when you brought up Crump because I wanted to see where you were going with the story. I ran into Billy years ago. He wasn't so aboveboard then. Has a couple shady dealings in his past. As I said, I'll give him a call. You have his current number?"

I nodded. "It's in my phone. "What makes you think he'll tell you who he's investigating?"

"Let's just say I was the one who convinced him to go straight, get his PI license, and live like an honest man."

I adjusted the wheel a little more and spun it again. "Can you tell me what his shady business was?"

"No. It happened long ago, and it's between him and me. But it'll give me a little, shall we say, leverage with him."

* * *

Abo Reba strode—as much as really short legs can stride—in the front door of the shop at a few minutes past eleven. I waved at her from the repair area. Norland had been busy for an hour with rental and retail customers, and I'd gotten in a couple of new repair jobs, too. The shop was only now quiet and empty of customers again.

"I'm here to woman the desk again," she announced. "Hey, Norland. Mac's got you working here now, does she? Retirement too boring for you?" She plopped her bag down behind the rental counter and slid off her hat.

"Thought I'd help out," Norland said. "But as you well know, Reba, retirement's not a bit boring."

Her eyes twinkled. "I was pulling your leg. So, Mac, what's going on? Do you need me?" Abo Reba strolled toward my half of the shop.

A man holding a little boy's hand walked in and started speaking with Norland about renting bikes. I wiped the grease off my hands with a rag and waited for my grandmother to come closer before I spoke.

"You heard the news?" I murmured.

She lowered her voice to match mine. "Joseph told me all about your brother." She shook her head in a brisk move. "Sounds like you found him just in time."

"I guess I did." I must have looked worried, because she reached up a hand gnarled from arthritis and stroked my cheek.

"Now, honey. He's going to be fine. That was only a momentary hiccup for him. You listen to your Abo. Life is full of little glitches like that. We get through them, with the help of family and friends, and just keep on keeping on. Do you think I got this old without having a few setbacks?"

I smiled at her wisdom. "I don't suppose you did,

no." I wasn't sure if being a person of interest in a murder was a little glitch or a major threat in Derrick's life. Following her advice, I resolved to work on getting through the situation and keep on going. Worrying never helped anybody.

She tapped the workbench. "So will Derrick be in today or not?"

"He said he would, after lunch. I don't know how long Norland can stay."

"Don't you worry about a thing. I cleared a few hours in my schedule." She grinned. "It wasn't easy. I had to put off a lunch with the president of the Garden Club."

"Isn't she the one who's always trying to make you do work you have no interest in?"

"The very same. Avoiding a meeting with her wasn't much of a hardship, as you can imagine. I told her family comes first. And it does."

"Well, once again I appreciate your help. As you can see, Orlean didn't make it in today."

"What's going on with that girl?" Abo Reba narrowed her eyes.

"Abo, she's over forty! Hardly a girl."

She grinned. "When you're eighty, every female's a girl."

"Anyway, I don't know what's going on with her. She texted me that she's sick. I can't argue with that, but I wonder if it's more her ex-husband she's sick from than her health. He seems to be giving her problems. I didn't want to pry, but I really need her in the shop."

"Leave it to me. Maybe I can find out."

"Abo Ree, do you still have that PI's card?"

She nodded and fished it out of her bag. "Why? You decided to talk to him, after all?"

"Can you give it to Norland? He says he knows Crump. He'll give the guy a call." I hadn't had a minute to find the number on my cell.

A group of seven fresh-cheeked young adults entered. "Looks like I'm on." Abo Reba hurried toward the rental side.

An hour later, after Norland had left with Crump's number entered into his phone, my mom swept through the back door of the shop.

"Hi, honey," she called out.

At least I was pretty sure it was my mom. I couldn't see her, because my head was down, peering at my greasy hands and this morning's latest problem, a thoroughly messed-up derailleur. My nose was full of the sweet smell of metal, oil, and rubber, my favorite scents in the universe. But what in the world had the guy who'd dropped off the bike done to cause this kind of screwed-up-ness? The highly useful term was one I'd learned from the Voc-Tech teacher in high school, the man I'd first learned bike repair from.

"Hi, Mom." I greeted her without looking up, since I didn't want to lose my place and the client had insisted he have it back by three this afternoon. I hadn't promised anything.

"Tim sent over scones from the bakery for all of us," Mom went on in her ever-cheery voice.

All of us? Her, me, and my grandmother? Not exactly a cast of thousands.

"And I brought a new friend I want you to meet. Can you spare a few minutes to take a break and have a snack?"

No, I can't, is what I wanted to say. Instead, I straightened, wiped my hands on the rag in my apron pocket, and turned. "All of us" turned out to be my mother and Katherine Deloit. My mouth started to fall open before I caught it. Was this who she meant by her new friend?

Then I caught myself and mustered a smile. "Nice to see you again, Katherine. So you've met my mother." I could swear I'd told Ms. Deloit I owned the bike shop. But maybe I hadn't, or if I had, maybe she hadn't remembered.

Mom looked from Katherine to me and back. "You've been introduced before?"

I nodded. "I'd shake hands, but . . ." I held two blue latex gloves with grease-blackened palms in the air.

Katherine, dressed today in a more casual outfit of a tasteful blue-striped top and Dockers-type navy pants with red espadrilles, smiled calmly. "Yes, we did run into each other out at the Point a few mornings ago. I simply hadn't made the connection between your daughter Mackenzie and Mac, here." Holding the coffee she'd carried in, and with a red leather handbag in the crook of her elbow, she gazed around the shop. "You have quite an establishment. Business is good, I trust?"

The other day I hadn't noticed how nasal her voice was. "Thank you. Yes, the business is thriving." I turned to Mom. "So you're buying from Tim, now?"

"Of course, my dear. Such a dear man. I happened to strike up a conversation with Katherine while she was doctoring her coffee. She's coming over to get her chart read!"

Huh? This was not computing. A powerhouse businesswoman wanted to know what her astrological makeup was? You can't explain human nature.

"That's lovely," I said. "And thanks so much, Mom, for bringing the scones. But I really can't spare the time. Orlean is sick, Abo Reba is on the other side, and I have to get this job done by noon-thirty so I can start another urgent one." I watched my mom's face fall. "I'm sorry, but that's the life of an independent business-woman. Right, Katherine? You said you're in business." I mentally crossed my fingers she'd back me up on this, being Mom's new best bud and all.

She didn't disappoint. "Absolutely. I'm sorry we interrupted you."

"My grandma loves scones, though. Abo Ree," I called. "When you can, come have a scone with Mom and her friend." I walked close to my mom and turned my back on Katherine. "Sorry, Mom. Next time, okay?"

She nodded. "Baker Brunelle doesn't look like he's going anywhere." She smiled and nudged me. "I'm sure he'll bake more scones."

I had to hand to it my mom. I'd disappointed her before, but she never held a grudge, and she didn't do guilt trips. Both were awesome traits and I hoped I'd inherited at least a portion of them. "You rock for picking up a new client, too."

Abo Reba sauntered in, all four foot eleven of her. "Did somebody say scones?" She pulled up short, the smile sliding off her face as she blinked at Katherine. It was almost like my grandmother knew who she was. Then she mustered up her smile again.

"I think scones sound about perfect." She greeted Mom and shook Katherine's hand, introducing herself.

"Let's eat outside, shall we?" Mom suggested.

Abo Reba plucked a scone out of the bag and nodded even as she popped half of it in her mouth. For someone so tiny, she had an impressive appetite. She liked to say she had both the metabolism of a humming-bird and a digestive system that didn't absorb calories.

More power to her. And I knew I'd inherited those genes. I'd never had to worry for a minute about packing on extra pounds.

I watched the three of them take the baked goods out back and then returned to my repair. Did I need to warn Mom about Katherine Deloit? I didn't have any logical reason to think the visiting businesswoman was dangerous, any more than Suzanne or Gin's Wes Farnham were. Or Pa's tattooed accountant Edwin, or even the mysterious sad girl. Katherine had said she was visiting a college friend, hadn't she? But it was that tiny little feeling way back beyond my consciousness that nagged at me about all of them. Even the mysterious sad girl. I would look the fool, however, if I took Mom aside and told her not to be alone with Katherine while she ran her chart and explained the influences of the planets and stars on Katherine's personality. So I didn't.

Chapter Twenty-three

I'd finished cleaning up the bike and was scrubbing my hands when Abo Reba came back in. I peered behind her. "Where'd Mom go?"

She frowned. "Off to read that woman's chart. Bunch of bull twaddle, if you ask me. Not that I would say as much to your mother's face, but really. Some far-off stars can affect your personality and govern how you act? As if." She tilted her head, regarding me. "What do you think?"

"I agree completely." I laughed. "But hey, it makes Mom happy, and I guess she makes some money at it, too." I focused on the repair note, jotting down what I'd done, the prices for parts I'd replaced, and the labor costs. When I was finished, I said, "Abo Ree, tell me something. You got a funny look on your face when you saw Katherine Deloit. Had you already met her?"

She shook her head fast and furious. "Never. Didn't know her name."

"What did you all talk about, you and Mom and her?"

"Little bit of this, little bit of that. Nothing important. But I saw the woman through my scope yesterday."

"Oh? And she was simply walking down the street, or what?"

"Not just walking down the street." Abo Reba narrowed her eyes as if examining the past. "It was the oddest thing. I saw her all dolled up in her heels and fancy skirt looking at something through a pair of binoculars."

"Haven't you heard, Abo Ree? It's the latest in birding-wear." I tilted my head and smiled.

She snorted. "She wasn't looking at birds. Unless she was trying to identify Belle."

"You mean she was checking out my house?" A frisson of unease rippled through me. Katherine spying on my residence with binoculars was downright creepy.

"Maybe. It was a little hard to tell, but she was in front of the post office and looking across the street."

My grandmother lived in an apartment reserved for senior citizens above a row of shops on the far side of the post office, almost across from Pa's church. My shop and my house behind it were five properties in the opposite direction on the other side of the street.

"She couldn't have seen behind the shop to my house." I frowned. "But why was she using binoculars when she could go a little farther and walk by the shop up close?"

She shrugged. "I guess I could have asked her while she was here what she was looking for, but it seemed a bit rude to butt into her private life."

A family wanting rentals strolled in, so I left them to Abo Reba and went to find my lunch. As I munched, I shook my head. Katherine's behavior had to have a more reasonable explanation. A Californian real estate agent had no reason to be checking out the town with binoculars, my house or any other. Maybe she was a birder and a rare species had stopped by Westham. Or not.

"Titi Mac," Cokey called out, skipping into the shop half an hour later.

Derrick followed close behind her, a bright pink mini-backpack slung over his broad shoulder.

"Yes, favorite niece number one?" I smiled at my only niece. I knelt and opened my arms wide. I wasn't exactly longing for a kid of my own, but squeezing this curly-haired darling, inhaling her energy and her little-girl scent, was one of the best things in my life right now.

She squeezed back, then planted a miniature kiss on my cheek before pulling away. She grabbed her pack from her dad and ran to Abo Reba for a repeat of hugging. I pushed up to standing.

Derrick looked tentative. "Okay that I brought her in? Cokey's ready to work, at least that's what she claimed."

"And you didn't want to be apart from her." I spoke softly.

He nodded.

"Don't worry." I patted his shoulder. "It's fine. We're a family business, right?" I glanced over at Cokey, who now perched on the high stool behind the rental counter, her great-grandmother hovering to make sure she didn't fall off. "Was Coke okay with you being away and then back?"

"She normally spends so much time with Pa and Mom, I'm not sure she even noticed. But I need to ask one more favor of you."

I took a deep breath. I didn't have a real positive feeling about this. "What is it?"

"I found an AA meeting at two o'clock in Falmouth. Can you and Abo watch her for an hour? I'll come straight back."

My feeling swung instantly to the Very Positive edge of the dial. "I don't know Abo's schedule. But my answer is yes." Anything to get my brother back on the sobriety track. "Go." I gave him a little push.

"I'll be back in an hour, sweetie," he called to Cokey, blowing her a kiss. "*Txau*, Cokey."

Cokey barely looked up from the paper she was bent over, crayon in hand, to wave at him. "*Txau*, Daddy."

I watched him hurry out the door. Derrick had been through a lot, and it wasn't over yet. But this was a good sign. A very good sign.

However, today was Friday. I had a shop to keep open all weekend from now until October. Sure, we got plenty of tourist traffic on weekdays. But weekend warriors who wanted to tool around on a two-wheeler and serious cyclists from out of town who had exactly Saturday to Sunday to explore the entire Cape bikeway network? For them I needed to be open, with bikes tuned up and available. And for that I needed people. I seriously didn't want to be here working seven days a week. Derrick was now struggling with his addiction again—which meant both that he needed to get to an AA meeting every day and also spend time with his little girl. And I couldn't keep relying on drop-in help like Norland or even Abo Reba, much as she seemed to enjoy the work.

I had really counted on Orlean for this season. I pressed her number, which went straight to voice mail. I hoped she was okay, but I still needed help in the shop. Now what?

"Titi," Cokey called to me, waving a sheet of paper. "Look what I drawed."

Watching her gave me an idea. "Wait a sec, *kretzeu*." I turned my back and pressed Pa's speed dial, instead. When he picked up, I said, "Pa, is Edwin with you?"

"No, why?" He sounded suitably confused.

"I wondered if he might want a few bike shop hours on the weekends. Maybe he's all set, but you said he rides and in case he'd like a little extra income . . ." I let my voice trail off. Voiced, my brainstorm sounded foolish. Why would an accountant want to work in a bike shop even if he was a cyclist? If he were really serious about a biking hobby, the employee discount would be nice, but—"

"I like the way you think." Pa rattled off Edwin's number. "He's a freelancer, so he could be out anywhere. I'm awfully glad I found him to do the books for the church. Edwin has one sharp brain."

I jotted down the numbers. "So why would he want to work part-time renting bicycles?" I hunched my shoulders, wincing at how I'd probably managed to sabotage my own suggestion.

"Call him. Let him decide." My father said he had to run and disconnected.

That sounded a lot like yet one more case of the minister knowing more than he could ever let on. But what the heck? I might as well give Edwin a try. What was the worst that could happen? He could say no, and I'd be in exactly the same place I was now. I took a minute to put Edwin's number into my Contacts list.

Now for Cokey. I hurried to her side. "Show me that drawing."

Abo Reba slid off her stool. "Going to use the ladies' while you're here to watch her." She trundled to the back of the store.

My niece cocked her head and considered her art with tiny furrows in her brow. "Well, now I'm drawing somebody else," she lisped. "See, there's the lighthouse. And there's the lady who came back cuz she losted her purse."

"A lady came back to the lighthouse because she losted her purse?" I asked, mostly to clarify if I'd heard correctly through the lisp. I gave my head a little shake, smiling. "I mean, lost her purse?" If I wasn't careful, I'd be talking like a preschooler, too.

"You got it, Mac." Cokey nodded, staying serious.

I, on the other hand, had a lot of trouble not cracking up. She was such a little adult, lisp and all.

"You know, Daddy does tours of the lighthouse," she went on.

I stroked her angel curls. "And this lady went on a tour but she left her purse inside?"

Cokey nodded somberly, her head bent so far over her drawing I couldn't see her cheek.

"Did she go back in the lighthouse to look for it?" I prodded.

Cokey didn't speak for another couple of minutes, pressing crayons with the fervor of any artist into the paper I kept with the crayons on a kid-accessible shelf.

She sat up straight and pointed to the paper. "See? There's the lighthouse, and there's the lady. She finded her purse."

I leaned over and examined the artwork, which my niece had executed in bold strokes of black, blue, and red. I saw a big head with two bent stick arms and two stick legs poking out of it. The mouth on the head had been colored bright red and the eyes were two circles of blue, giving the figure a blank stare. One arm had an iconic red purse hanging in the crook of the elbow— well, a red rectangle with an arc of red hanging over the arm. It looked like an iconic purse to me. Cokey added a scribble of red along the lower edge of the face, with a tail extending off to the right outside the head.

A rectangle of black enclosed the legs directly under the head. I pointed to it. "Is this her body?" I asked.

"No!" Cokey was indignant. "That's her skirt. Like a skinny person's skirt. And she wore a red scarf, too."

The thing with the tail was a red scarf. The black rectangle a skinny person's skirt. A skirt like the one Gin and I had seen Katherine Deloit wearing, and the purse identical with the bag she'd been carrying a couple of hours ago.

Had Cokey seen Katherine tour the lighthouse? She must have. Nobody dressed like that on the Cape in June. And Cokey must have watched her reenter afterward because she'd ostensibly left her purse inside. No woman leaves her handbag lying around in a public place unless she has dementia or is seriously distracted by something like a newborn or a cry of, "Fire!" I couldn't think of any plausible reason for our West Coast real estate agent to have "losted" her purse. But if Katherine happened to have slipped a knife inside said handbag while she was alone in the lighthouse, now that would be a reason.

"Can I keep your drawing, honey?" I asked. "I love it."

"Will you put it on your fridge?" Her face lit up.

"You got it."

Chapter Twenty-four

By 6:10, I was home with my feet up, a parrot on the arm of the couch, and a glass of cold Pilsner in my hand. My legs tingled with the message that says, *We've been standing all day, ya know. Thanks for finally sitting down, boss, about three hours too late.* No kidding.

Orlean had never appeared, nor had she returned my call. I could only assume she wouldn't show tomorrow, either, and I wasn't about to drive down Cape to look for her. Abo Reba had had to leave when Derrick returned, and he'd taken Cokey out to the playground when she got antsy and wanted to start trying out every kid's bike in the shop.

Me, I ran my tush off until six o'clock, logging in returns, fixing a couple of flats, selling biking shirts and gloves, and checking out a total of twenty-two weeklong rental bikes. My bank account was going to be happy, that was certain. I'd phoned Edwin but he didn't pick up, so I'd left a message, simply asking him to call me back. I wasn't going to use voice mail to describe the details of the mess I was in.

It was way past time to check the group text, see if anyone had posted anything new. I swiped into it. The people busy at day jobs—Flo, Zane, Stephen, Gin—hadn't responded, and Norland's only contribution was that he hadn't been able to learn a thing. Gin had been working all day, too, so I wasn't surprised she hadn't contributed.

I'd left Cokey's portrait of the lady with the losted purse on the little kitchen table at the other end of the house. I moved the few steps there and sat to study it. "What do you think, Belle? Is this our friend Katherine? Did she k—?" I cut myself off. I didn't want my parrot buddy learning words like "kill" or "murder." I started again with, "Do think she did away with Jake?"

"Oh, yeah. Oh, yeah." Belle nodded, uttering one of her stock phrases. One of her previous owners must have been from Minnesota, because Belle said the phrase with a super long "oh," and the word "yeah" sounded more like a Scandinavian "ya."

When Belle added, "Ya, you betcha," I laughed out loud. She wasn't much of a jury, though. The smile drifted off my face. Why would an apparently fastidious woman like Katherine Deloit stab a man? If she'd wanted to kill him, wouldn't she have obtained a lethal little pistol, or figured out some exotic untraceable poison? Beyond the sheer violence of it, stabbing had to result in a messy death. I shuddered at the thought. Whoever killed him must have had to get rid of a bloody outer garment somewhere.

I couldn't believe my brother had done the deed, though. So who had? It was time to get more details from Gin about her guest, and to find out more about the young woman. To figure out how Suzanne knew about the stabbing. Or maybe the killer had been someone entirely different, a man Jake was incarcerated with. A fellow inmate could have tracked down Jake post-release to settle an old debt, or to get revenge from a hurt, real or imagined.

Also, what Cokey had said about the lady on the lighthouse tour was bugging me. I gazed out at a cedar branch bobbing in the late afternoon light as if focusing my eyes would also focus my brain. Last night Derrick told the detective he'd led a couple of tours on Sunday, and that everyone signed the book. Haskins had said he would come and get the book today. Had he? I jabbed at Derrick's cell number.

"Ya miss me already?" was how he answered.

"No. I mean, sure. Listen, did the police come get the lighthouse tour book today? Where you said people sign their names? Did Haskins or one of his people stop by and pick it up?"

"As far as I know they didn't."

I heard Cokey's high voice in the background, and the clink of flatware on plates.

Derrick went on. "But I was out all afternoon, as you know. I'm still not home. Having dinner with the parents. Why? What's up?"

"When you go home, do me a favor and type those names from Sunday into an e-mail? Names, and any other information, if you have it."

He waited just long enough before speaking for me to know he was either suspicious of my motives or reluctant to comply.

"Please?" I added.

"I guess. I'd like to know what you want them for,

though. And that you're not trying to do the detective's work for him."

"I'm not, and I appreciate the favor. Glad you're back among the sober and living, Derrick. Sorry, gotta go." I disconnected in a hurry. I didn't want to answer any questions.

I slouched in my chair. Belle climbed over to her roost and set up a bobbing motion with her head. "I'm happy," she crooned, extending her wings and swaying side to side. I laughed out loud, always my reaction when she danced to her favorite tune. I found Pharrell Williams singing "Happy" on YouTube and let her rock out for the duration of the song.

When it was over, she pleaded, "Please? Please gimme a treat. I love you, Mac."

Belle could get me out of any emotional darkness I'd ever experienced. Why didn't counseling centers and psychologists prescribe owning a bird for depression? *Apply parrot wisdom, dancing, and questions daily. Pay attention to the bird, including feeding and cleaning.* That should remedy any blues on the planet. I twisted to look at Belle.

"Do you?" I asked. "Do you want a treat? That was good dancing." I drained my beer.

Belle hopped down and marched to the kitchen counter where I kept the cookie jar of seed-filled delicacies. I followed her over, of course. It didn't do much good for one's self-image to start making a bird happy and then foil their pleasure.

I'd just handed Belle her treat when my phone trilled.

She paused with the treat in one claw halfway to her black beak. "Just a sec! Just a sec!" she squawked.

I suppressed a smile. How many times had I'd said exactly that phrase when the phone rang while I was mid-shower?

"Telephone, Mac," she went on. "Telephone for Belle."

"It might be for me, you know."

"Hello?" I said.

"Edwin here." His deep voice resonated through the device. "You called me?"

How had I not remembered his voice? The man could get a job on the radio, or doing voice-overs for movie trailers.

"Hi, Edwin. This is Mac, Joseph's daughter. We met the other day."

"Yes, I remember. What can I do for you?" He kept his tone on the formal side.

And why not? I was the boss's daughter, after all. "I, um . . . well, I was wondering if you might, sort of, consider—"

I cut off my words. I was sure I was blowing this, big time. Why was I so nervous? Maybe because the shop was my life and livelihood? And because I couldn't imagine why he would say yes to the gig.

My phone rang again. The exact ring tone. I glared at Belle and shook my head firmly. She stopped imitating the tone and marched off to her cage, muttering, "Telephone for Belle. Belle's a bad bird."

"And you hoped I might go out with you, is that what you're trying to say?" Edwin asked.

Cripes. He thought I was flirting, trying to get a date with him. Thanks very much, Mr. Edwin accountant man, but no thanks.

"No, in fact, I wasn't angling for a date," I said.

"And I'm sure your dance ticket is fully booked. Um, so to speak."

"Fully booked. Yes, indeed." He sounded like he was barely suppressing chest-heaving waves of laughter.

I swallowed and told myself firmly to get on with it. "No, the reason I called is that I need some part-time help in the bike shop and I wondered if you'd be interested."

A moment of silence. Another one, broken only by Belle learning new words in the background, muttering, "Hi, Edwin. Hi, Edwin. Um, hello?" I could listen to her all day, but Edwin's lack of response was getting odd.

"Edwin? Did you hear me?"

He laughed with a low rumbling sound. "Yes, ma'am. I heard you. So you need help in the shop, and you're not even interested in potential applicants submitting their resumes? Just a tip, hon, but it's good business practice to make sure an applicant is qualified for a position before you go around offering jobs to people. That said, I'd love to work in the best bike shop up Cape."

"Really? That would be such a huge help. How does tomorrow look?" I crossed my fingers, and for good measure, crossed my eyes, too.

"What time?"

Chapter Twenty-five

Greta's Grains was rocking. On Friday nights Tim hosted Brews and Breads, or Bs & Bs, as it had come to be known. He hired musicians, served beer and wine, and made up various whole-grain flatbreads and other delicious baked munchies. It was a big success so far, with every seat taken on Friday evenings and plenty of people standing at the counter, too, the counter doubling tonight as a bar.

This week the music was provided by a group from Newburyport up in the northeast corner of the state. Also a touristy coastal town, it was friendly to artists and writers, and if Liz Frame and the Kickers were any indication, a whole lot of talent lived up that way. Liz set the style for the women in the group, who wore cowgirl boots with short skirts. A couple of men played in the background, but it was clearly a female-centric group. Liz, tall and energetic with cropped salt-and-pepper hair and a rich contralto, sang lyrics of her own creation and played guitar. A slight woman wearing a big smile worked a stand-up electric bass, and another younger woman played drums with enough energy to light the bakery for a year if it was harnessed.

I perched on a stool at the end of the bar and sipped from my glass of white, tapping my foot to the beat. Tim was working hard, pouring beverages, serving up slices, and schmoozing. His helper tonight was a multi-pierced high school kid with green hair who also worked in the bakery. She ran her feet off clearing tables, washing glasses, and bringing warm flatbreads out from the back. Tonight's offerings were an olive-with-caramelized-onion pie and a spicy Southwestern bread topped with chilies and jack cheese. Tim had also made gourmet pigs-in-a-bun and some kind of turnover stuffed with ground lamb and Middle Eastern seasonings.

Sounded like dinner to me. "I want one of each," I told Tim. I was definitely not a vegetarian, holding a particular place in my heart for hot dogs. I knew raising meat was not the best way to feed the world's population, but I justified my preferences by not eating much in the way of meat despite how much I loved it.

A minute later I had a mouth full of lamb pie when a person angled up to the counter next to me, his tattooed arm sliding onto the counter, fingers tapping a rapid beat on the polished wood.

"Can I get a Sam Summer?" the arm's owner asked Tim, referring to Sam Adams seasonal offering, the Summer Ale.

The deep voice was familiar. I looked up to see . . . almost Edwin. Huh? The extent of the tats on this man's arms matched Edwin's, and his face looked similar. He had the same black hair, the same lean build. And yet this wasn't my father's brainy accountant. He was older, more worn, in a plaid flannel shirt with the sleeves rolled up. But he had to be a blood relative, and likely a brother.

"Hi. Are you related to Edwin?" I asked after swallowing a bite of the best turnover I'd ever eaten.

He glanced at me for a second, dark eyes wide, and then looked away. His knee jittered, fast. "Never heard of him."

Really? "Sorry. You look a lot like him. I'm Mac Almeida." I wiped off my right hand and extended it for a handshake, but since the dude wasn't looking at me, that didn't happen. "I haven't seen you in here before."

He fixed his dark eyes on me. "And you can forget you did." His whole body quivered like he had to get out of there. He slid his arm off the bar, muttering, "Never should have . . ." He pushed through the crowd and disappeared out the front door.

Tim set a full and frosty Pilsner glass on the bar next to me. "Where'd the ink go?"

I shrugged. "He left." I gazed at the door and was about to tell Tim how I thought his lost customer was connected to my dad's accountant. Instead, someone at the other end of the bar called out for a Sam Summer. My boyfriend flashed me his sparkling smile and whisked the beer away. My encounter with Tattoo was certainly the shortest and oddest I'd had as long as Tim had been running Bs & Bs. Could the guy really not be related to Edwin? If he wasn't, why did introducing myself make him nervous enough to walk out so precipitously? And if he was related, why deny it? Could any of this be related to Jake's murder? I didn't know how, but so many odd things had been happening lately, it wouldn't surprise me.

My food was getting cold. I dug in, but my brain kept spinning.

Tim returned and leaned toward me. "What'd you do to scare that guy away, anyway?"

I frowned. "First I asked if he was Edwin's brother."

"Who's Edwin?"

"He's my dad's new accountant. I only met him a couple of days ago. He doesn't really look the part of a numbers man—he's got as much ink on his arms as our mystery man had." Plus a do-rag.

"Tattoos shouldn't affect a brain that's good at working with figures."

"Exactly. Pa says he's good at what he does, and that's all that counts. He's right, of course, as are you. Anyway, the dude who was in here denied he was related to Edwin, but they appeared and sounded so similar. And it was funny, he didn't look at me when he said he wasn't a relative. Then when I introduced myself—bam, he's gone."

"Maybe it was this Edwin's *doppelgänger*. His spirit twin," Tim said before being summoned elsewhere again.

Bs & Bs was always like this. My guy and I never got more than a few words together, but I liked to come, anyway. The atmosphere was fun and the eats were always great. Plus, frankly, the interactions were a lot more interesting than talking with Belle all evening. A girl with a vocabulary the size of hers? Conversation could only go so far. Also, I hadn't heard the word *doppelgänger* in a long time. But "spirit" twin? I thought it meant more like "evil" twin.

I was sitting contentedly sipping and munching when Lincoln Haskins appeared at the bar.

"Yo, Detective." I caught his eye.

He made his way toward me through the scrum of thirsty newcomers.

"Ms. Almeida. Enjoying yourself, by the looks of it."

"I am. It's Friday night. Buy you a beer?"

He gave me an inscrutable look. I wasn't sure if he was thinking, *Who is this idiot? Can't she see I'm on duty?* or *That was sweet of her. Wish I could.*

"Thanks, but no." He leaned on the wall next to me, shoved his hands in his pockets, and surveyed the crowd. "Did you happen to see a man in here with heavily inked arms? Black hair? Plaid shirt?"

"I did, a few minutes ago. He looked familiar. I thought he was the brother of a guy who works for my dad."

"Is he still here? The one I asked you about?"

I shook my head. "He left without staying. Actually, he split after I asked if he was Edwin's brother. That seemed to spook him somehow. It's just that Edwin has tattoos on his arms exactly like that guy's, and their voices sounded similar. They looked related in their faces, too."

Haskins tilted his head to the side and forward, gazing at me with the intensity of a laser. "Does this Edwin have a last name?"

"Germain."

Haskins's nostrils flared ever so slightly. I almost missed it. He blew out a breath.

"I met Edwin at my parents' place. You know, the parsonage. He's my father's accountant." I twisted in the direction of laughter coming from the area in front of the band. Someone had cleared a bit of a dance floor, and who should be holding beers and rocking out in the middle of it but Gin . . . and Edwin? I hadn't seen either of them come in, and didn't realize they even knew each other. I drained my wine, planning to join them. I never wanted to start the dancing alone. Once a group was on the floor I was happy to join in, and I didn't feel I had to bring a partner with me, either. Maybe Edwin could tell Haskins who his tattooed brother—or not-brother—was, too.

"See that guy dancing with Gin Malloy?" I said, gesturing with my chin. Abo Reba had ingrained in me that it's rude to point.

"See who? I don't know a Gin Malloy."

"That couple. She has thick chestnut-colored hair. The guy is Edwin. He's wearing long sleeves, but his arms have a lot of tattoos."

"Ahh." He folded his arms but didn't move.

"Are you going to talk with him now?"

Haskins shook his head.

"Then, if it's okay with you, I'm going to dance with them."

He nodded, but kept his eyes on Edwin.

When the band took a well-earned break, I joined Edwin and Gin at a small table. Edwin, *sans* do-rag tonight, turned out to have hair about as long as my one-inch style, and as curly. He wore a long-sleeved pressed shirt untucked over jeans and sandals. After I'd hit the dance floor, I'd seen Haskins take a seat at a small table on the far wall. He was still there.

"Another of the same?" Edwin gestured toward Gin's bottle.

"I'd love one, thanks."

"Mac?" he asked.

I felt Gin's gaze on me, questioning how he knew my name.

"A Cape Cod IPA, please." I pulled a twenty out of my bag.

Edwin held up a palm. "This round's on me."

After he headed to the bar, Gin leaned in my direction. "How does he know you?"

"He's Pa's new accountant. How do you know Edwin?"

"I don't. I just started dancing and he appeared."

"Really?"

"Yeah. Don't you think he's cute?"

"Uh, yeah, if you like cuties in their twenties." I wrinkled my nose. "Isn't he a little young for you?"

"Relax, Mac. I'm not going to do anything about it. I can look, can't I? Hey, did you hear about the owl?" Gin, a devoted birder, gazed at me with bright eyes.

"What owl?"

"There's an Eastern screech owl nesting in a dead tree right here behind the bakery. It's fabulous."

"Are they rare?"

"No, but they usually hide. Their feathers are speckled and they're hard to spot. This one is sitting in a hollow twenty-five feet up and doesn't seem to mind all kinds of people walking up and staring, taking pictures, exclaiming about it."

"Interesting." And that must have been exactly what Katherine Deloit had been checking out with her binoculars. Not my shop. The bakery was only four doors down from Mac's Bikes, after all. Maybe she wasn't exactly sure where the bird had taken up residence.

Gin surveyed the room, then leaned closer to me. "Who's that big guy sitting with his back to the wall? You were talking with him at the bar."

I didn't have to check out who she meant. "That's Detective Haskins. The one investigating Jake's death."

She nodded slowly. "Don't look, but he seems to have his eye on Edwin."

I couldn't help looking, of course. When I did, Haskins met my gaze. *Caught in the act.* I smiled and gave a little wave, then turned back to Gin.

Edwin returned with three open bottles. "Cheers," he said, sitting. "You ladies are chatting like you're old friends already."

"We are," I said. "This is Gin Malloy. Gin, Edwin Germain."

"Cool to meet you, Gin. I enjoyed dancing with you."

"Same here," Gin replied. "I hope the music starts up again soon so we can get back at it."

"Edwin's also a cyclist, and he's going to help me out in the shop part-time," I told Gin. I'd really lucked out with that stab in the dark, asking him if he was interested.

"That I am," he said. "I'm a pretty quick study. Shouldn't take me long to learn your system and what needs to be done."

I'd briefly outlined to him on the phone what I needed and why. We'd go into plenty more details tomorrow.

"I'll be at the shop tomorrow to walk you through it," I said. "But I don't want to have to be working every weekend all summer, and as I said, my employee seems to be a bit AWOL for now. Even if she reappears, I need to have at least two people working, especially on summer weekends."

"You got it," he said.

"So this band's pretty good, isn't it?" Gin asked.

I spied Suzanne coming in the front door, and turned away from the two of them as they started talking about the music. Suzanne was followed in by a tall, silver-haired woman I thought for a fantasy moment was the uber-bestselling Canadian mystery author Louise Penny. It would be exactly like Suzanne to flaunt a guest of her caliber in public and not tell the Cozy Capers of her visit. Not that Penny's books were cozies, exactly, despite featuring an enchanting fictional village in Quebec. But she certainly wrote traditional mysteries, of which cozies were a subset. On second look I realized it was only a tall, silver-haired woman with a kind, congenial smile. She'd come in with the bookstore manager, who now took a perch at the bar next to her.

I was dying to ask Suzanne how she knew about Jake's stabbing. But how could I? I'd never been famed for thinking fast on my feet, and now proved no exception. I couldn't think of a single excuse for inquiring, so I turned back to my drinking pals. Edwin, looking as warm as I felt in the overcrowded space, was in the process of neatly folding back each cuff of his shirt. He then folded the sleeves back again, revealing the ink on his arms.

Gin gaped. "That's a lot of tattooing. Doesn't it hurt when you get those?"

I looked closely, as well. I hadn't really had a chance in Pa's yard to examine exactly what was stenciled into his skin. Now I spied a fanciful dragon in three colors disappearing up one sleeve, and a basket of animated numbers on the other arm. "Yes, isn't it painful?" I forced my gaze away from the artwork and my thoughts away from the man I'd seen who I was certain was his brother.

"A bit, but you get used to it. Hurts more on sensitive skin." He turned the inside of his also tattooed forearm face up and stroked it. "Like here, for example." He turned his arm over again and took a swig from the beer. "This is a pretty cool event. You been here before, Gin?"

"Almost every week. I keep telling Mac she ought to get me the friends-and-family discount, but so far it hasn't come through."

It was Edwin's turn to give me a quizzical look. "You run this place?"

I laughed, shaking my head. "No, but my boyfriend, Tim, does." I gestured with my thumb. "The tall one behind the counter. It's his bakery and his Friday night pop-up bar. Sorry, Malloy. No discounts."

"Wait." Edwin looked from me to Gin and back. "You really are friends, aren't you?"

"Yup," she said. "Known each other half our lives so far."

"Speaking of knowing people for a long time, do you have an older brother who really resembles you?" I asked Edwin. "A guy came in earlier I could swear was your brother. And it wasn't simply his tattooed arms that made me think so. He looked a lot like you, and his voice sounded like yours, too, except older."

Edwin froze. He placed his beer on the table so slowly I wondered if somebody had just switched the film of our lives to run at half speed. But I wasn't in a movie theater.

Liz Frame and her Kickers meandered back to their instruments. A few chords, a few strums and the start of a tune began. "Thanks for sticking around, everybody," Frame said into the mike. "We have an even better set for the second half of our show tonight, including a brand-new song written by yours truly. Never before performed, and you can say you heard it first here at Greta's Grains!"

Edwin frowned at me, his face pale, both hands clamped on the edge of the table. "What did you say?"

"I said a guy was in here who reminded me of you, just an older version."

He swore under his breath and stood so fast he bumped the table. "Excuse me, ladies." His beer bottle teetered on its axis until it tipped over, spilling amber liquid out between Gin and me, narrowly missing both of us. He didn't seem to notice. I watched him make for the door. Detective Haskins stood and hurried after him. Gin's mouth hung open.

"What in heck was that about?" she finally whispered.

"I have no idea."

The music took over all available airwaves while the beer dripped silently into a puddle on the floor.

Chapter Twenty-six

Gin and I didn't end up dancing again at Bs & Bs. Edwin leaving so abruptly had been a shock to her, I think. Me, I was curious about why Haskins was interested enough in my dad's accountant to follow him out. I doubted if he'd tell me. We finished our beer and enjoyed the music, but didn't talk much more, either, since it was too loud to conduct a reasonable conversation.

"I'm going to head home," I said when one song ended. "You?"

She nodded and followed me to the bar, where we said goodnight to Tim. Outside, Gin said, "Do you think that other guy you saw was Edwin's brother?"

"I don't know. Edwin sure acted like something was up. Maybe he didn't know the brother was in town, or hadn't seen him in a while."

"The detective went out right after him."

"I noticed." I yawned. "Sorry. I'm beat."

"Me, too. Call me when you get home, all right?" She held her thumb and pinkie up to her ear.

"Will do. Or you. Whoever's first." It seemed the prudent thing to do with a murderer at large.

"Yep. See you in the morning."

We exchanged a hug and each walked home in our opposite directions. Our pact seemed a little foolish, since it was only ten o'clock and a number of tourists still strolled the sidewalks of town on this mild night, checking out storefronts, grabbing a late ice cream, or inhaling some evening air. Mine was the furthest thing from a lonely, dark, scary night's walk, since it was only four stores away.

I fully intended to dutifully call her and report in after my door was locked behind me. Except when I arrived, key at the ready, a folded piece of paper extended from the slit between the door and the frame. Who would leave me a note instead of texting me? And if it was store business, they would leave a message at the bike shop, not back here at my personal residence. Wouldn't they?

A chill set in and unsteadied me. The night instantly seemed darker, more full of creepy, spooky noises. And I instantly was completely alone in a scary scenario. I'd found Jake's body only yards from here. Was I to be the next victim? A note stuck in a door was the kind of thing that happened in mystery novels. The protagonist gets a threatening note, warning her off the case— or else. Huh. Was I the protagonist in this story? The whole book group was looking into the murder, not only me. I silently scolded myself. I guess I'd see what the message actually said before I jumped to any more conclusions.

I again fished in my pocket for a tissue and used it to extract the paper. I gave a quick heart-pounding glance around, then unlocked my door and hurried inside, turning the deadbolt until I heard its reassuring *thunk*.

I switched on the lights, laid the note on the kitchen table, and nudged the fold open with a pen. I gasped and stepped back, my hand coming to my mouth in an involuntary move.

STAY OUT OF WHAT ISN'T YOUR BUSINESS
OR ELSE

The note was typed in italicized all caps on regular-sized white paper. It must have been printed from a computer. But who was threatening me? And when did they leave it? No, I knew when. Sometime between seven and now. It would be easy to discern when I wasn't home. All they'd have to do would be watch Main Street. Or watch my door. This wasn't fiction. This was real.

My phone trilled with a call. I'd been targeted with a note. Was this the author, calling to warn me in a different way? I glanced at the display, ready to learn the killer's number. I laughed out loud, albeit a bit shakily, and connected the call.

"Gin, I'm so glad it's you."

"Why? We agreed we'd call each other when we got in, right?" She sounded suitably confused.

I lowered my voice. "I got a note. In the door."

"What are you talking about?"

"A note threatening me away from the investigation. Exactly like in the books we read."

Her harsh intake of breath matched my own from a minute ago. "What did it say?"

I read the words.

"OMG," Gin breathed. "You need to call that Haskins guy. Or Victoria. Or someone."

"I will. I was really careful and only touched it with a tissue."

"Ooh, smart move. How are you feeling? Are you scared? Do you want me to come over?"

"I'm okay. You know, I've always felt safe here in Westham. I walk around at night, I live alone. I mean, I lock my door when I go out, but half the time it's wide open when I'm inside." I didn't really live alone, of course. I gazed at Belle's cage. I'd put her in and covered her home for the night before I went out, so she knew it was sleeping time and hadn't woken to hear our conversation. My side of it, anyway.

"I hear you," she said. "I feel the same way."

"I didn't even worry after I found Jake dead on the path. But now? I'm kind of terrified." But was I scared enough to want her to come and keep me company? Babysit me? No. "I'll be fine alone, though. And I'm going to call in the note as soon as we get off the phone."

"Okay, if you promise."

"I do." I wasn't messing around with a threat. Taking it straight to the authorities was the only way to go.

"I'll sleep with my phone next to my bed and I'll keep the sound turned up. You need me in the night, you ring."

"Will do, Gin. Thanks. You rock."

After our call ended, I debated only a moment. Victoria or Haskins? The note had to be about the murder investigation, so I went looking for the detective's card. Good thing I'd retrieved it from my back pocket that day he'd given it to me and slid it under H in my business card holder. I hit the number. He'd said to contact him without hesitation, and I was going to go ahead and interpret that as meaning at any time of the day or night. I definitely didn't want to ever get another ominous note stuck in my door.

"So pick up already," I muttered, drumming my fingers on the table next to the note.

When he finally answered, he was both terse and so soft-spoken I could hardly hear him. "Haskins. What is it, Ms. Almeida?"

Whoa. Down, boy. "A threatening note was stuck in the door of my house when I got home from the bakery tonight. You told me to contact you without hesitation. So I did. I mean, I am."

He didn't respond. After maybe twenty seconds I heard voices through the phone, the crackle of static, the *thunk* of a car door closing. I waited. Maybe he'd been able to track the other Tattoo Man. Maybe he was on a bust, or whatever they called them in real life. Or a stakeout. Or a different case entirely.

"Mac, do you feel safe where you are?" When the detective finally spoke, he kept his voice low.

Did I? His question echoed the dispatcher's from when I'd called about Jake. I thought for only a moment, then answered honestly. "Yes." I didn't think he'd ever called me by my first name before, so this must be serious.

"Good. I need you to use a handkerchief or something to pick up the note with. Put the note into a new sealable bag. Someone will get it tomorrow. Make sure your doors and windows are locked."

"I will. Should I bring the bag to my shop? I'll be in by nine."

"Yes. Gotta go." He disconnected.

I virtually patted myself on the back for doing the right thing by holding the note with a tissue. After it was secured in the clear bag, I went around to my super energy-efficient windows and locked the latches. At this time of year I usually kept one or more open at the top, because I liked sleeping in cool temperatures. For now I made sure no openings remained on the ground floor, and followed up by closing all the blinds, too. The transom-type clerestory window in the loft could stay open. It was too high and too narrow for a person to ever climb through, anyway.

I marveled at how I hadn't heard a peep from Belle during all that talking. African Greys needed a lot of sleep, and she rarely stirred once she'd entered dreamland. Good. I didn't want her to learn phrases like "dead on the path" and "threatening note."

The threatening note someone had brazenly left in my door. Or was it a brazen move? My house faced back toward the marsh and the coast, and my tiny backyard was rimmed with *Rosa Rugosa*. My neighbor on one side was the path to the Shining Sea trail, and on the other it was the yard behind Tulia's. Anybody could have darted back here and stuck a piece of paper in the door without being seen, especially after dark.

I wiped down the surfaces in the kitchen and bathroom, not that they needed it. I wasn't sure I'd be able to sleep, and I was pretty sure I wouldn't find a murder mystery comforting reading tonight, cozy notwithstanding. I poured half a glass of port and moseyed around my house, which didn't take long. Everything was already tidy and in its place. Sinking down on the couch, I checked the group text again. *Darn*. A couple of messages but nothing really new.

Chapter Twenty-seven

It was Gin's turn to be late for our walk the next morning. I stretched my hamstrings in front of her candy store, admiring the sunlight prancing through the fresh tulip-tree leaves above even as I yawned. My sleep had not been a restful one. I'd turned over as many times as my mind had, considering possibilities for Jake's killer, thinking about Edwin and the other tattooed man, picking up and tossing down all the bits in the group text, and worrying about who had authored my note of warning.

"Hurry up, Gin," I said to her store front. I wanted to get walking and, more important, talking.

"I'm here, already," she said, hurrying around the side of the building, her hands securing her hair into a knot on top of her head.

I laughed. "Sorry about that. One of the perils of living alone is that I get used to talking to myself. Ready to roll?"

She nodded and we headed out.

"Sorry I'm late. No excuse, really. Well, okay, I slept in. So shoot me!" She aimed a smile at me but didn't break her stride. "What did the police say about your note?"

"Haskins was kind of distracted when I called. He told me to put the note in a bag, and to lock my doors. Done, and done." I patted the pocket holding my house key.

"Is being threatened going to stop you from nosing around about Jake's murder?" she asked. "Because we don't have to, you know. We can tell the group to forget about it."

I glanced at her face, which showed new worry lines around her mouth. "I don't plan to stop. But nobody else has to be involved, you know, especially not you. Really. I'm not worried about the "or else" part of the threat. That doesn't mean that others aren't concerned for their own safety. I understand that completely."

"Hey," Gin said as we swung onto the trail from the access path. "If you're in, I'm in. We'll just be careful, right?"

"Right. And turn any information we learn directly over to the detective." I snapped my fingers. "Remind me when we're done, and I'll add his cell number to the group message."

"Good idea. And speaking of the group, I was a little late because I was adding something new I learned about Wes, my lodger."

New information could only round out the picture. "What is it?"

"I happened to casually bring up Tuesday afternoon. I asked him if he'd gotten a chance to visit the photography exhibit at the Cape Museum of Fine Arts, because that was its last day and he'd said he was interested."

"And?"

"The guy said he'd taken himself for a long walk, instead. On the Shining Sea trail, Mac."

"Okay. That's information. And unless he can find someone who saw him on the trail, he doesn't have an alibi for the murder, is that what you're saying?"

Gin nodded. "Because that's where Jake was killed."

We passed over the marshy area bridge, waving in return to a group of white-haired power walkers we often saw.

"What about last evening? Do you know where he was while we were at the bakery?" I asked.

"He said he had dinner in Falmouth with old friends. So he could be lying, or could have left early and stuck that note in your door."

I faced her for a moment. "Isn't the bigger problem figuring out why in the world he would murder Jake?"

"Yes, that is a tiny problem. Maybe Jake did something nasty to him when they were kids and Wes has never forgiven him. He could have stolen money from him."

"Or hurt his sister," I added. "Maybe. Too bad we don't have time to go investigate in Providence."

"I know. Who else do we have?"

"I'm sure the police will want to know where Derrick was last evening, but that won't be hard. He'll have been with Cokey." I crossed my fingers surreptitiously. He better have been. "And then we have Suzanne. Did you see her at Bs & Bs last night?"

Gin nodded. "But only for part of the time. What would be her motive for murder?"

I hunched my shoulders and let them drop. "That's the sticky part of all this. Except for Derrick, we don't know why anyone would want Jake dead."

"That's sticky, all right."

We strode in silence for a couple of minutes until we reached the branch-off to the point. "Shall we?" I gestured toward the point extension.

"Absolutely. And this reminds me of Katherine Deloit. That's where we talked to her. Did you see that Norland learned where she's staying?"

"She's in that Victorian B&B in Falmouth. He said he was going to go poke around, find out where she was on Tuesday." I inhaled the briny air. Just the smell of it made me feel healthier. "I guess I should tell the gang about my note, so people can be looking into alibis for Friday night between seven and ten."

"We don't know why Ms. Deloit would kill Jake either, do we?" Gin asked.

I let a sigh float onto the wind. "No. My mom befriended her yesterday. They came into the shop and then were going off so my mother could read and interpret Katherine's chart."

"Make sure you ask Astra if she noticed a tendency toward violence in it." Gin was much more a believer in astrology than I was.

I agreed and challenged her to race-walk to the point again. We didn't speak until we stretched, breathless, at the lookout. A windsurfer rode the waves wearing a black wet suit, her arms pulling on the arched green-and-white sail full of wind.

"That sport is not for me," I said, shuddering. "Just imagine what could go wrong."

"You could imagine the speed and thrill involved, too. Not that I would attempt it, mind you." Gin raised her eyebrows. "So what about that mystery girl you and Zane saw?" She kicked her foot back and grabbed it, pulling it up and back to stretch her quads on that side. "You know, the one who was happy while Jake was alive and sad after he was killed."

"Didn't Zane put something about her in the text?" I nodded, dug my phone out of my bag, and swiped through the message, which was getting longer every few hours, it seemed. I shook my head. "No, I guess not. I don't see anything new. The timing could be purely coincidental, of course." We headed back down the trail. I picked up the pace and swung my bent arms to get my heart rate back into cardio range. "I doubt it's related to the murder, but didn't you think Edwin's reaction to my question last night was overblown?"

"Of course I do. What's the harm in asking if you know somebody?"

"It's been bugging me since I saw the lookalike. Neither he nor Edwin wanted to talk. It makes me really wonder about their past, if in fact they're related."

"What if they've been estranged for a decade?" Gin asked. "Edwin hears his brother is back and he's not sure how to deal with it. Or maybe he has an idea of where his brother is staying and couldn't wait to go and see him."

"Or maybe it is related to Jake's death." What if Jake, Derrick, and Edwin's brother had all been in prison together? What if the brother had come back, killed Jake for some wrong in their past, and decided to look up Edwin now that he was here in town? I opened my mouth . . . and shut it in the nick of time. I couldn't mention that I knew Jake had been in prison with Derrick. That would break Derrick's confidence. I had to keep remembering it was his story to tell.

"How?" Gin asked.

"Hmm." I didn't have to go into anything about Derrick, or knowing that Jake had been incarcerated. "Stranger comes to town. Has a past with Jake. Finds him, stabs him." I scrunched my nose and glanced at her. "It's plausible, right?"

"I guess. Sounds kind of like fiction to me."

She was right.

Chapter Twenty-eight

I hung out the OPEN flag at ten before nine. I'd had to scurry to get ready in time, but Edwin was due any minute. If he showed, that is. His abrupt departure from the bakery last night had almost exactly mimicked that of the man who looked like him. I wouldn't bet money on Edwin explaining why he left like that and who the guy was, but I hoped he would.

I'd carefully stashed a big envelope holding the bag with the note in my desk drawer when I first came in, and I'd locked the desk. The desk key now kept company with the rest of my keys on a ring clipped onto a belt loop of my shorts. I'd also included Cokey's drawing in the envelope, with a note explaining what it portrayed and said I'd explain what it could mean. I wanted the detective to follow up on Katherine Deloit, and this was the first real clue I'd run across that she might have been up to something worse than bad.

By nine thirty, I had five repair customers growing impatient and eleven point five rental prospectives (the

point five being a toddler needing a trailer) itching to
get out into this fine sunny Cape day. I didn't blame them,
but I was still alone in the shop. And ready to scream.
This was not part of my business plan. From the corner
of my eye I saw someone hurry in the door and make
for the repair side. The person definitely didn't fit Edwin's profile.

I excused myself to the waiting rentals and made it
around the other side, where I saw Orlean stashing her
lunch in the fridge and throwing on a repair apron.
Glory be to whatever kind spirit moved my employee
get her rear end in here.

"Glad you could . . ." I stopped myself before I said
something rude in front of customers. "Glad you could
make it in after all this morning, Orlean." I pasted on a
smile. "These nice folks have been very patient, and all
have either urgent repair needs or something to leave."

"I'm on it, Mac." Orlean didn't quite mutter, but almost. At a look from me, she cleared her throat and
mustered her own version of a smile. It wasn't much,
but it would have to do. "Who's first here?" she asked
as I headed back to my clutch of tourists.

By ten-thirty we almost had things under control.
Orlean was greasing and tuning like crazy, with her favorite Emmy Lou Harris CD playing in the background. On my side I was banking rental deposits and
selling biking clothes at an equal pace. Things could be
worse. I'd find a moment free to talk with Orlean
sometime before the end of the day. We really needed
to hash through the scheduling nightmares that a no-
show caused, or a late arrival. For the moment I had a
lull in walk-ins, but I knew she was hurrying to finish a
bike for someone who insisted he had to have it by
eleven. Now would not be a good time to have our lit-

tle chat. I did want to tell her I thought I had hired someone new, but it could wait. And maybe I hadn't, after all, since Edwin himself was a no-show so far.

A motorcycle needing a muffler putted past outside. At least the driver was taking it slow through town. Whenever I heard Harley-Davidson engines revving, it always made me think of the oldie song, "Leader of the Pack," that Mom used to sing along to in the car when I was little. And it was an oldie then.

I was tidying the stack of rental agreements when the no-show himself appeared backlit in the open back door. At least, I hoped it was Edwin and not his mysterious spirit twin. From here, with the sunlight behind him, I couldn't quite tell. I waited for the man to come all the way in, but he didn't.

"Edwin, I thought we agreed you'd be here at nine."

"I only wanted to tell her I'm sorry."

That wasn't Edwin's voice. Was it? I slid off my stool, approaching the figure until I could see it wasn't Edwin, in fact.

"Who are you? Who did you want to apologize to?" And what have you done with Edwin?

He finally moved in enough for me to see that it was the inked guy from last night. "My name is Corwin Germain. I'm Edwin's older brother." His voice was deeper, a bit rough, like I'd remembered it, but still so similar to Edwin's.

"I thought so. I tried to introduce myself last night." Once again I held out my hand. "I'm Mac Almeida, and this is my shop."

He shook hands. "Sorry about that. Last night, I mean. I couldn't stick around." His short-sleeved black shirt revealed even more of the tattoos than had shown last night. One was the same dragon as on Edwin's left arm.

"Edwin was going to start working here this morning, but I haven't seen him," I said. "Would you have any idea where he is?"

Corwin turned away without speaking, jamming his hands into the pockets of his jeans.

"Is Edwin all right?" I raised my voice. He'd better be. I chided myself. Of course he was. Haskins had followed him out last night. I didn't know where he lived, though, and didn't have time to call Pa and ask him.

The brother faced me again. "Edwin's fine. I think he's fine, I mean. I don't know why he's late. Does Orlean Brown work for you?"

I almost staggered from the whiplash. Why was he asking me about her all of a sudden? "Um, yes. She does. Why?" If he took ten more steps he'd see her himself.

"She's my wife. Or was."

Aha. The mysterious "ex." I was surprised she hadn't heard Corwin's voice but Emmy Lou's haunting voice must have masked it.

"I wanted to tell her I'm sorry." He spread his hands.

A hand-holding couple in matching Hawaiian shirts strolled up to the counter. I smiled and told them I'd be with them in a second. I faced Corwin.

"Would you mind waiting out back at the picnic table?" I gestured through the open door. "I'll see if Orlean is free."

His eyes flew wide open. "She's here working? Now?" He took a step toward me, trying to peer into the rest of the shop.

I held my ground, and firmly steered him out through the door behind him. "Wait there." I folded my arms and filled the doorway so he'd know I was serious. I wasn't letting him loose on Orlean without first making sure she wanted to see him. From the way she'd referred to the "ex" a couple of days ago, I wasn't sure. If she didn't want to talk with him, it was going to be bye-bye Corwin, at least off my property, at least for now. My employees came first, no matter how difficult they were.

After I helped my rental couple and sent them on their way grinning atop a yellow tandem, I scooted around the corner to Orlean. She was head down and working in the repair area. I cleared my throat and waited until she looked up.

"Yeah?" she asked, in her taciturn shortcut for, 'what do you want?'

"A man named Corwin Germain just came in asking for you."

"My ex." Her face, never one to sport a rosy glow, went paler than usual. She blinked, waiting.

"That's what he said."

She nodded once, slowly, down and up.

When she didn't add anything, I went on. "He'd like to speak with you. I sent him out back to the picnic table."

She opened her mouth, but only blew out a breath that sounded exasperated.

I went on. "When he first came in, all he said was that he wanted to tell you that he's sorry. I told him that if you want to talk to him, I'll send you out. But that it's up to you."

"Jeemus H. Crackers, Mac," Orlean said after staring at me for a long few seconds. "I've been a lousy employee, and here you're doing me a favor?"

"Hey. I know you. I hired you because I trusted you and I needed help. I don't know this dude Corwin from a hole in the ground."

Orlean nodded, kind of like she didn't trust herself to speak. As I watched, her eyes went saucer-ish. I turned to see a sheepish Edwin in the doorway.

"Man, Mac, I'm really sorry. I know I'm three hours late, and I can explain everything." He looked at Orlean and smiled shyly. "Hey, Orlean. Long time."

I glanced from him to Orlean and back. She stood stock-still. She looked like she'd never met him, but he was her brother-in-law. She must have.

"Edwin, you know Orlean?"

"She and Cor . . ."

I saw the light of recognition come into Orlean's eyes. "Edwin?" she screeched. "You've changed, kiddo."

His eyes, on the other hand, grew sad. "You thought I looked like my brother, didn't you?"

"Exactly," she replied. "You sound like him, too."

Same as what I'd thought last night.

"You were still a kid last time I saw you," Orlean went on.

"Yeah. I was fifteen, but I was late to mature."

He'd made up for lost time, with that low voice and beard growth.

"Have you seen him?" Edwin asked Orlean. "Mac here said he was in town. I mean, last night she asked me if I had a brother. I've been looking everywhere for him."

Orlean pressed her lips into a grim line. "He's been calling me over the last few days. I said no way. The dumbass got himself incarcerated. I divorced him. I don't want nothing more to do with him." She dusted off her hands with a slapping motion. "Good riddance. I'm sorry, Eddie, I know he's your big brother. But I can't have a husband like that."

Mentally I reeled from this new information, which was also the most words my taciturn mechanic had strung together since I'd met her. What she said explained her mood and her absences recently, however. And Corwin had been in prison. With Derrick? With Jake? And for what? This wasn't the time to ask.

"Mac says your brother," she spat out the word like it was poison, "is out back, wanting to tell me he's sorry."

Edwin's eyebrows and whole face lifted. That hadn't been his reaction last night. What had changed?

"He's been telling me he's sorry since he got out," Orlean continued. "I don't care, and you can tell him that for me."

Edwin glanced at me as if seeking confirmation.

I nodded. "He was out back a few minutes ago. Go see if you want."

"Thanks. Orlean, I'll be right back." He started for the door.

"Kid?" She held out a hand. "I'm happy to see you, and I always will be. Want you to know that."

Edwin turned back. He grabbed her hand and drew her in, planting a kiss on her cheek. "Likewise, sis."

I shot one glance at Orlean, but she was lost in her job again, albeit with pinkened cheeks. I hurried after Edwin and caught him before he went out.

"Orlean said your brother was incarcerated."

"Yes, but—"

"I don't care. Would you do me a favor and ask him if he knew my brother Derrick Searle . . ." I had been about to say *while he was in prison* but caught myself in time. Edwin didn't know Derrick had been incarcerated. "I mean, if he's ever spent time with Derrick. In the past."

Edwin narrowed his eyes at me. "What do you mean, ever spent time with him? Like hanging out?"

I nodded, fingers crossed behind my back. I shouldn't get my hopes up, anyway. There were prisons everywhere.

"Okay. I'll ask him." He headed out the door.

"And find out where he's staying," I called after him. He nodded without looking back.

As I crossed to the rental counter, I glimpsed Corwin sitting on one of the picnic table benches, back to the shop, arms folded, legs extended. Like someone who could wait all day. If he'd been in prison for a few years, he had to be good at waiting.

A flurry of new customers kept me from looking again, and fifteen minutes must have passed before Edwin came back in with more spirit in his step than before. He hung out browsing the shelves of merchandise, checking the prices on bikes, and reading my rental information sheet until I had a free moment.

"Please let me apologize again for being so late," Edwin began. "I can explain   "

"Don't." I cut him off with a stop-sign hand. "Just don't be late again. I need to have prompt employees. My business would collapse if it opened late, closed too early, or simply wasn't open at all on a Saturday morning, especially during the season. Got it?"

He stood up a little taller. "Got it."

"You all set with your brother?"

Edwin pursed his lips but said he was.

"Did he leave?"

"Yeah. But I know where he is. He got a room in Bourne."

"Good. I might need to get that information from you later. Now, let me explain the rental system." The two of us hunkered over the info sheet on the counter, me pointing out the rules and the prices, him asking the occasional question. Of course I was dying to know the whole story—where Corwin had been, if he'd known Derrick in prison, where he was now—but that was going to have to wait. It wasn't properly a workplace discussion. As Orlean's past with him wasn't, either.

"Let's go around to the side and I'll show you the categories of rentals." I caught sight of the clock. "Oh, geez, it's already after noon. Let me see if Orlean wants to take her lunch now. Meet you over there."

I made my way to the repair side. Orlean straightened from writing on a repair ticket and faced me. Tears stained her face. She swiped at them with the back of her hand.

"I'm sorry, Orlean." I paused, not sure whether to go to her or keep my distance. But heck, I like human touch when I'm upset, so I kept going and put my hand on her bony shoulder. "Can I do anything?"

She sniffed. "Nope. Nothing nobody can do. It's just, seeing Eddie's face all young and hopeful like that. That's how my Cor's was. Before." Her voice turned cynical on the last word and she turned away.

I was about to say, "You don't think you can give

him a second chance?" when Edwin moved in on
graceful cat feet. He took my place next to her. He also
took my words.

"Won't you give him a second chance, sis?" he murmured to her. "Will you consider it? I think he's
changed."

I tapped my hands on my legs. I wasn't quite sure
whether to leave Orlean and Edwin alone, tell her to go
eat lunch, or pretend nothing had happened.

Derrick bustling in solved that little problem for me.
He took in the scene. Orlean turned toward the tool
bench and started straightening the tools she'd been
using.

If my brother had known Corwin in prison, was he
going to have the same reaction to seeing Edwin as I'd
had seeing Corwin after meeting his brother first? But,
no. Surely Derrick and Edwin had met at Pa's before.
Derrick was around my parents' place a lot more often
than I was because of Cokey. So either Derrick hadn't
known Corwin, or he'd kept his thoughts about a re-
semblance to himself.

Sure enough, Derrick and Edwin exchanged some
kind of complicated guy handshake. My brother looked
at me. "Cokey's on a play date and I have the afternoon. Want me to take over the rentals and retail?"

My mind raced at everything I could do with a free
afternoon, possibly including a bit of sleuthing. "You
bet. I was training Edwin here to help out. Looks like
you guys already know each other. Can you keep
showing him the ropes?"

"Of course," Derrick said as Edwin nodded. "Come
on, dude. Let's learn some wheels." The two men
headed over to rentals and retail.

"And Orlean, I'll cover repair while you get lunch. Good?"

"Thanks."

"You okay?" I didn't have vocabulary like *dude* or *man* to soften a phrase for women. *Girlfriend,* maybe. But that was the kind of word I'd use with Gin, not to Orlean. I left my question unsoftened.

"I will be," she muttered. She grabbed her bag lunch out of the fridge and disappeared out the front door.

Chapter Twenty-nine

Half an hour later Orlean was back on the job, working on a maintenance issue with a rental, and the guys were each helping customers. Edwin was a quick study, exactly as I'd thought he'd be. I hoped Orlean and Corwin could come to a peaceful understanding, but I also knew it was completely out of my hands, and rightly so.

Nobody from the police had come to pick up my threatening note, so I thought I might as well deliver it. Too bad nobody thought it held much urgency. Maybe I could get a few bits of information out of the detective while I was at the station, too.

I checked the wall clock, which read a quarter to one. Good. I could take a few hours if I needed them. "I have to run some errands in town, gang," I called out to my crew. "Be back before closing."

"Go. We got it covered." Derrick waved me toward the door.

"Call me if something comes up." I held thumb and pinky to my ear.

Orlean only nodded. I stuffed the envelope in my small backpack and headed down the street.

My first stop was Greta's Grains. I'd invited Tim for dinner tonight. Our quiet evening for two on Thursday had been thoroughly disrupted by rescuing Derrick, and I was looking forward to reconstructing it. Tulia sold fresh cooked lobster meat at the Shack, and I could assemble a mean lobster salad with the best of them. Add a baguette from Tim, a bag of salad greens, a chocolate hangover cake from the patisserie, and bingo—homemade dinner involving zero cooking. My kind of hostessing.

When I moseyed in the bakery's back door and looked around the kitchen, though, my man wasn't in evidence. I peeked into the front, where Greenhair from last night was wiping off a table.

"Tim gone already?" I asked her.

She ignored me and kept on wiping. At least I thought she ignored me until I saw the telltale earbud wires. I moved into her field of vision, waving one hand. She pulled one bud out.

"Is Tim gone already?" I repeated.

"He's out on a delivery."

"Thanks." I scanned the shelf of breads behind the counter but the baguette basket was empty. They must have sold out, and most of the rest of the breads were sweet. So much for my dinner baguette. But I'd be willing to bet Tim had some in reserve in a freezer either here or at his house.

I took in the sun-filled room. Funny how different it looked at night when it was full of musicians, drinkers,

and dancers: bigger, darker, more exotic. I headed out
the back and was about to aim myself for the police
station a couple of doors down when I veered course
and crossed the street to the Book Nook, the bookstore
Suzanne managed. Last week I'd seen a picture book
called *My Daddy* featuring gorgeous hand-drawn artwork and lovely, simple words about all the things a
daddy does for his child. I thought Cokey might like it,
and frankly that Derrick would, too. He could use
some positive reinforcement these days.

Thinking of the night-and-day difference in the bakery's front room reminded me of the note in my bag.
The full light of a June Saturday on the Cape sure
made the words on a piece of paper feel a lot less
threatening than they had last night when I was alone
in the dark. How could I be in danger right here in the
middle of town? I was across the street from the police
station, no less. The sunny air was mild, not yet too
hot, and smelled of roses in bloom and a touch of seaweed, exactly like it should. It also sounded like a
clutch of motorcycle nuts was cruising the Cape. I'd
know that deep loud roar in the distance anywhere.
With any luck they'd pass by Westham and keep on
going. Riders who discarded their helmets the minute
they crossed the line into New Hampshire (motto:
"Live Free and Die" in my version) weren't my fa-
vorites.

A few minutes later I emerged from the bookshop
wearing the kind of smile only an avid reader can. Not
only did I now hold Cokey's book in my hand, I also
had an armful of four new cozies in a paper bag. Despite Suzanne's disapproval, I'd indulged my addiction
to justice-is-restored, nothing-offensive village mys-

teries. She was a shopkeeper who'd never heard of the principle of, *The customer is always right.* Or, more likely, simply didn't care to follow it.

I didn't see a car coming from either direction, so I stepped off the curb to cross over to the police station. From just beyond Cape King Distillery down the block, a huge Harley-Davidson, all black and chrome, sprang to life. The driver revved the engine in a burst of noise. I silently cursed motorcycle owners who drove muffler-free. Our sweet town didn't need that kind of noise pollution.

As I frowned, the machine roared directly at me. What? What was the driver doing? I yelled and waved my arms. The motorcycle didn't stop, didn't swerve. Its deep vibrating noise deafened me. The decibels bounced off the brick of the police station opposite.

"Mac!" someone yelled.

I couldn't see who'd called out a warning. The black-leather-suited driver and the death machine was almost on top of me. I stepped backward and tripped onto the sidewalk. The Harley sped past, spinning dust and gravel into the air. Its heat burned my bare legs. The smell of exhaust filled my nostrils.

Chapter Thirty

I lay panting on the pavement, heart athud, throat thick. The Harley was gone. The afternoon fell silent. My elbow smarted, scraped raw from where I'd landed on it, and my head pounded. My new books lay scattered on the pavement, covered with black bits of gravel. And I hadn't even gotten a look at the license plate. Some amateur sleuth I was.

Victoria dashed across the street. I pushed up to sitting as a customer hurried out of the Book Nook, followed by a slower-moving Suzanne.

"Are you all right?" Victoria asked. "I saw that Harley try to run you down." She extended a hand to help me up but I waved her off.

"Thanks, but I'll sit here for a minute if that's okay. Did you get the plate?"

"No, it happened too fast," she said. "And I'm pretty sure the cameras in front of the station don't reach over here."

A Cape Rescue ambulance roared up from a scant thirty yards down the street. I knew I was okay when I caught myself thinking that the EMTs should have just walked. I sat on the sidewalk in my daze, picturing the motorcycle coming at me, then tearing away after I hit the pavement just out of reach. I'd seen something, some flash of color. I gaped in the direction it had disappeared.

"I think I saw a logo of some kind," I said.

"An identifying mark?" Victoria asked. She knelt in front of me. "Like a sticker?"

"It happened too fast to really see. But I saw some orange lines, I know that. Like a spray of them."

She nodded. "It could be anything, of course. A Harley club or a cause. But it's most likely to be from the dealership. They would decal the bikes they sell."

My thoughts seemed to be in a random jumble. I'd moved on from orange bits to Victoria. "Did you just happen to be standing in front of the station?" I gazed at her, with her Nordic hair aflame in the sunshine. "How'd you get over here so quick?"

"I was walking out to grab some lunch."

"Was it you who yelled to me?" I asked.

Victoria smiled. "It was. Really glad you weren't seriously hurt."

I blinked at her. That might have been the first nice thing she'd ever said to me, and one of the first genuine smiles.

Suzanne squatted next to me. "You okay, Mac? That guy looked like he was gunning right for you."

"I know. I think I'm okay." I rubbed my elbow. "You said 'guy.' Did you see that it was a man?" The attack had happened so fast I couldn't picture the driver's face. As with the cyclist who nearly clipped Gin and me on the trail the other day, I thought the driver today had been slender. My attacker hadn't been a stocky person. Could it be the same as the possibly malicious bicyclist?

"No, I think you're right." Suzanne shook her head. "I was watching through the window but I couldn't see if it was a man or a woman. Usually women don't own those huge machines, but some do. That was a big honking helmet, tinted face shield and all."

"Right. The driver wasn't wearing a little Harley helmet, the ones that don't do anything to protect from brain damage." Victoria pressed her lips together and gave her head a little shake.

"The ones that look like Nazi helmets," I added.

Two EMTs were hovering but I waved them off. "I'm fine. I didn't hit my head, and I can put a bandage on my scraped elbow at home."

"Permission to leave, Chief?" one asked Victoria.

"You're released," she said.

"While you're here, I have something to tell you," I said to Victoria as the EMTs climbed back into the ambulance. "I was coming across the street to give you a letter. I might as well give it to you now."

Suzanne straightened from her squat but remained in place, her arms folded across her chest.

"A letter?" the chief asked.

"It's actually for Detective Haskins." I stuck my hand out for her to give me a boost up to standing, and dusted off my rear end once I was on my feet. "Someone left a threatening letter in my door last night," I murmured. Suzanne edged forward a few inches with studied casualness. Oh, well. The news would be all over town soon enough. I went on. "I called Haskins at the time. He was pretty busy and said an officer would pick it up at the shop this morning. But nobody did, so I thought I'd deliver it." I shrugged off my pack and extracted the now-rumpled envelope.

Victoria took the envelope. She lifted the flap and Suzanne moved even closer. Victoria closed the envelope and faced the station across the street, turning her back on Suzanne.

"Thanks, Mac," the chief said. "We'll enter this as evidence."

"I put something else in the envelope that Haskins is going to want to see," I said. "But I'll need to explain it to him."

Victoria waited as if I was going to explain Cokey's drawing to her.

I shook my head. "I'm going to have to tell him myself. In person. Could you please ask him to call me when he gets it?"

Victoria lifted one pale eyebrow. "All right, whatever. You're sure you don't need assistance here?"

I shook my head. "But thanks." After she hightailed it back across the street, I turned to gaze at the mess on the ground behind me. "Give me a hand with these books, Suzanne?" I stooped to pick one up.

Suzanne retrieved the others. "Sit down for a minute." She sat on the wooden bench in front of the store and patted the place next to her.

Wow. So friendly all of a sudden, and to a cozy fan, no less. I sat, figuring I might as well take advantage of the outreach, plus my legs were a bit wobbly from the attack. I was pretty sure she wanted to get information out of me, but the info swap street could go in two directions.

"So what did that letter say?" Suzanne asked without looking at me. "What was the threat?"

"It was a kind of vague warning. No big deal."

"Then why did you give it to Laitinen?"

"I was told to. Maybe the police can trace who wrote it, who left it. It's not very nice to find a belligerent note stuck in your door." I twisted to look at her. "I saw you at Bs & Bs last night."

She blinked. "Where?"

"At the bakery. At Brews and Breads."

"Right. I saw you dancing for a while. Good band."

"They are. How late did you stay?" At the rumble of an engine, I cringed without meaning to. But it was only a big macho truck cruising through town, and it stayed firmly in its own lane on the other side of the road.

"Until they closed at midnight." Now Suzanne regarded me. "What, do you think I left you that note? Why would I do something like that?"

She could have stuck it in my door before she went to the bakery. "I don't know, why?"

"No reason in the world. I didn't kill Jake, you know. And I think it's ridiculous that you and your 'cozy' group think you're the sleuths in a book all of a sudden."

"Too bad about the way he died, wasn't it?" I asked, with what I hoped was unstudied casualness.

"Stabbing's gotta be bad for the victim. You see it coming, and the death must be slow." She hugged herself.

Should I ask her? Why not? "How did you know Jake was stabbed?" We were in the sun across from a dozen or two police officers. What was she going to do to me? Although that attitude hadn't exactly kept me safe from getting run down a few minutes ago. "The way he was killed wasn't public knowledge."

"Sure it was," Suzanne scoffed.

"Maybe the method has leaked out by now, but you knew about it the day after Jake was killed. The police had kept it secret. The only way I know is that I saw the knife in him." I shivered despite the warm day.

She sighed. "Okay, so I have a source. My friend Gail works with the District Attorney's office."

"Where the state police homicide unit operates out of."

"Exactly. She hears everything. And sometimes she tells me stuff."

So much for my great theory. "Is Gail the one who looks like Louise Penny?"

Suzanne looked puzzled for a second, then laughed. "She's the one. You saw her last night?"

"Had me going there for a minute when you two came in."

"Don't worry, she's not a Canadian author. And I keep what she tells me under my hat," Suzanne said. "Usually."

It being Saturday, I expected Flo wouldn't be working at the library today. She was one of the people I wanted to talk to, though, so I headed down Main Street to where I could conduct a few phone conversations in relative privacy, or at least not under Suzanne's nose. I crossed side streets very, very cautiously, and stayed on the sidewalks as far away from the curb as I could. My legs were still shaky from the attack, and another sudden gun of an engine made me flinch right out in public. I was already creeped out simply knowing somebody somewhere was watching what I did, tracking who I talked to. Did I want to let that threat of "or else" stop me? I thought about it as I walked. No, I didn't.

I perched on a shady bench under a tree in front of Town Hall and texted Flo. I waited a few moments, but no immediate response was forthcoming. Next I called Tulia at the Lobstah Shack and reserved my claw and tail meat to pick up later.

"How late are you open?" I asked after I put in my order.

"Six, hon."

"Thanks. By the way, have you learned anything about Jake's murder?" I asked, after checking around to make sure no disc-throwing youth lurked nearby.

"Not about his murder, exactly. Did you see in the group text that I volunteered to find out where Deloit was on Tuesday?"

"That's right, I forgot." Or maybe I hadn't checked the message thread lately. "Any luck?"

"Somebody saw her at Jimmy's Harborside at around seven that night. And she was in the gift shop at two o'clock buying starfish earrings."

Which didn't sound like Katherine's style of jewelry. Maybe she had a daughter or a niece at home who loved starfish. Jimmy's Harborside was a conventional seafood restaurant, popular with tourists looking for fried fish, surf and turf, and the whole lobster experience, complete with nutcrackers and bibs.

"Good fact finding, Tulia. Do you know if she was eating alone at Jimmy's?"

"No," Tulia said. "It was a customer who told me. She was remarking on a woman who'd been borderline rude to her and when she described the woman, I knew it was this Deloit character. I didn't want to ask if she'd been with anyone else."

"But nobody knows where she was between two and seven?" I asked.

"Nope. At least not that any of us have found out."

"Was one of us supposed to be checking into who that young woman was?"

"I don't remember." A crash sounded in the background and Tulia swore in language only a sailor might utter. "Gotta go, Mac. Later."

I started to say "Later" but she'd already hung up. I opened my notes file and tapped in that information. Then focused on the list. The column under the question mark was still way longer than the list under the Truth heading. Checking alibis and mysterious person identities was supposed to be the job of the police. At least I hoped they were working on that. Were we duplicating their efforts? Or trying to?

I called Norland next, but he didn't pick up. He was likely out at a grandkid's game or revarnishing his sailboat. What about Corwin? Mysterious stranger comes back to town. Sure, he and Orlean had a past to work out. But if he'd been incarcerated with Jake, he was surely on Haskins's person-of-interest list. Or was he?

It was time to bite the bullet, so to speak. I pressed the detective's number. He didn't have to pick up if he didn't want to. For whatever reason, he actually did.

"Detective, would you have a few minutes to chat?" I swore I could hear the swooshing sound of his eyes rolling. I continued before he could refuse. "I gave Victoria my threatening note to pass along to you, and another thing in the same envelope I think you're going to want to know about. I happen to be free right now."

The sigh was unmistakable. Still, he asked me to

meet him at the station in twenty minutes. I had just enough time to grab an ice cream cone from Neptune's. Except it was one-thirty and, as far as I remembered, I hadn't had lunch. Good thing ice cream cones included three of the four major food groups: cream, chocolate, and cookie. The only one missing was champagne, with beer allowed if you were hard up.

Chapter Thirty-one

I was munching the last bite of my sugar cone when Haskins met me in the police station lobby. He gazed with sorrow at the chocolate on my fingers.

"Sorry I didn't get you one," I said. "It's my lunch."

"That's okay. According to my doctor, I'm off all that delicious stuff, anyway. Milk, sugar, wheat. Everything that brings joy in eating."

I gazed up at him. "You don't look very happy with those constraints. Tell me about it."

"No time to whine. We need to talk about this note." He led me back to a small office devoid of wall decorations but with a white board covered in names familiar from this week, starting with Derrick Searle. I winced to see it. He gestured to a chair in front of the desk and took the seat across from me. He spread my bagged note flat on the desk before he spoke. "You called me about this at a little after ten last night, correct?"

"That's right. As soon as I got home and saw it. I

mean, as soon as I got inside and locked the door."
Strictly speaking that was true, even though I'd spoken
with Gin before I called him.

"Have you been looking into the crime?" he asked,
tapping the note in time with the words.

"A little. I'm only trying to help. I'm sure you and
the rest of the department have your hands full. Can it
really hurt if some of us divvy up tasks and learn who
was where, and so on?"

"Some of us?" His voice rose. "Who else?"

"It's this mystery book group I'm in. Tulia at the
Lobstah Shack, Gin, Zane King from the distillery,
Florence Wolanski, a few others. Oh, and Norland Gif-
ford."

Haskins's expression darkened, quite possibly at
hearing that a former police chief was in the book
group.

I swallowed and hurried on "For example, Tulia just
told me she learned that Katherine Deloit was at the
gift shop at two o'clock on Tuesday afternoon and at
Jimmy's Harborside at seven, but nobody knows
where she was in between. Which is when the murder
must have been committed, right?"

Haskins opened his mouth, shut it with a frustrated-
sounding exhale, and opened it again. "I can see how
you might not think it could 'hurt' anything to ask a
few questions here and there. But may I remind you an
actual murderer is walking around out here? This person has not yet been apprehended, and might be feeling
safe, maybe getting sloppy. Imagine this, Ms. Almeida.
What if this person sees you and your group going
around town making inquiries? Your actions are now
threatening a killer— an actual real-life murderer—and
he or she decides to do away with you, too. That would

hurt a lot. It would hurt you and it would hurt me." He stared at me over the top of his glasses like he already knew I'd nearly been run down by a motorcycle three times my size. Victoria would have told him when she handed over the letter.

"When you put it that way, I guess you have a point," I said. "So what have you and yours figured out so far?" I kept my voice upbeat and cheery, not sure if he'd respond to that approach, but it was worth a try.

He folded his arms, ignoring my question. "Will you promise you'll stop this amateurish sleuthing you're doing? And convince your friends to do the same?"

"All right." I doubt this murderer would try to kill off an entire cozy mystery book group, but I had no choice but to agree.

"Good. We do have a team checking alibis. It's our job."

"I know. I promised, didn't I? At least let me tell you what else I've learned." I waited for his almost imperceptible nod before continuing. "Corwin Germain was married to Orlean Brown, my bike mechanic. She apparently divorced him after he was incarcerated. He came in this morning and wanted to apologize to her. Edwin came in a little later and talked to his brother. He told me Corwin is staying in Bourne." I caught the detective briefly raising his eyebrows at that last bit. "I don't know yet if he was in prison with Jake or not. If he was, he could have followed him here to settle an old wrong or a debt, or get revenge."

"Thank you. Anything else?"

"Do you have that picture my niece drew?" I asked.

He pulled it out of the envelope and spread it on the desk next to the letter.

"So Derrick told you he gives tours of the lighthouse on weekends. Cokey—that's his daughter—was with him on Sunday. She told me a lady lost her purse inside and had to go back in to look for it. Everybody else was outside. The picture Cokey drew looked exactly like Katherine Deloit, at least seen through a four-year-old artist's hand, it did. Deloit could have gone back in and stolen Derrick's gutting knife."

Haskins stretched out his long legs and clasped his hands behind his head. The big yawn that came next made me wonder if he was planning to nap on my information. Through the open window I spied a gull land on the roof of Neptune's Ice Cream next door and begin a plaintive rising and falling *weow* cry.

"What reason would this Deloit woman have to kill Mr. Lacey?" he finally asked.

"We haven't quite figured that out yet." I hated to admit it, but it was the truth.

"Maybe your brother did away with Lacey." He tented his fingers.

"No! I know he didn't."

"Maybe he fed his daughter that story about Deloit and her so-called lost purse."

"No." I tapped my foot. "Cokey is reliable, I'm sure of it." On the other hand, four-year-olds could be swayed by suggestions, at least as far as I'd read.

He glanced sideways at me. "Do you have any other suspects up your sleeve?"

This was so frustrating. "Not really. I texted you about Wesley Farnham, the rich guy Gin Malloy has staying in her B&B, who was interested in custom fishing knives. The one who knew Jake growing up. And we've seen a young woman around town somewhere who looked happy before Jake's death and devastated afterward. But we haven't been able to locate her."

"Welcome to my life, Ms. Almeida. Investigating a homicide is not safe, easy, or straightforward." He sat up straight again. "But I beg you, leave the investigation to me and my team. You don't want the next attempt on your life to be successful."

Chapter Thirty-two

I trotted down the steps in front of the station. "The next attempt" was definitely a reference to my encounter with the Harley-Davidson. The detective really, really didn't want me—or any of the Capers—to be poking around. I most certainly didn't want to be the second murder victim in a week. And yet . . . no, no "yet," I scolded myself. It was time to take this business seriously. I sat on a step, pulled out my phone, and opened the group text.

Big Harley almost ran me down in front of Book Nook today. Apparently on purpose. Someone delivered threatening note to my door last pm. Det. Huskins told us to stop investigating. We don't want a Caper to be next victim, right? Sadly, cease and desist, O sleuths.

I hit Send, even though I didn't want to. Leaning against the iron railing at the bottom of the steps, I bumped my scraped elbow. The attack by the Harley raced up to the top of my consciousness and I shivered, as if it was charging at me all over again. My heart jackhammered in my chest, my hands turned sweaty, and I wanted to leap off the steps and hide. I forced myself to breathe deeply. I looked around, admonishing myself. I stood in front of the town police department, after all. I should be safe here, at least from attacking motorcycles.

When I'd talked myself down, I pictured those orange stripes again. Or were they lines spraying out from something? How could I ever figure out what they were part of? Would it really be so bad if I put the Capers on the case? Not by asking questions in public, of course. It had to be safe, however, to do an Internet hunt for a motorcycle logo with a spray of orange. I returned to the text.

Saw small spray of orange lines on Harley. Dealer logo? Motorcycle club? Can one of you search? Internet only, tho. Not in public.

There. That was done. I supposed it was time to get back to the shop. Not pop into the distillery and ask Zane what else he'd learned. Not swing by Gin's and do the same. Not call Flo again and see where I could meet her. I swore under my breath, but Haskins was right. Public snooping was exactly that—public. If I was being watched, it would be clear what I was doing. At least it would be clear to the person who'd threatened me twice.

"Ms. Almeida," a man's voice hailed me from down the block. I whipped my head in that direction to see Wesley Farnham. Had any of us ever learned anything useful about him? I shook my head. *Not our job, not our job.* I had to internalize that mantra. I stood and waited for him to approach. He was outfitted in the same vein as the first time I'd met him, except in a traffic cone motif: orange shirt and white pants. When he got close I saw a sailboat logo on his shirt instead of the upended whale.

"How's your house search going?" I asked.

"I believe I have found my cottage." He beamed. "A modest abode up in Pocasset."

A modest abode. With his apparent riches? "That's great."

"I'll be gutting and adding onto it, of course, but it's a scenic setting."

Of course.

"It's just what I wanted." The smile slid off his face. "I was deeply troubled to hear of my old friend's death. Poor Jacob." He shook his head. "And by a violent hand, to boot."

"It's really awful."

"The police," he waved his ringed hand at the building behind us, "somehow discovered my past connection with Jacob and paid me a visit. I didn't mind a bit, and told them all I knew about my old friend. And I said if there was anything further I could do to assist, they should not hesitate to ask me." He lifted his chin blinking solemnly, looking like the serious businessman he must be, or at least probably thought of himself as.

"When were you friends? High school?" Maybe my Google search had missed something.

His smile was a sad one. "We were next-door neighbors. Inseparable as boys. But we grew apart, had different goals in life. Jacob dropped out of high school, and I went on to Yale." He gazed up at a small airplane droning by. "You get to my age, Ms. Almeida, and you're seized with the urge to look up people who knew you when you were young. I missed my chance with Jacob."

"I'm sorry you didn't get to visit with him before he died."

"I, as well. Good to chat with you. I must be off." He held out his hand.

I shook it and watched him head briskly in the direction of Salty Taffy's. Was he telling the truth? I didn't have any real reason to believe he wasn't. On the other hand, there were plenty of great liars out there. And at least one right here in Westham.

I needed to be off, too. But before I could start walking, the telltale rumbling putts of overpowered motorcycles grew louder from the north end of town. My heart revved up. I glanced in all directions. I could hardly swallow, my throat was so thick. I wiped my hands on my shorts as they grew nearer and nearer. All I wanted to do was dash behind the building, or better, run back inside, lock the door behind me, and cower.

"Mackenzie, calm down," I admonished myself out loud. Was an entire club of Harley owners going to race up on the sidewalk and go after me on the steps of the police station? Of course not. The riders came into view, a rumble of ten or more. Black leather vests, bare arms pushed back from Easy Rider handlebars, and sure enough, little Hitler helmets. They rode right on past me. Of course they did. My being attacked once didn't mean every Harley on the Cape was out to get me. Far from it. Still, I didn't let myself relax until their backs and taillights were in view.

I whacked myself on the head. Because of my panic attack, I'd missed a primo opportunity to glimpse any decals on these Harleys, to look for that spray of orange. The motorcycles had been going nice and slow, too. *Shoot*. I peered down the street. My spirits lifted with my eyebrows when I saw the motorcycles slow and turn off one by one. The noise fell silent, too. I squinted. If I wasn't mistaken, they'd just filled the parking lot next to the Lobstah Shack.

It was clearly time for me to go back to my shop. And if I happened to admire a few monster two-wheeled machines on my way, who could blame me?

Chapter Thirty-three

Dejected, I turned toward Mac's Bikes. I'd strolled through the parking lot and casually examined the motorcycles, admiring them, taking a couple of pictures with my phone. But I hadn't seen a single decal like the one I thought I'd seen on the attack Harley. With any luck, one of the Capers would dig it out of the vast library of images that was the Internet, instead. I glanced across at Zane's. I really did need to pick up a bottle of wine for dinner. Even if the villain was watching me, it would appear to be a reasonable shopping stop, especially if I actually came out holding an elongated paper bag.

Once again looking both ways, and keeping my ears alert for any motorcycle noises, I hurried across Main Street. But when my gaze fell on Yoshinoya, the Japanese restaurant, my thoughts fell on the young woman none of us had identified. The one I'd seen weeping. The one Zane's husband Stephen had seen eating a happy dinner with Jake in this very restaurant on when? Had it been Monday? The idea of including a Japanese appetizer in tonight's meal occurred to me, so I detoured into the doorway, which stood open to the summery air.

Blue and white rectangles of curtains that hung down to chin level in the doorway to the back were decorated with bold white slashes of characters. The glass front of the sushi bar showed a dozen slabs of fish, all nestled neatly in crushed ice. The air smelled delectably of seafood, seaweed, and soy, with a tang of vinegar in the background. I definitely needed to get over here for a full meal one day soon. I saw only two customers, a couple at a small table in the front window. By their smiles and mostly empty plates they seemed to be enjoying their late lunch of tempura and fat *nori* rolls while splitting a liter of Sapporo.

I strolled up to the sushi bar and waited until a young woman in a kimono-style jacket over skinny jeans ducked through the curtains.

"Can I help you?" Her features looked like she might be part Asian but her English was a hundred percent American.

"I wanted to get a takeout order of seaweed salad, one cucumber *nori* roll, and an order of *inari*." I had a real weakness for *inari,* the moist, slightly sweet pockets of fried tofu stuffed with sushi rice.

"Certainly." She jotted down the items on an order pad.

"How long will the wait be?" I could pop over to Zane's and get my wine if it was going to take a while.

"Not very long. It'll be right up." She called out something I didn't understand and started to head to the back.

"Excuse me," I said. "My name is Mac Almeida. I own Mac's Bikes here in town. Could I ask you a question?"

She smiled and nodded.

I kept my voice low, on the extremely rare chance that one of the diners was the murderer. "I am trying to find a young woman who ate dinner here on Monday. Were you working that day?"

"Monday." She frowned. "Yes, of course."

"She's slender with long light hair, and was with a man maybe twenty years older. Pointed chin, straw-colored hair, also thin."

The waitress gazed around the nearly empty restaurant as if thinking. "Yes, I remember them," she finally said.

"Do you happen to know who they were?" I asked.

"I think I have seen him around town. Not her, and I don't think he's ever eaten here before. And I heard her call him Dad."

Dad? Jake was her father? I didn't know he even had a family. They certainly didn't live here in Westham or I was sure I would have heard of them.

"Did you happen to hear him address her by name?" I asked.

"Yes, he called her Wendy. They shared a bottle of sake. They both seemed kind of, I don't know. Happy, but cautious about it. Like they couldn't quite trust the feeling. Does that make sense?"

"Sure," I replied, although I wasn't sure it did. What did make sense was that this Wendy would be weeping after she heard of Jake's death. Who wouldn't weep at learning of their father's murder? Maybe not Oedipus, but I was willing to bet Wendy had neither the desire to kill Jake nor the strength to actually plunge a knife into him. She was only a little bit of a thing.

A man in a white chef's tunic and a white cap hurried in behind the sushi bar, nodded at me, and proceeded to assemble my *nori* roll with speedy dexterity. Without looking up he barked something at the waitress.

"Excuse me. I'll have your order ready in a minute." She disappeared behind the curtains.

The chef handed me a small plate holding a single serving of sushi rice topped with *tamago*, the slice of distinctly Japanese omelet, complete with its tiny nori belt. "On za house."

I thanked him and popped the complimentary treat into my mouth, savoring the perfect combination of savory and sweet. As I chewed, I watched the chef without really seeing him. *Wendy.* Wendy Lacey? Why would she be cautious about seeing her father? Maybe they hadn't seen each other in a while. Maybe she lived out of state and this was their first visit in years. Or they'd been estranged and finally were able to get beyond whatever the hurt had been. Or had she been given up for adoption and just found her birth father? No matter the reason, the shock at Jake's death must have struck his daughter doubly hard if she hadn't seen him in a while and had seemed happy about finally reuniting. I shook my head. I could spin fantasy tales forever but they wouldn't get me the truth.

I was about to take out my phone and do a search on her name, assuming she shared the surname Lacey with Jake, when the waitress reappeared with a paper bag. I abandoned that project, instead paying my bill in cash. I thanked both her and the chef and made my way out.

I had no idea how Wendy was important to the murder investigation. But it was information, and that had to count.

A minute later I was inside Zane's store. I didn't see him at first glance, so I once again browsed the wine selection. The store seemed empty. Maybe a sunny day like today drew boaters and cookout chefs to the beer store instead of here. I selected an Alexander Valley pinot noir and brought my bottle to the register.

When no one appeared, I called, "Hello?"

A woman of about fifty hurried in from the back. "I'm sorry to keep you waiting. Did you find everything you needed?" Her smile signaled welcome, but she most certainly wasn't my friend, the proprietor.

"Where's Zane?"

"He takes weekends off." She lifted the wine. "Will this be all?"

Darn. I was glad Zane had carved out time for himself. But it meant I wouldn't be huddling with him to solve the mystery of Wendy Maybe-Lacey after all. Not now, not here, anyway.

I should have cut my sleuthing short earlier. Mac's Bikes was hopping with Saturday business when I eased in the back door at about three thirty. I'd taken a minute to stop by my house, drop off the wine and Japanese treats, and say hi to Belle. I also washed and bandaged my elbow and hung out at the house long enough to add a note to the Capers' group message thread. I told them about discovering Wendy's identity as Jake's daughter, and asked if anyone had seen her in the last couple of days. None of the group had added any new information, but folks were probably enjoying their weekends or working. I was sure Gin's candy shop was also a whirlwind today.

I also dutifully sent Detective Haskins a text giving him the Yoshinoya waitress's name and telling him what she'd told me about Wendy's name and her addressing Jake as her father. I mentioned, in an only slight white lie, that the waitress had volunteered the information when I was in the restaurant ordering takeout.

Now I was in the middle of my own whirlwind. Orlean looked frazzled as two customers waited with increasingly impatient body language for her to fix a flat and a slipped chain. I would have jumped in to help her, but we had only the one workstation. Which was possibly poor planning on my part.

"We'll be right with you, folks," I said in my most reassuring owner voice.

Over on the rental/retail side, Edwin looked like he'd always worked here, talking up customers and demoing bikes. Derrick, on the other hand, perched atop the high stool behind the counter and worked his phone.

"How's it going, bro?" I asked, sidling up next to him.

"Mac." He glanced at the phone in his hand and pressed something before sliding it into his back pocket. "I was checking on Cokey. She's been invited to stay for dinner at her little friend's. I told the mother it was fine." He smiled a little wistfully. "That's a first, her being asked to dinner. What's next? The prom? Her moving out? This childhood thing is racing by way too fast."

I punched his arm lightly. "And you're enjoying every minute of it."

"Doing my best." His eyes looked haunted, but his shoulders were squared and he looked ready to take on the world. "She's the number one reason I have to stay sober, I'll tell you."

I was gladder than glad to hear him say that. "For sure. So has it been this busy the whole time I was gone?" I vaguely gestured at the room and the family Edwin was currently engaged with.

"Pretty much." He narrowed his eyes at me. "Were you out being Girl Detective?"

I scrunched up my nose. "A little. Until a big-ass motorcycle tried to run me down." I kept my voice low so I didn't scare off the customers.

"Mac, are you all right?" The alarm on his face was obvious.

"I am. I only scraped my elbow." I held it up in evidence. "Later I met with the detective for a little bit, too."

"Haskins?"

"The very one. He basically told me—the whole group—to cease and desist investigating. He said next time I could be hurt a lot worse. I agreed. But . . ."

"But what?"

"I can't seem to help myself. I stopped into Yoshinoya to get a couple appetizers for dinner. I asked the waitress about a young woman Stephen saw eating there with Jake on Monday. The same one who looked devastated a few days later. Turns out her name is Wendy, and she addressed Jake as Dad."

Derrick's eyebrows zoomed up. He whistled. "Wait a second." He tapped the counter. "What does she look like?"

"Slim, long light hair. I didn't see her up close so I don't know her eye color or anything. I don't think she was wearing glasses."

He nodded in slow motion. "I think I saw her talking to Pa yesterday."

"To Pa?" My voice zoomed up almost as fast as Derrick's eyebrows had. "Why?"

"I suppose in his role as pastoral counselor. You know, all kinds of people come to him with their concerns."

"True. People who aren't interested in going to confession at Our Lady of the Sea but still need somebody wise to talk to. And Pa's nothing if not both wise and a good listener. I wonder if he'd talk to me about her."

Derrick gave me one of his "Are-you-an-idiot?" looks. "Mackie. As if. You know how he holds confidences sacred."

"You're right. Of course he does."

A cheerful noisy group of a dozen young adults swept in, helmets in hand, sunburned cheeks and wind-blown hair all. The smell of beer breath swept in right along with them. They'd each signed my standard form saying they wouldn't ride a Mac's Bikes rental while intoxicated, but of course I had no way to enforce the rule. Or any way to discover if they had unless someone got in an accident with the bike and the police got involved.

My chat time with Derrick was over. He started doing intake on the group's bikes and I headed over to the other side to help Orlean with repairs. But what I really wanted to do was drop in on my father and convince him to talk with me about Wendy. Or at least tell me how to find her.

Chapter Thirty-four

After I locked the shop at five thirty—one of these days I should simply change my closing time on the sign to correspond to reality—I power-walked down the sidewalk toward the UU church and my parents' house. I'd extracted promises from both Derrick and Orlean that they would run Mac's Bikes tomorrow, and I'd left it all tidy and squared away.

Now I had to see if Pa would talk with me about Wendy, despite Derrick's caution that he wouldn't. I was pretty sure he would keep her confidences, but I felt driven to give it a try. I could grab the lobster meat from Tulia's on my way back, and I should have time if I hurried. I'd invited Tim for six thirty. It didn't matter if everything wasn't ready ahead of time. Tim was always happy to help me cook, or even take over the meal preparation, which suited me just fine.

I was forced to dodge tourists right and left. Tourists holding maps. Tourists licking ice cream cones. Tourists laughing as they walked out of the pub. Tourists everywhere. They were key to the success of my business, but they definitely got in the way when you wanted to get somewhere in a hurry.

I slowed as I approached the big white church. The parsonage occupied the property on the far side, and Pa's office was in a low building that looked like an afterthought, stuck onto the side of the church between it and the parsonage. On a whim, I trotted up the wide granite steps of the church first. Ever since I was little I'd loved to sit in a back pew of the sanctuary when it was empty. The sounds of the world were muted, distant. The spiritual space had brought me peace and solace on many an occasion when I'd needed it. Even when I didn't, I still appreciated the solid construction, the scent of antique woodwork, and the little creaks and emanations of a building a hundred and fifty years old. Light flowed in from the tall windows on both sides and from the high windows in the front. In spring and summer the sunlight danced with the leaves outside, and in late fall and winter it was clean and pure with nothing but bare branches to block it.

Pulling open the heavy door, I slipped into the foyer and closed it softly behind me. Pa always left the front door unlocked during daylight hours, wanting the public to feel welcome. So far that public hadn't betrayed his trust; the church had never been vandalized. The door to the sanctuary stood open, so I walked in on cloud feet, a term Cokey used to describe walking softly. I gazed up at the balcony that ran on three sides of the church, its floors slanting gently up to the wall behind so all pews had a view of the altar. Derrick and I and our friends had sometimes played hide-and-seek up there while Pa was writing sermons.

I was about to slide into a pew at the side when I

glimpsed movement. My senses went on alert. Had I been I followed here? Was this the next scene of attack, as sacrilegious as that would be? I absolutely did not want to be alone in a church with a murderer. I'd better get out while I could. I grabbed my phone out of my bag. And halted.

I peered at the front pew. I heard a sniff and saw hair the color of Cape sand. That was no murderer at prayer, no Harley driver pretending to worship. That was Jake's daughter. Exactly who I wanted to see. I cleared my throat.

"Hello?" I kept my voice light and friendly as I walked up the center aisle until I came to a slight figure bent over with her elbows on her knees. "Excuse me." I waited.

She sniffed again and swiped at her eyes. She gazed over at me. "I'm sorry. Do I need to leave?" Her green-gray eyes were rimmed with the red of a crying jag.

I glanced down at my Macs Bikes polo shirt and navy shorts. Did I look like a minister? "No, of course not. Are you all right? Can I do anything?" I perched on the end of the pew, twisted half toward her.

She gazed down. "I'm sorry," she repeated.

"Don't be. We all go through tough times. And isn't this the best place to be?" I gestured at the sanctuary. "My name is Mac Almeida. I've spent my whole life coming in here, sitting alone, finding peace when I needed it. It's perfectly fine for you to do that, too."

"Almeida?" She looked at me as if for the first time. "You're related to Joseph?"

I smiled. "His daughter." Now that I was near her, I could spot ways she resembled her own father. Her slim build, the color of her hair, although she had rounded cheeks where Jake's had been lean. And on her Jake's pointy chin was softer, and made her face look heart-shaped.

"Joseph has been so helpful to me, since . . ." Her voice trailed off and she sniffed again, looking like full-blown tears were about to spill over.

"He's like that. Did something bad happen to you recently?" Pretending my way into the conversation wasn't my finest moment, but it didn't seem like a huge crime.

"The worst." She swallowed. "I didn't grow up with a father, not like you. I just found him. Only last week. And now he's dead."

"I'm so sorry, um . . . what's your name?"

"Wendy. Wendy Rawson."

"I'm so sorry, Wendy." I reached over and patted her hand where she'd rested it on the seat. "A man died here in town this week. Was your father Jake Lacey?" Why did she have a different last name? Maybe her mom had remarried.

She nodded. "We had dinner together Monday. I'd been looking for him for a long time and finally made contact. I took the bus here from Fall River where I live. We made plans to spend more time with each other." She blew her nose, and exhaled. Maybe the tears weren't on the surface, after all. "He made me laugh, and I immediately forgave him for deserting Mom and me when I was a baby. That's why I have my mom's last name, not his. But now he's gone."

What a shame. I couldn't even imagine her pain. As dysfunctional as Jake was, still, he'd met with Wendy, was kind to her, and clearly wanted to establish a father-daughter relationship.

"He said he'd learned that he'd inherited some

wealth recently, enough to get him back on his feet," Wendy went on. "That was the way he put it."

"He'd told me he was coming into some money, too." But not that he'd inherited it. From whom? And who did he learn about it from? Maybe Jake had been the target of the private investigator hanging around town. "Did you happen to talk to the police yet?" I asked.

"No. Your father said I should, but . . ." She picked at a thread on her jeans with a ragged nail. "Mac, it's all so hard."

"I know. But I think you're going to have to. The detective, Lincoln Haskins, is a good guy. He won't be mean or anything." He'd better not be. "Would you like me to go with you? Or better, my dad?"

"I guess. Joseph already offered, too, and he said he knows the guy's phone number." She sat up a little straighter. "Joseph said it might help them find the person who, who killed my dad."

Should I tell her I was the one who found Jake's body? I decided to. If she heard it from anyone else, she'd know I'd held out on her. I reached over and patted her hand.

"I should tell you that I was actually the person who discovered Jake was dead."

Her intake of breath was sudden and harsh. She brought her hand to her mouth, staring at me. "You were?"

I nodded.

Her eyes searched my face. "Will you, could you, tell me what happened? I think I need to know. All I've heard was that he was murdered."

"Are you sure?"

"Yes. Please." Her face calmed, and she folded her hands in her lap, giving me all her attention.

I took a deep breath. "I was coming home that night on the bike trail, and he was lying on the ground. He was already gone."

She nodded slowly, now studying her hands.

Outside the church bell rang six times. Because it was a hundred feet and many layers of building above our head, the sound was muted, but it still said six o'clock.

Tulia's closing time. *Rats.* There went my lobster salad.

"It's six." Wendy stood. "Your parents asked me to dinner. They're awfully nice, and I don't want to be late."

"Where are you staying?" I knew Detective Haskins was going to want to know.

"I'm staying at the Seaview Motel. It's not that great, but all I could afford. I'd better get over to the parsonage now."

"Go, then." I stood, too. "I'm so glad we got a chance to meet and to talk."

"Me too, Mac." She reached out and hugged me. "Thank you. I promise I'll call the police tonight."

Chapter Thirty-five

The normalcy of being home with Belle and Tim had never been so comforting.

By means of a near sprint, I'd managed to snag my lobster meat from Tulia before she closed, so we weren't going to have to eat hot dogs or some other last-minute dinner solution. I'd taken a minute to text Haskins about Wendy Rawson, in case she chickened out about contacting him. I didn't want to be accused of withholding information. I set a new personal best in the high-speed-shower event and was in a slim-cut aqua t-shirt and a long Indian skirt chopping celery when Tim arrived.

Belle, who watched from her perch on a wall sconce, squawked, "Say hi to Belle, Tim. Say hi to Belle, Tim." A wolf whistle followed.

Tim kissed the back of my neck and obediently said, "Hi, Belle." To me he added, "Hi, beautiful." From behind his back he flourished a fat bunch of red carnations.

Belle echoed, "Hi, beautiful." This time her wolf whistle made sense.

"Ooh, my favorite flowers. Hi, yourself." I smiled up at him, then focused on my chopping. Losing a fingertip was not on tonight's agenda.

From a green cloth shopping bag he unpacked the requested baguette, a glistening bottle of Pinot Gris, and a quart of hand-made Provincetown Pistachio ice cream from Cape Cod Creamery.

"Shoot," I said, laying down the knife. "I'm glad you brought the ice cream. I was going to pick up a couple of slices of hangover cake and totally forgot. I would so fail as a caterer."

"Westham Market carries Creamery ice cream now, so you don't even have to drive far to get it. You like pistachio, don't you?" He looked relaxed and extra handsome tonight, in loose white linen pants and a squared-off cream-colored cotton shirt with embroidery that looked Mexican or maybe from India.

"Of course. Do you think fudge sauce would work on top of it? I have a jar from Josie's Fudge."

"Worth a try. Now, what can I do?" He stroked my neck.

Which made it impossible not to drop the knife, throw my arms around him, and accomplish a proper greeting. We pulled apart after a minute when my stomach growled audibly.

Tim laughed. "I get the message."

"Sorry. It was a long day and I think I only had ice cream for lunch."

"Gimme some ice cream please?" Belle asked, cocking her head.

"Later, Bellita." She didn't much like my response,

but at least we didn't get a repeat performance of the car alarm adagio.

By seven we sat at my little patio table outside in the early-evening light, with still an hour until sunset. We'd devoured the appetizers while we assembled the meal. The sea-scented air was mild but starting to cool, so I'd thrown on a sweater. Belle perched on the back of one of the wrought-iron chairs, content to cock her head and watch us eat. A fat candle flickered in a glass chimney that prevented a stray breeze from blowing it out. Our plastic wine glasses were full of the chilled white and the bread was warm and crusty. The salad was full of fat lobster chunks, crunchy celery, minced chives, bits of sweet yellow pepper, and a gourmet mayonnaise sauce. I'd served it on a bed of pre-washed greens and to me it tasted just about perfect.

"Tell me about your long day." Tim spread a forkful of salad on a chunk of the crusty bread and popped it into his mouth.

"Where do I start?" I took a sip of wine before telling him about Edwin, Orlean, and Corwin. "It's complicated, but Edwin seems to think Corwin means well and that he's a different person now he's out of prison."

"Did he say what he was in for?"

"No, and I didn't get a chance to ask. But I do wonder."

"Funny that you hired Edwin without knowing he was Orlean's brother-in-law. Or former brother-in-law, I guess."

"Right? And you should have seen her face. I guess the last time she'd cast eyes on him he was a young teenager. He hadn't finished growing, getting facial hair, an adult voice, the works."

"That would explain her not recognizing him. Corwin applied for a job at the bakery today."

"He did?" I was surprised, but of course he would need a job now that he was out of prison.

"Yes. He said he learned to bake in prison and has a knack for it." Tim sipped his own wine.

"Are you going to hire him?"

"I'm going to give him a try." He reached over and stroked my hand. "I'm tired of handling the early shift on weekends. I'd much rather be sleeping in with you, so I hope Corwin works out. I could use a second baker. Plus, he was honest and told me he'd been incarcerated. I think he expected me to kick him out at that point."

"So you didn't ask him why he'd been in prison, either."

He shook his head. "I don't care. He did say it wasn't for murder. And as long as he obeys the law now, that's all that matters. He's got quite the ride, though."

I cocked my head. "What do you mean?"

"His hog." Tim gazed at me and laughed. "You know, his Harley."

A chill crept through me that had nothing to do with being outside. "He rides a Harley?"

"A monster of a motorcycle. Said he was inside so long that now he doesn't even want to be inside a car."

I hugged myself despite my sweater.

"What's wrong, hon?" He rubbed my calf with his bare foot.

"I was nearly killed by a Harley today in front of the bookstore. It came straight at me."

"No! Are you all right? You seem fine."

"I'm fine." I patted my sleeve. "Only scraped my elbow."

"I wish you'd told me."

"I was getting to it. But, Tim, what if Corwin was incarcerated with Jake? What if he came here to kill him?"

"What if I just hired a murderer, you mean?"

Chapter Thirty-six

By eight thirty Tim and I sat holding hands on the couch listening to a Mozart sonata playing softly in the background. I was comfortably full from dinner, and two dishes holding only traces of ice cream sat on the coffee table. Belle snoozed in Tim's lap.

But my orderly—obsessed?—mind couldn't escape thinking about the murder. I'd discovered who the mystery girl was. But who had attacked me with a Harley? Was it Corwin? Had he left the threatening note? And who had hired Billy Crump, PI?

I sat up straight, looked at Tim, and said, "I have to do something."

He raised his eyebrows but smiled fondly. "Be my guest."

A moment later I was at the little kitchen table at the other end of the house. I must not have clicked Save after I'd entered Crump's number on my phone. It was nowhere, but I knew where I could get it. "It's not too late to call, is it, Abo Ree?"

She laughed. "Of course not, honey. Don't you know old ladies don't sleep much? What can I do for you?"

The tinkling sound of her laugh always made me smile. "Do you have the card that guy gave you, the private investigator we talked to?"

"Mr. Crump? I believe I do. Hold on."

After sounds of rummaging and a few mild swear words, she came back on the line. "Got it." She read me the number. "Are you going to ask him to help with the investigation?" She sounded excited at the prospect.

"Sort of. I feel like I need to know who hired him, and what he's learned, if anything."

"Good luck, Mac, darling. Oops, gotta go. My show's coming on."

I said goodbye and disconnected. I was about to press Crump's number before I ran out of momentum when a text came in from Flo.

Bourne Motor Sports rents motorcycles.

I sat up straight. A lead?

Orange swish logo. Called them but no way to pin down who rented the one that attacked you, if it was rented. Will convey to detective.

I slumped again. So much for that bright idea. I tapped back my thanks and disconnected. Corwin had a Harley, too. It wouldn't be hard to examine it for an orange logo. If he'd bought it from the Bourne shop, it should bear their symbol, too. Edwin had said Corwin was living in Bourne, so he might have bought the motorcycle from that dealer, if he didn't pick one up off of Craigslist. I couldn't go traipsing around looking for a Harley tonight, though. I should, however, let Haskins know Corwin drove a Harley. A quick text accomplished that.

I returned to my plan to call the private detective. I glanced at Tim while the call connected, but he'd joined Belle in an apparently blissful dreamland. The poor guy got up so early, I didn't blame him. And his snoozing left me free to do a little sleuthing. I grabbed a notepad and pen and sat at the tiny kitchen table. Crump finally picked up.

"Mr. Crump, this is Mackenzie Almeida. You stopped by my bike shop the other day and I'm afraid I didn't have time to speak with you."

"Call me Billy, please. You have time to talk now, I gather." The drone of a television in the background alternately blared and ebbed.

"Yes, and please call me Mac. I wondered if you'd be willing to share information with me on what you've discovered."

Silence. *Rats*. Was he going to return my unfriendly behavior? The TV fell silent, too. Maybe he'd only been searching for the Mute button.

"Frankly, Mac, I haven't made much headway and my client isn't a bit happy."

"I haven't learned much either, and was attacked for my efforts."

"I'm sorry to hear that. No idea who was behind the attacks?"

"No. I called you because, well, I was still wondering who hired you."

He sighed noisily, deep, and long. "I might as well tell you. The executor of an estate hired me. A recently deceased woman—who died of old age, I might mention—was a distant cousin to Jake Lacey. He was her only living relative, and she left him a sizable and valuable piece of property. Property right here in Westham. I was hired to find him and let him know."

"So that's what he was talking about. You had a chance to tell him?"

"I did. One brief chance on the telephone a few days before he was killed. He told you about inheriting the property?"

"He only said he was not going to be needing money soon, and he seemed quite happy at the news."

"I should think so." Billy cleared his throat. "The question remains as to whether his inheritance was the reason he was murdered."

It was my turn for silence as I turned over this new piece of information. "But . . ."

"But what?"

"Do you know about his daughter?" I asked.

"Daughter?" He nearly screeched.

"I met her this afternoon. Wendy Rawson. He had left her and her mom when she was a baby, and she tracked him down only a day or two before his death."

Billy whistled. "How old is she?"

"I don't know, exactly. I'd say over eighteen but maybe not by much."

"Strong? Capable of murder?"

"What?" The word started out as my own screech but I tried to keep it down so I didn't wake Tim and Belle. "No way. She was devastated that she'd found her father and then lost him again, this time permanently. Also, she's quite slight."

"Okay, maybe not her. But what if her mother found out about the property and did the deed? She could certainly have cause to hate the victim, and would benefit from the daughter's inheritance."

How could a voice sound like hands rubbing together in glee? I shook my head. But it was a perfectly reasonable suggestion, even though it hadn't occurred to me.

"I really don't know anything about Wendy's mother." Now my brain was in overdrive. "I have seen a stranger around town, though, a Katherine Deloit. Not a tourist. She's slim like Wendy. Katherine says she's a real estate agent from California here to close a deal for a client out West. What if she's actually Wendy's mother and she and Wendy haven't yet crossed paths here?" Was that even possible in our small town? Could Katherine have been lying about everything to throw people off her track? And did she drive a Harley?

"Or perhaps they are in cahoots."

Wow. PIs actually said "cahoots."

Billy went on. "Do you know where each of these ladies is staying while they're here?"

"Wendy is at the Seaview Motel," I said. "I think Katherine is in a Victorian B&B in Falmouth." I supposed they might not have run into each other here in town, whether they were related or not.

"I'm on it. Surveillance is boring work, but sometimes it's the only way to find out what I'm hired to find out. And right now my client wants me to find out who murdered his client's beneficiary."

Chapter Thirty-seven

Standing in front of Gin's candy shop, I checked my phone again. Seven fifteen? My friend was super late for our walk this morning and I'd done all the stretching I needed to. After a delightful early-morning wakeup, Tim had left me rosy-cheeked and cozied up in bed at four. I wouldn't mind at all if Germain worked out as a weekend open-the-bakery kind of employee. And I might have to cancel my own Sunday morning walks, too.

I glanced around the side of Salty Taffy's into Gin's driveway, but her little red Honda was parked in the back. Was she sleeping in again? Too sick to cancel? I hadn't missed a seasonal time change. That was back in March. We hadn't confirmed our walk, but we never did. We only contacted each other if one of us couldn't make it.

I texted Gin but got nothing in return. I was getting a bad feeling about this. When was Haskins going to finally catch Jake's murderer so we all could stop worrying about it, stop watching our backs?

As I waited, I thought about my chat with Billy Crump last night. Jake's circumstances certainly would have changed if he owned valuable real estate. He could have sold it. Or he could have sold most of it but built a house on a small parcel and not have to worry about either money or homelessness ever again, as long as he managed the funds well. It was all theoretical now, though. Had he had time to get a will written and notarized in the few days since he'd met Wendy? She would probably inherit the property, anyway, being his next of kin. Stephen had seen Jake at the county courthouse—but it had been with Katherine, not with Wendy. Had the older woman, if she was Wendy's mother, been trying to convince him to hand over the property to Wendy now? He'd refused and she'd killed him? But how had she learned he'd inherited it? Too many questions, not enough answers. After my walk, maybe I'd see if I could pay Katherine a visit, myself.

The sunlight caught a glint of silver in the municipal parking lot next door to Gin's driveway and postage-stamp backyard garden. Only a couple of trees and a low flower bed separated her property from the lot. I peered at the silver vehicle, then sauntered closer, trying to look casual. Was that Katherine Deloit's car? It was the same color, and the same make as the one she'd had out on the Point. Then I spied the Cape Luxury Rentals decal. She was up and about early. Maybe she was at a coffee meeting with a real estate counterpart from this area closing the deal for her international client. I snapped a picture of the license plate on the back and texted it to Haskins in case he'd want to see it. I added a quick message.

Thought you'd be interested. Deloit car in municipal lot next to Salty Taffy's.

But if she was Wendy's mom and was hard up for money, why in the world would she rent a luxury car? Why hadn't she simply driven over from Fall River in her own car? The working-class town was south of Providence west of here. The car was much more consistent with Katherine being the California real estate wheeler-dealer she acted—and dressed—like.

I glanced around the lot, wondering if Billy was lurking in the vicinity keeping an eye on Katherine. I didn't see him anywhere. I supposed a good detective would have no problem staying out of sight while on surveillance. I headed back to the sidewalk in front of the shop. A brisk breeze made it chilly to stand in the shade, and I pulled my jacket sleeves down over my hands. I picked a sunny spot to stand in while I decided whether to wait longer or head out for my own walk. I shot Gin one more text before I left. This time she answered.

Delayed in shop kitchen. Door open.

I laughed at myself and slid the phone back into my bag. I hadn't even tried the front door of the candy store. She usually didn't open until eleven on Sundays.

I'd rarely been inside when the shop was closed and was impressed by how quiet it was. The air hung onto scent memories of sweetness, butter, chocolate. Twenty bins of colorful wrapped taffy lined up in a candy-lover's dream. Behind gleaming glass cases blocks of fudge of all varieties waited patiently to be cut into cubes. Truffles in seashell shapes were displayed in boxes with cellophane windows. An earthenware crock held giant spiral lollypops. The tidy organization, clean floor, and polished surfaces were a dream to an OCDer like me.

"Gin? I'm here," I called out as I pushed through the swinging door to the kitchen. Usually the candy-making room was busy with Gin hard at work in it making sweets.

She was in the kitchen, except she wasn't stirring a vat of fudge. She wasn't working ropes of taffy. She wasn't rolling rum balls in cocoa. Straight ahead of me across the room my friend sat in an office chair. Her wrists were bound to the chair arms with heavy clear tape and a wide strip of it covered her mouth. Her wide eyes held terror.

Chapter Thirty-eight

"Gin, what happened?" I rushed to her side.

She shook her head quick, then jerked her head backward and sideways. She moved her eyes in that direction, too, so I looked. The only thing that way was the back door.

"Are you telling me whoever did this went out the back? Hang on a second." I extended my fingers toward the tape covering her mouth.

Gin made a sound behind the tape that sounded like she was objecting.

"Hands off, Mackenzie."

I froze at the voice from behind me. A nasal voice. A woman's voice.

I turned slowly. Katherine Deloit leaned against the tall stainless refrigerator on the wall next to the door I'd just come through. She pointed a compact black gun at us with a steady hand. My breath rushed in with a rasp when I saw the weapon.

"You don't take a hint, do you?" Katherine's lips were even redder today, her face paler. "I tried to warn you off, but you kept digging."

"You left me the note?"

"Obviously. I've been watching you, you know. Poking into business that wasn't yours."

The binoculars. So she had been watching me, in fact, not the owl. "What do you mean?" My throat was almost too thick to speak. Ice water had replaced my blood.

"You know what I mean. You and your cozy amateurs looking into Lacey's death. I heard all about it from that nutty mother of yours. You didn't really think I was interested in astrology, did you? You're in my way, Mackenzie, you and candy girl here. And nobody stands in Katherine Deloit's way."

"We were only trying to help the detective." I tried to keep my voice steady. "Did you kill Jake?"

Her laugh came out harsh and short. "Nice try. I'm not telling you anything."

I swallowed down my fear. "I guess you did it for Wendy."

"Who?" What sounded like genuine puzzlement mixed with disdain in her voice, like I was an idiot for asking about somebody she didn't know. "What fantasy are you trying to distract me with? It's not going to work, regardless."

So she was, in fact, a ruthless real estate dealer, not Wendy's mom. She must have thought if Jake died without family, she could buy the property for Mr. Wu from the state or the town or whoever it defaulted to. Jake couldn't have told her about his daughter or Katherine wouldn't have reacted the way she did. And Wendy would be dead by now, too.

None of that mattered if Gin and I didn't get out of here alive. Thoughts raced through my brain at supersonic speed. If Billy was tailing Katherine, had he seen me go in? Would he realize she had Gin and me hostage? Unlikely. He didn't know Katherine had a gun. What about Haskins? Would he figure out Jake's killer and rescue us? No way. Anyway, in the mysteries our book group read, the resourceful and self-reliant protagonist always managed to rescue herself. That's why we liked her. She didn't need any brave white knight swooping in. I would have welcomed one, but I knew Gin and I were on our own here.

"You," Katherine barked, gesturing at me with the gun. "Get that stool and put it next to her."

A stainless steel stool sat at the far end of the long candy counter, but it was half-hidden by the big red taffy-pulling machine on top of the counter. The stool was the only other seat in the room. She was going to tape me up, too, and then probably shoot us both. My heart beat a terrified fist against my sternum. What could I do? I didn't spy a tool anywhere. Nothing heavy and unanchored I could throw at her. No knives in evidence. I had my EpiPens, but it would take too long and be too obvious to grab one out of my bag and take off the safety cover. Anyway, if I got close enough to attack Katherine, she'd shoot me in the process. Or worse, the defenseless Gin.

"Move," Katherine ordered, her pitch rising like she was losing her cool, getting desperate.

Wait. Why didn't she simply shoot us now and

leave? Why order me to get tied up, too? If I rushed her, would she shoot then? Maybe she didn't have any bullets in that thing. Heck, maybe it was a fake gun. She could be stalling. She might figure if she left us tied up, we wouldn't be discovered here for a long, long time. I knew Katherine was never going to get that property, but she didn't.

"Relax. I'm going." I sidled toward the stool but I kept my eyes on Katherine. As I moved, the weight in my right pocket reminded me I did carry a weapon. Or at least a tool, albeit a very tiny one. As I passed the red taffy machine, I flipped the switch to ON. A din filled the room. The noise of the rotating arms caromed off the walls.

Her eyes wide, Katherine let out a string of obscenities. "What is that? What did you do?" Her gun-holding hand wavered.

The machine hid the lower part of my body as I passed behind it. I eased out my Swiss Army knife and opened the tiny—but wicked sharp—blade, then palmed it as I grabbed the stool with my other hand.

"The taffy machine must be on a timer." I carried the stool as close to Gin as I could get and sat. "Right, Gin?" I cleared my throat.

Gin nodded. Her eyes signaled something to me. Possibly gratitude.

Katherine pressed her lips together and shot me a glance burning with vile. She moved slowly, cautiously toward us, skirting the counter on the other end from the machine. "No crazy moves, got it?" She pointed the weapon at my head and grabbed the wide tape dispenser off the counter. Sweat made little rivulets in the makeup on her forehead. She stepped back, breathing hard. "Put your hands together in front of you. Like you're praying." Another barking laugh. "You're going to need all the prayers you can get, especially once I light a match to the joint."

A match? She was going to burn us up with no way out? Not on my watch, she wasn't. She wasn't exactly an experienced criminal. Both me and Gin with our hands in front and our legs free? *Bad move, Katherine.* She gestured with the gun, so I complied, sliding my palms together, willing my hands not to shake. I took care not to reveal the knife as she moved toward me, the dispenser in her left hand.

The sticky tape hit my left wrist. I heard a shout from outside. Katherine glanced in that direction. I gripped the knife and jabbed it into the tender veined skin of her inner wrist.

She cried out, dropping the gun and the dispenser. She grabbed her wrist with her other hand. I pushed up from the stool. With the heels of my hands I used all my strength to push her. She staggered back. Her head hit the counter and she crumpled to the floor.

I could barely breathe, my heart beat so hard. Katherine didn't move. The red handle of the little knife stuck out of her wrist. Blood trickled out around it.

I shot a wide-eyed glance at Gin. "We have to get out of here, but let me find the gun first." I whipped my head around but didn't see it on the floor.

Katherine moved her arm and moaned. At least I hadn't killed her. But if she woke up we had to worry about her attacking again.

I swore. Gin shook her head frantically. She pedaled her feet, aiming the wheeled chair toward the back door.

The gun lay on the floor under where her chair had been. I gingerly grabbed the weapon. I didn't think I could push her and safely hold it, too, so I laid it in Gin's lap. As the empty taffy machine clattered on, I hurried Gin, her chair, and me outside to freedom.

Chapter Thirty-nine

Heads spun in our direction as we emerged into sunlight. Two Westham police cars hovered in the public parking lot, lights flashing, with a couple of state police cars nearby in the same condition. Victoria, clad in a thick black vest, stood to the left of the building, weapon drawn and extended with both hands. When she saw us, she lowered it.

"Hey, Victoria." My heart rate started to slow, ever so slightly. We'd made it.

"Hey, Mac," she said. "Glad you got out." The two similarly dressed officers behind her nodded. "We were about to go in."

I knew what that meant from all the mysteries I'd read. This was way closer to a scene from a thriller than I was comfortable with.

"Ms. Almeida, are you all right?" Haskins hurried toward me from the parking lot, with Billy Crump close behind.

An ambulance rumbled into the parking lot, too, lights strobing but *sans* siren. Two EMTs jumped out.

"We're both all right. Katherine Deloit is on the floor inside, though." I pointed to the gun in Gin's lap. "I believe Katherine killed Jake, and she threatened us with that."

Haskins's eyebrows went up. He pulled a blue glove out of his blazer pocket and pulled it on. "Excuse me, Ms. Malloy." He lifted the gun with great care and handed it to a uniformed statie, also gloved. "That was the only weapon you saw?"

"Yes." I swallowed. "I stabbed her wrist with my little knife, then pushed her."

Billy, who stood hovering behind Haskins, gave a soft whistle.

A small smile flirted with Haskins's lips. "Did you, now? Good work."

"I think she hit her head on the metal counter before she fell," I went on. "But she was starting to move and make sounds, so be careful when you go in."

"Got it. Ms. Malloy, we'll get you freed up right away." Haskins called to one of the EMTs, who hastened over with a pair of surgical scissors. First he loosened a corner of the tape on her mouth.

"I'm sorry, ma'am, this is going to hurt." He eased it off with a gentle expertise, then clipped the tape on both of Gin's wrists.

Gin thanked the EMT. "I'm glad to get out of that mess." She flexed her fingers and rolled her wrists, then stood. Her normally pink cheeks matched her cream-colored shirt. When she swayed, I grabbed her arm.

"Do you need medical attention, ma'am?" the EMT asked her, taking her other arm.

"I don't think so. Now that I'm not a prisoner to the chair, I'm fine," Gin said. She took a deep breath and blew it out. "But thanks. And thanks, Mac. My legs just felt like jelly all of a sudden. I'll be fine."

"If you're sure." The EMT looked at me.

I shook my head. "No, I'm good, thanks."

"Detective, my Airbnb tenant is upstairs, Wesley Farnham," Gin said, worry in her voice. "He won't get hurt, will he?"

Haskins appeared to swear under his breath. "Is there an outer egress to the second floor?"

"Of course." Gin pointed to the back of the building. "A set of stairs just around the corner there."

"Good. I'll send someone up."

He turned away and spoke into his communication device. A few seconds later an officer made her way toward the back of the building.

"A favor, please?" Haskins spoke to the EMT as he pointed to the chair. "If you could roll this into the lot behind the cruisers, I'd appreciate it. Keep the gloves on, and then stand by for instructions."

"Sure, sir." Gin's ride clattered off with him across the uneven pavement.

"Ladies, Mr. Crump, I'll need you to wait over there, too."

Haskins led us and Billy into the lot behind a double row of cruisers. "Stay here, okay? I'll be back soon." The detective beckoned to more staties. They strode over to Victoria and the officers and conferred.

"I saw Deloit enter through the back door," Billy said. "I was about to call to you when I saw you go in the front, so I called Haskins."

"Thank you. I was kind of hoping you were watching from somewhere. You hide pretty well."

He laughed softly. "It is my business, after all."

"Gin, how did Katherine get in your kitchen?" I asked.

"I was coming out the back door and there she was. She pushed me back inside. When that gun came out, I wasn't going to argue with her. Then she made me return your text. I didn't want to, believe me." With a down-turned mouth, she said, "I'm really sorry. She said she'd shoot me if I didn't."

"Don't worry about it." I frowned. "But I don't understand why she attacked you and didn't go straight for me. I'm the one she threatened more than once."

"I'd say she was using Gin to get to you," Billy offered, raising one eyebrow. "If she'd been watching you, she knew you two went walking every morning."

"I guess she wanted to get us out of circulation because she thought we were getting closer to the truth about her." I kept my eye on the police activity. One officer now stood at the ready near the front of the shop, and Victoria and her gang of uniforms looked like they were about to storm the Bastille.

"But were we?" Gin asked. "I didn't think so."

"Hey, a person reckless enough to kill someone to get a piece of land has to be at least a little paranoid, right?" I asked.

"You did a good job of escaping. Did you really stab Deloit?" Billy asked, admiration tinting his voice.

I nodded. "The knife is only two inches long, but it's wicked sharp. I had no desire to end up with both of us trapped inside. She said was planning to set the kitchen on fire before she left, too." I shuddered and my knees suddenly turned rubbery, too. "I'm going to sit down for a sec." I headed to the curb at the far edge of the lot and sank down.

"Good idea." Gin joined me on the curb. "That woman would have burned up Wes sleeping upstairs, too. What an evil person, or deeply disturbed, at least. Good thing she wasn't that bright." From our seats we could see Wes staring out the window at the police vehicles. The officer must have warned him to stay put. Our position also gave us a vantage point for the show that followed.

Three officers with weapons raised, led by Victoria, burst into the building. Haskins stayed outside but held some kind of communication device in front of his mouth. I couldn't see from where we sat if the officer in front had gone in that way, or not. At some directive, in a couple of minutes the EMTs followed. They wheeled a stretcher, its bright yellow metal frame contrasting with a somber black pad.

We waited. My head pounded. Gin's face was still pale. Billy kept quiet, standing next to us. The house was quiet, too. No gunshots. No yelling.

An officer emerged from the house and held the door open. An EMT was next, at the foot of the stretcher, which held Katherine Deloit.

"I didn't do anything. Those women tricked me. I demand you let me up from here!" Her nasal voice was strident and shrill. She thrashed on the stretcher but couldn't get far.

Even from here I could see her left wrist wrapped in white bandages. The wrapping wasn't too thick for a handcuff to be fastened around it, though. And the second cuff of the set was locked into the yellow-and-black railing at her side.

Chapter Forty

An hour later Gin and I had finished giving Haskins our accounts of the morning in a conference room at the police station. Gin, Billy, and I sat next to each other, and across the table were Haskins, Victoria, and a young officer I didn't know. After tourists drawn by the lights and the commotion had started to crowd around, Haskins had directed us to the station. Victoria had sent somebody out for decent, non-police coffee, which had gone a long way toward restoring Gin and me to a semblance of normalcy.

"I thought people were always separated when you interviewed them about a crime," I'd said, once again drawing solely on my reading experience for my knowledge.

"That's for suspects," Victoria replied. "Not quite the case here."

Now we were done telling our stories for the record. Billy had contributed what he knew and had seen, and Haskins hadn't objected. He'd even thanked Billy for contacting him this morning. Finally the detective had declared the formal interview over. Our empty cups sat on the long table, and the young officer must have had pages of notes to submit, since he'd typed into a small laptop throughout the interview.

"Is she still insisting she did nothing wrong?" I asked Haskins.

"That's right. Often criminals like her have a long history of refusing to take responsibility for their own actions. Particularly when it comes to murder."

I frowned. "I asked her directly if she killed Jake, since she was on our suspect list, but she wouldn't admit it. You can find evidence now that you know it was her, I hope."

Haskins tented his fingers. "We're working on that. At least we have cause to get a search warrant. We'll go through her room, the car, her phone, and other possessions. I feel confident we can bring a murder one case. And no way she's getting out of the assault charges."

"That's good." The color in Gin's face was starting to return. She glanced at the wall clock and stood. "Can I be getting home? Sunday is one of my busiest days."

Haskins nodded. "That's fine."

"Are you all right to start work so soon?" I asked her as I stood, too.

"It'll help, frankly."

I gave her a hug and watched her go. I turned back to Haskins. "I told you Derrick was innocent, didn't I?" I sat again.

"You did. And you were correct."

"At least it wasn't Corwin," I said, almost to myself.

"No, it wasn't. I haven't found any evidence that he

was involved, although he did know both Lacey and your brother in prison. He appears to be working hard at establishing a crime-free life for himself."

"Good. So were you ever able to talk with Wendy, Jake's daughter?"

"I did," Victoria chimed in. "She came in at a time when Detective Haskins was unavailable. I took her statement about her reputed father."

Reputed. Did Victoria not believe Wendy? I wasn't going there now.

Haskins sat back in his chair, stretching out his long legs and fixed his gaze on me. "What are your theories about Deloit's motivation to kill Mr. Lacey?"

Now he wanted me to be an amateur sleuth? Fine with me. "I think she wanted desperately to buy Jake's new inheritance, that piece of undeveloped land out on the Point."

"The one I was hired to tell Jake about," Billy added.

"Right. Deloit had a rich international customer, a Mr. Wu." I narrowed my eyes, trying to remember her exact words. "Gin and I overheard her talking to him. She mentioned there would be no issues going forward, and that an obstacle had been something or other."

Victoria leaned forward. "Something or other?"

"The wind shifted and I couldn't hear the end of the sentence. I think she must have said the obstacle had been removed, or taken care of. It was after Jake's death."

"But since Mr. Lacey had already spoken with his daughter, he likely wanted to keep the land for her, is that your idea?" Haskins asked.

"Yes," I said. "Maybe Deloit thought by killing Jake the land would be available to buy. She must not have known about Wendy at all. I had a thought she might be Wendy's mother, but when I said Wendy's name to her she looked at me like she'd never heard it before." I shook my head. "She might be a top real estate agent, but she was kind of a stupid criminal. Taping our hands in front of us and leaving our feet free. That would never happen in the mysteries I read."

Haskins laughed. "Stupid criminals make our jobs a lot simpler, believe me." He stood and extended his hand to me. "You both have been a great help. Thank you." After we shook, he and Billy did the same. "Glad to see you doing well for yourself, Crump."

"Yes, thanks, to you both." Victoria smiled at me, but it was pinched, like she'd had to dig for it and put rusty smile muscles to a rare use. "And Mac? Glad you weren't harmed this morning."

Would wonders never cease?

Chapter Forty-one

I sat in a patio chair with my family, plus a few, behind the parsonage at the end of the day. My formerly growling stomach was well-sated by the picnic dinner I'd just consumed. Pa had barbecued his signature marinated ribs, with hot dogs and chicken breasts for those not inclined to pork. Mom had served her spicy Asian noodle salad, with smooth soba, crunchy bits of carrot and cabbage, and a sweet-and-tangy dressing that included sesame oil, rice vinegar, soy sauce, and I wasn't sure what else. I only knew I loved it. Tim had brought fresh ciabatta and a stick of Irish butter, and Gin contributed a plate of fudge.

The five o'clock sunlight slanted into my eyes, so I nudged my chair a few degrees to the left on the grass. As chickadees zipped from branch to branch, making their tiny beeping calls, I watched Tim push Cokey in the swing, her yellow top now stained with barbecue sauce. That kid was the furthest thing from a picky eater. Gin sat chatting with my father. Abo Reba returned from the drinks table carrying a sangria refill of her blue plastic margarita glass in one hand and a beer for me in the other. Nobody had delved into my morning's excitement except to hug me and tell me they were glad I was all right.

I'd taken a few minutes after I'd gotten home from the station to finish up the Cozy Capers' group text with the bare bones of the candy shop attack and Katherine's arrest, and said I'd give a more complete report Tuesday at our meeting. Norland texted back within the minute, writing only, "Congrats!"

Writing to the Capers had reminded me I hadn't read a word of the next book. I decided I deserved a day off, what with the events of this week up to and including this morning. After checking in that all was well at the shop, I'd packed up the book and a towel. A sandwich, a beer, and a bottle of water in a lunch cooler also accompanied me to Chapoquoit Beach for the day. Watching the water, I'd reflected on how, just like in the books we read, justice had been restored to our small community. After our kitchen ordeal on top of the week's happenings—threatening note, motorcycle attack, suspicious strangers—I decided I'd much rather stick with fictional murder investigations.

Now, between the beach, this meal, and another beer, I was more relaxed than a slowly pedaled ride on level ground.

Abo Reba broke the streak of picnic peace by gazing at me with bright eyes. "Okay. Tell me all about it."

I sighed, but I couldn't refuse my grandma. I outlined the events as briefly as I could.

"Were you afraid she would shoot you?" she asked.

"Of course. The thing is, I don't know why she didn't. It seemed weird that she was going to tie us up and then I guess she was going to leave. I still don't know why she didn't fire the gun. Maybe it was fake, or she didn't actually have any ammunition."

Mom appeared at my side. "She had a built-in opposition to explosions. That's why." She sat cross-legged in front of us, her back erect, her purply pink dress spreading out around her like the skirt of a fuchsia.

"What do you mean?" I asked.

"I saw it in her chart," my mother said. "She didn't mind stabbing poor Jake, but when it came to explosive devices like a gun, she couldn't tolerate it."

I mentally rolled my eyes but made sure Mom didn't see me actually doing it. Somehow I wasn't sure about that explanation, but now wasn't a time I wanted to argue with anyone about anything.

"Linc, come and join us," Abo Reba called, waving.

Lincoln Haskins had just appeared around the corner of the house from the front. He paused to shake hands with Derrick and Pa before making his way to where we sat.

"Good afternoon, ladies. I hope I'm not intruding. Joseph invited me to stop by."

"The drinks are on the table, Detective, and there's plenty of food." I smiled at him. "Please help yourself."

He hesitated, then laughed. "Oh, why not? I'm off duty." He returned with a frosty Sam Adams in his hand. He sank to sitting on the grass next to Astra, also cross-legged and with a fluid grace that surprised me in such a large man. He must have seen my reaction.

"I'm Wampanoag, you know. We never outgrow joining ourselves with the Earth that sustains us." He sipped from the beer then cradled it in both hands.

"I don't want to make you talk shop," I began.

"But you're going to," Abo Reba said with a gentle elbow jab that didn't quite reach me.

"Go ahead," the detective said. "I don't mind."

"I wondered if you've found any definitive evidence." I took a good long swig from my own bottle.

"You don't need to worry. It's early, yet, but we've already found notes in Katherine Deloit's room about Jake, his property, and his schedule, not to mention a rental receipt from Bourne Motor Sports."

"So it was her on the Harley. Wow. And she knew Jake had inherited the land?" I asked.

He nodded, his dark eyes thoughtful. "Looks like it. I don't yet know how or where she uncovered that. Crump says he didn't tell her. Could be she overheard Lacey talking to someone about it. We'll find out. We also unearthed a bloodstained coat balled up in a Falmouth dumpster near Deloit's lodging. She wasn't a very devious bad guy, as you saw. The coat was missing a button, too. The others matched that button you found near where Lacey was killed."

I blew out a long breath and slumped back in my chair. I watched Cokey again. *The woman who losted her purse.* "But stealing the knife from Derrick. That seems so random."

"It might have been opportunistic," he said. "Surely she could find a knife anywhere, but once she spied that unique one, she knew killing Lacey with it would automatically cast suspicion on your brother."

"I guess. Seems unnecessarily cruel, though. She didn't even know Derrick."

"Mac, she's a ruthless murderer," Abo Reba said in a gentle voice. "Cruel comes with the territory, I'd say."

I gazed at her. Of course it did.

Haskins cleared his throat. "Now, as I said earlier, Ms. Almeida—"

I held up a hand. "Oh, please. Call me Mac."

"Mac, then. And I'm Lincoln. You should know how much I appreciate your digging up helpful information. But you also got a taste of the very real danger involved."

I nodded. "And I promise, I'm going to let the group know we're sticking strictly to fiction in the future. Don't worry, Lincoln."

He only cocked his head and gave a nod, but it came with one of those looks that says, "I'll believe that when I see it."

"Titi Mac!" Cokey called. "Come push me. Tio Tim is all tired out."

This was a sign not to be ignored. Off I went to be an auntie. It was one of the most important jobs in my life, and I was grateful I was alive to push a little girl in a swing.

RECIPES

Stephen's Killer Pizza

Cozy Capers member Stephen Duke made this pizza the week the book group read Sherry Harris's *I Know What You Bid Last Summer*, in honor of Angelo's Pizza in the book.

Note: Start the dough a day ahead for a stretchier pull.

Ingredients:
1 cup warm water
1 packet or tablespoon yeast
2½ to 3 cups unbleached white flour
3 Tablespoons olive oil
1 teaspoon salt
2–3 cups grated mozzarella
Fresh Parmesan cheese
Tomato sauce (homemade or from a jar)
Dried oregano
Toppings as desired; including pitted Kalamata olives, sliced sweet peppers, sliced mushrooms, caramelized onions, ham, fresh basil leaves, crumbled goat cheese, pepperoni or other sausage.

Directions:
Twenty-four hours before you want to eat the pizza, sprinkle the yeast over the warm water in a mixing bowl. Stir it in, and then stir in one cup of flour. Add 2 tablespoons of olive oil and the salt, and continue to add flour until the dough stands up as a lump.

Flour a countertop or table and turn out the dough, making sure to scrape all the dough off the sides and spoon. Rub the remaining oil all over the inside of the bowl and set aside.

Knead the dough, turning a quarter turn each time, until smooth. Lay it in the oiled bowl smooth side down and press with the back of your hand, then turn it over. Cover the bowl with plastic wrap and refrigerate. Before you go to bed, punch the dough down twenty times, cover, and refrigerate again.

The next morning, punch the dough down and refrigerate again. Four hours before you want to eat the pizza, remove the dough from the refrigerator. Let it warm and rise until doubled.

Preheat oven to 500 degrees Fahrenheit.

Divide dough into two balls.

Option: Skip the preceding steps and buy pizza dough at the grocery store.

Lightly grease two large pizza pans or baking sheets. Roll and gently stretch out one ball of dough on one pan, being careful not to tear the dough. Spread a thin layer of tomato sauce. Add toppings. Sprinkle with mozzarella. Finish with a grating of Parmesan and a sprinkle of oregano.

Bake for 12-15 minutes, watching carefully that the pizza doesn't get too brown. Repeat for the second ball of dough.

Serve hot, and enjoy your pizza with a green salad, a glass of red wine, and your favorite cozy mystery.

Note: You can skip the overnight refrigeration. In that case, instead of refrigerating, let the dough rise until doubled and proceed from preheating the oven.

Tim's Cranberry-Orange Bread

Baker Tim Brunelle makes this yummy quick bread for Greta's Grains. Make a day ahead of time for easiest slicing.

Ingredients:
2 cups unbleached white flour
¾ cup sugar
1½ teaspoons baking powder
½ teaspoon baking soda
Zest and juice of one orange. If juice doesn't equal
    ¾ cup, add orange or cranberry juice to supplement
¾ cup buttermilk
1 egg
3 Tablespoons vegetable oil
1 cup cranberries (fresh or frozen)
½ cup chopped nuts (optional)

Directions:
Preheat oven to 350 degrees. Grease a 9" x 5" loaf pan with butter.

Chop cranberries in a food processor or by hand.

In a large bowl, mix flour, sugar, baking powder, baking soda, and salt.

Make a well in the center and stir in the egg with a fork. Add the juice, buttermilk, oil, cranberries, and nuts, and stir until just mixed. Do not beat or overmix.

Pour batter into the loaf pan. Bake for 55 to 65 minutes, until a knife or toothpick inserted into the center of the loaf comes out clean and the bread starts to pull away from the edges of the pan. Remove it from the oven and let cool on a rack for fifteen minutes, then turn it out of the pan to cool completely.

Enjoy with butter or cream cheese and a cup of your favorite coffee.

Cape Cod Wine Spritzer

Mac makes this to relax at home. Adjust proportions up or down depending on sweetness and degree of alcohol you like in your spritzer.

Ingredients:
6 ounces Pinot Grigio
4 ounces cranberry juice (I use an all-juice cranberry-apple mix but you can also use cranberry juice cocktail)
1 Tablespoon Grenadine syrup
¼ lime, squeezed
Lime seltzer

Directions:
Combine ingredients in large-bowl wine glass. Add ice cubes and top up with seltzer. Adjust up or down on the juice and Grenadine to make it more or less sweet, and the seltzer to dilute it.

Tim's Seared Scallops

Mac's boyfriend Tim whips these up in a few minutes after they return home from rescuing her brother.

Ingredients:
1 pound large sea scallops
Salt and pepper
1 Tablespoon olive oil
1 Tablespoon butter
1 clove garlic, pressed
Juice of half a lemon
½ cup dry white wine
2 Tablespoons fresh dill, minced

Directions:
Pat scallops dry with paper towels. Season one side with salt and pepper.

Heat oil and butter in a wide skillet on medium-high heat until butter foams. Lay scallops seasoned side down in skillet and let sear without touching for two minutes. Turn and add the garlic. Cook another minute and a half. Sprinkle with lemon juice and remove to a warm platter. Add wine and de-glaze the pan until the sauce thickens. Serve over scallops with a sprinkle of dill. Serve on a bed of buttered pasta, over brown rice, or next to buttered, herbed potatoes.

Connect with Us

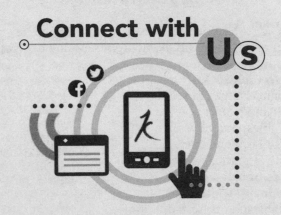

Romantic Suspense from
Lisa Jackson

Absolute Fear	0-8217-7936-2	$7.99US/$9.99CAN
Afraid to Die	1-4201-1850-1	$7.99US/$9.99CAN
Almost Dead	0-8217-7579-0	$7.99US/$10.99CAN
Born to Die	1-4201-0278-8	$7.99US/$9.99CAN
Chosen to Die	1-4201-0277-X	$7.99US/$10.99CAN
Cold Blooded	1-4201-2581-8	$7.99US/$8.99CAN
Deep Freeze	0-8217-7296-1	$7.99US/$10.99CAN
Devious	1-4201-0275-3	$7.99US/$9.99CAN
Fatal Burn	0-8217-7577-4	$7.99US/$10.99CAN
Final Scream	0-8217-7712-2	$7.99US/$10.99CAN
Hot Blooded	1-4201-0678-3	$7.99US/$9.49CAN
If She Only Knew	1-4201-3241-5	$7.99US/$9.99CAN
Left to Die	1-4201-0276-1	$7.99US/$10.99CAN
Lost Souls	0-8217-7938-9	$7.99US/$10.99CAN
Malice	0-8217-7940-0	$7.99US/$10.99CAN
The Morning After	1-4201-3370-5	$7.99US/$9.99CAN
The Night Before	1-4201-3371-3	$7.99US/$9.99CAN
Ready to Die	1-4201-1851-X	$7.99US/$9.99CAN
Running Scared	1-4201-0182-X	$7.99US/$10.99CAN
See How She Dies	1-4201-2584-2	$7.99US/$8.99CAN
Shiver	0-8217-7578-2	$7.99US/$10.99CAN
Tell Me	1-4201-1854-4	$7.99US/$9.99CAN
Twice Kissed	0-8217-7944-3	$7.99US/$9.99CAN
Unspoken	1-4201-0093-9	$7.99US/$9.99CAN
Whispers	1-4201-5158-4	$7.99US/$9.99CAN
Wicked Game	1-4201-0338-5	$7.99US/$9.99CAN
Wicked Lies	1-4201-0339-3	$7.99US/$9.99CAN
Without Mercy	1-4201-0274-5	$7.99US/$10.99CAN
You Don't Want to Know	1-4201-1853-6	$7.99US/$9.99CAN

Available Wherever Books Are Sold!
Visit our website at **www.kensingtonbooks.com**

Books by Bestselling Author
Fern Michaels

Available Wherever Books Are Sold!
Check out our website at **www.kensingtonbooks.com**